MORE PRAISE FOR *THE HOLLOWER*:

"SanGiovanni hits a multi-sensory home run with her evocative language…the imagery is…nightmarish and vivid…. This is the type of book that's worthy of repeat readings."

—FearZone

"Once SanGiovanni drops you into her reality, she never relinquishes her iron grip on your attention."

—*Dead Reckoning*, Fall 2007

"Although the cover of Mary SanGiovanni's debut novel *The Hollower* may look like another entry into the invisibility genre, it's actually one in the psychological horror, with nothing disappearing except the sanity of its various characters."

—Bookgasm

YOU CAN RUN BUT YOU CAN'T HIDE

The figure Sally saw dulled all sense of thought or flight. She opened her mouth to say something, and then closed it. The strength had gone out of her hands. The Hollower leaned casually against the wall as if waiting for someone (waiting for *her*), without really touching the wall at all. Its arms were crossed over its chest. A black fedora tilted low on its bald, earless head, which was bent down as if it dozed. It wore a long black trench, and featureless black clothes beneath. Its shoes blended into the gloom gathered at its feet.

It picked up its head to look at her.

The smooth blank plane beneath the hat was utterly featureless. It had no face whatsoever, yet she felt it watching her, even felt it smiling. It uncrossed its arms and extended one out in front of it. Its black glove closed in a fist. From between the fingers, blood pattered to the tiles in the center of the hallway. On its own, the blood ran off along the tiles, racing toward her. She stepped back but it formed an irregular circle around her feet. The Hollower laughed, drawing her gaze back up to it.

Like a magician palming a coin that had disappeared, it presented an open, bloodless palm to her with a flourish. Then it waved at her.

"Found you," it told her in a throaty voice. "Now die."

Other *Leisure* books by Mary SanGiovanni:

THE HOLLOWER

MARY SANGIOVANNI

FOUND YOU

LEISURE BOOKS NEW YORK CITY

*This book is dedicated to my mother, who taught me
the saving grace of relying on one's own inner strength.*

A LEISURE BOOK®

October 2008

Published by

Dorchester Publishing Co., Inc.
200 Madison Avenue
New York, NY 10016

ISBN 10: 0-8439-6110-4
ISBN 13: 978-0-8439-6110-2

Printed in the United States of America.

10 9 8 7 6 5 4 3 2

Visit us on the web at www.dorchesterpub.com.

ACKNOWLEDGMENTS

Thanks to my first readers: Heidi Ruby Miller, Jason Jack Miller, Christopher Paul Carey, and Meghan Knierim.

Thanks to Don D'Auria and all the fine hard-working staff at Leisure, and also Frank Weimann and Jaimee Garabacik and The Literary Group International.

Thanks also Jim Moore, Dallas Mayr, Gary Braunbeck, and Gary Frank, for keeping me sane.

Thanks to Laura Mazzarone and Pete Markson for letting me bounce ideas off them, and for providing me with research information.

Thanks especially to Adam SanGiovanni, Michael and Suzanne SanGiovanni, Michele and Christy San-Giovanni, and to Jason D'Accardi for patience, love, and understanding during the completion of this book.

FOUND YOU

CHAPTER ONE

The night had drawn long shadows across the room in Oak Hill. It was the first thing Sally noticed after the flinch that took her out of sleep. She rubbed her eyes with a small white fist. When she looked around the room, she saw a different kind of dark.

In the *usual* dark of her room, the dresser squatted, keeping guard over her while she slept. The blankets spread in a miniature hilly landscape that reached to her chest. The orange pill bottles that kept the voices out of her head and the strange sights away from her eyes stood neatly arranged on the night table beside her bed. The closet door, always closed, still stood against the chair propped beneath the knob. The door to her bedroom also remained closed and locked. Her room, her safe place, where no furnaces hissed threats of boiling skin and no snow chilled the snug corners. No Bad Thing could take that room away from her and make her scared. That's what her brother Dave had told her. Dr. Fiorello told her the same thing. And she believed them. They had never lied to her. She trusted them.

But the way the moonlight came into the room, long and sideways as if hoping to sneak in without her notice—that didn't feel right. It made her safe place look crooked, piece-y, like slabs of light and shadow had been pulled apart to distort her view.

She sat up and looked at the window. Through it she could hear the soft concert of tree frogs and crickets, a rhythm that reminded her of vacations in Seaside with her mother and Dave. Back then, they'd slept with the shore house's windows open. The ocean breeze, a scent of salt and sand and dissipating heat, carried the faint sounds of boardwalk rides and prize booths and laughter and the dull roar of the water. It also drew in the croaking and chirping of the night creatures outside. She'd liked those sounds once—back when open windows and fresh air meant good things. Back before The Bad Thing made her scared to have too much easy access to the outside world, or for it to have too easy an access to her.

Sally frowned, feeling the night air blow across her. Goosebumps rose on her skin. She brushed a shy arm over her chest to quell the tingling there. The storm window was up, the screen down.

She never left her window open. She had, in fact, closed it before she'd lain down for her nap that afternoon.

Sally tossed back the covers and swung her feet to the floor. She shivered, wrapping thin arms around her narrow ribs, and got up, scowling at the window. She might have slept straight through until morning without the safety of a pane of glass between her and the night, if not for the bad dream. Outside, the rolling expanse of lawn that covered the quad between the buildings of Oak Hill

Assisted Living was empty. Trees stretched their black-fingered shadows over the hills. A red rubber ball lay cupped by grass. A green bench stood to the side of the path leading out to the parking lot.

Nothing there, and yet she wished Dave was with her. Something about the emptiness didn't feel right. Something about it reminded her . . .

. . . *of scraping and chattering and whips and blades and The Bad Thing she wasn't supposed to talk about because it was dead and wasn't ever coming back. But what if, what if it did . . . The Bad Thing without a face that hated her and showed her blood and wanted her to die, die, die!*

In the dream, she'd been scared because she'd been alone. It found her like before and hurt her in the head because she'd been alone. But then Dave came and fought it and it had run away.

She spent a lot of time alone now, at least after the others in the community had gone in for the night, and usually she didn't mind. But something, now, about the yard, the window, the quiet, the—

The red ball rolled toward her window, fighting the breeze uphill. It struck her as strange. Wrong, but the reasons why were difficult to frame in her mind. The throaty sounds of the crickets and frogs sounded now a little to her like laughter.

Dave told her not to talk about It, not even to think about It. It was dead, after all. They'd killed It, hadn't they? She closed the window, cutting off the weird from outside.

But not completely. Some of the weird had leaked into her room. She felt it as she turned around. Her place,

3

her safe place, had changed. It wasn't anything she could quite put her finger on, but . . .

The blankets. She'd folded them back when she got out of bed, but they were pulled up to the pillow now. Something beneath them bulged—not the impression of her body, not caved inward, but swelling outward. The shape formed a headless body, the neck aligned with the edge of the blanket. And where the chest would have been, the blankets steadily rose and fell.

Oh no. No no no. Blankets can't do that. I don't think . . .

Her heart felt cold and heavy, thumping against the fragile bones of her chest and echoing through her ribs. She made small fists with her hands, and her fingertips felt cold against her palm. She crept to the side of the bed. The bulge beneath the blankets moved as if turning on its side. She jumped, letting out a little squeak, and paused. It kept on with its light breathing, but otherwise lay still. She moved forward again.

When she reached the side of the bed, the breathing stopped. Sally felt her own breath hitch in her chest. She swallowed, her hand diving in slow motion toward the covers. The blanket felt stiff beneath her fingers, but they closed around it anyway, and she yanked the covers back.

No body. Nothing at all but a red smear on the sheets, dark like blood, in the shape of an arrow. It pointed to the door of her bedroom. She looked up. The door stood slightly open, not even enough to see the hallway, but open all the same.

And a nagging thought, *Dave said, he promised, if I just forgot about The Bad Thing*, half crushed between the broken gears of her mind, struggled to gain hold but was lost.

She skirted carefully around the foot of her bed and softly stepped toward the door. A chill spread across the back of her neck, down her arms, across her breasts, down her legs. She eased open the door.

The hallway outside was not her hallway. Cement walls, flaking stucco, and what looked like rust or paint formed a long corridor that turned sharply to the left about twenty feet down. Chipped tile littered the broken floor, and what little light hit it from her bedroom window lit the broken glass in tiny glittering patches.

"Saaa-lleeee . . ."

A spark of recognition made her reel a little where she stood, feeling sick. The voice from the shadows at the end of the hall, both male and female braided together, made her skin crawl. She remembered.

Tears blurred the hallway for a moment before spilling, first hot then cold, down her cheeks.

She remembered the voice of The Bad Thing without the face. They called it the Hollower. It was ageless, it had told her, and it would never die.

But they'd killed it. They'd watched it die. She knew that. Didn't she? Wasn't that what Dave had told her— that the shuddering husk wailing a siren into the strange dawn of River Falls Road stopped moving, stopped being altogether? Wasn't that why they had come through the rip . . .

The tears came stronger. There had been others. Three others. And one of them . . . one of them had looked right at them.

"Found you . . ." The multi-voice laughed in the darkness, and the sound made Sally think of strangled tree frogs and crickets crushed under the heels of black shoes, or in the fists of black gloves.

"Leave me alone," she whispered, her voice thick with crying. "Please go away."

"You go." Its voice floated over her shoulder, close to her ear, and made her jump. "Run, Sally! Run!"

She ran, plunging headlong into the gloom of the strange hall. Anything to get away from the voice, anything to move her muscles and warm her body from the cold hate the Hollower brought with it. Anything to escape.

She turned left and skidded to a stop in front of a grandfather clock, all polished brass and mahogany wood, set up against a dead-end wall. The hands made a patient sweep backward, the minute hand trailing the hour hand around a blank and numberless face. But that didn't bother Sally. What made her cringe, what made her scalp tingle and her tiny fists clench was the blood that dripped from the top of the face down, pooling in the plastic cover, filling up the face until the hands floated, useless. And it began to chime—clear, melancholy gongs that echoed in the underground hallway.

Sally backed away, shaking her head slowly, soundless words forgotten on her lips. She turned to run again.

Behind her came the high whine of claws scraping concrete and the glassy clink of whips hitting tiles. Its laughter, a crowd of mirth, was louder still. Her own whimpering got lost beneath it. Hot tears blurred her vision, and she blinked hard to clear them.

"I'm going to break you, Sally. I'm going to drive you right over the edge." The Hollower's voice again sounded close to her ear, right over her shoulder, and she shrank away from it as she ran.

Sally turned sharply right and then left, the tiles slanting down beneath her feet. The sounds behind her drove her farther, deeper underground. She remembered what Mr. Wranker in 305B said about the catacombs beneath Oak Hill, back when there had been a hospital on those grounds and not a halfway house, about how dangerous the weak foundations beneath the off-limits "old spot" were . . . and how haunted . . . full of asbestos and crumbling floors that fell to sublevels so deep in the earth that no one would ever find you. How the air was thin and polluted with mold. All this flittered through her mind in a few seconds, her feet carrying her without thought, the faint light that came from no place growing dimmer the farther down she went. Then the hallway opened up. She slowed to a stop in the middle of a room, her breath coming in little pants, and looked around.

Those little breaths caught and stuck in her chest. She felt the air, chilly and difficult to draw into her lungs, and panic ran in tiny threads through her veins. Cold white stone walls and ceiling entombed a tiled floor, and fluorescent ceiling fixtures cast a harsh light over the grimy tables. On the tables lay rows of large metal tools like corroded jaws of strange animals, long and sharp and lined with teeth. One of the walls featured rows of metal doors, an immense filing cabinet cut into the stone. And in the center of the room . . .

Sally shivered. Mr. Wranker never mentioned a morgue beneath Oak Hill.

She didn't want to go, but her feet carried her a little way into the room. It felt almost as if she needed to see them better, to take all of them in, to be sure that what she was seeing, what she was understanding, was what was really there. It wasn't always, even when she took her pills.

But she could smell them, and what she thought might be on them, covered by sheets. Then she thought—this made her tingle inside her skin—that she heard one of the wheels squeak along the dirty, grouted tiles.

Rusted gurneys formed a half-circle around her, draped in dirty, stained sheets. Beneath each of the sheets was a form very much like a headless body, just as she'd found in her bed. Some looked like women-bodies, some bodies of men. Two looked no bigger than children. Sally's breaths loosened a bit and became little sobs. And as if on cue, just as the one in her bedroom had done, the chest of each began to rise and fall.

"Join us, Sally." The words came from one of the gurneys to her far left—one where a blood corona stained the place where the head should have been. It sounded like Max's voice.

Max Feinstein, who had taken off the back of his head with a shotgun because he couldn't bear to deal with the Hollower for even one more day. Max Feinstein, whose funeral had given Sally the first opportunity to see for herself the Hollower monster that stalked her brother.

"Sally," the dead man's voice spoke again from beneath

the filthy sheet. "Just lie down and die, girl. Just lie down with us right here and die, you bitch."

Sally uttered a cry that echoed back to her ears. Her legs felt weak and tingly beneath her, but she made them move, made them take her away from the awful place, back the way she'd come.

But it wasn't the same hallway she stumbled back into. Even lost and confused, she knew the floor beneath her wasn't sloping up toward the apartments, up toward her room and safety. Instead, it rose, plateaued, and dipped again deeper into the earth, turning all the wrong ways as she continued on. The mold patterns and piles of debris were different in these corridors. The dank patches beneath the chipped concrete here sometimes looked like faces, sometimes like words she could almost make out. One bloody handprint, which looked to Sally like someone had smacked the wall sideways to support rising weight, dripped long scarlet claws from the fingertips. In a crevice where a chunk of concrete had come loose, Sally thought she saw a couple of bloody teeth.

She made a turn at the end of the corridor and a cement wall, glazed wet and spotted with black mold, blocked her way. Unable to stop short enough, she tumbled into it, throwing up her arms to protect her face and scraping them from wrist to elbow.

Sudden sharp, jarring pain speared her skull as well as her arm.

"Damn." She whispered the word, afraid of it, afraid of the hopelessness contained in it. She backed away from the wall slowly, step by step, her chest heaving, her face pinched tight in a grimace from the throbbing in her head. Clouds in her mind obscured logical thoughts. She could hear echoes and voices that made it hard to concentrate. She wasn't sure now if they were outside her skull, bouncing around the hallway, stray threads of sound from the Hollower, or in her head. She counted steps in reverse, the skin around her eyes tight from fighting off tears. She stopped when sharp cold whipped down the neck of her nightgown, across the backs of her arms, and lifted her hair. Sally turned around.

The figure she saw dulled all sense of thought or flight. She opened her mouth to say something and then closed it. The strength had gone out of her hands, but they flexed open and closed at the sides of her nightgown with weak deliberateness anyway. The Hollower leaned casually against the wall as if waiting for someone (waiting for *her*), without really touching the wall at all. Its arms were crossed over its chest. A fedora so black it was almost blue tilted low on its bald, earless head, which was bent down as if it dozed. It wore a long black trench of the same hue and featureless black clothes beneath. Its shoes blended into the gloom gathered at its feet.

It picked up its head to look at her.

The smooth blank plane beneath the hat was utterly featureless. It had no face whatsoever, yet she felt it watching her, even felt it smiling—something about the trick of light and shade from somewhere inside it, the wrong kind of dark and light, like in her room. It uncrossed its arms and extended one out in front of it. Its black glove closed in a fist. Between the fingers, blood pattered to the tiles in the center of the hallway. On its own, the blood ran off along the tiles, racing toward her. She stepped back, but it formed an irregular circle around her feet. The Hollower laughed, drawing her gaze back up to it.

Like a magician palming a coin that has disappeared, it presented an open, bloodless palm to her with a flourish. Then it waved at her.

"Found you," it told her in throaty voices. She offered nothing but a miserable sob. It gravitated away from the wall and stood in front of her, blocking her way. "Now, die."

She spun around and lunged forward. Suddenly her feet felt light, so light she couldn't feel the floor beneath her. Her stomach bottomed out. Air whooshed up and tugged her hair, and she realized she was falling, gaining speed as the walls rushed by her, her nightgown tangling up around her waist. She couldn't scream; the air pressing against her chest made her scared, too scared to inhale. She twisted midair, her arms flailing to try to slow her fall, her hands grasping at anything to hold on to and finding nothing. She saw the glowing white faceless thing, its hat tipped low, growing smaller as it looked down.

Sally hit the bottom of the concrete shaft hard enough to loosen her teeth when they smashed together. She didn't feel that, nor did she feel her hip or elbow shattering against the tile floor, because the impact broke her back first. She didn't feel her leg twisted up under her like a deer mangled along the side of the highway. She had less than a second's sense of its wrongness, its bulgy poppingness. She bounced once and then landed hard again. This time she didn't feel the jagged tile that broke her neck bury itself straight through from the base of her skull to her throat.

But she thought she heard Dave's borrowed voice giggling high and strained, before the darkness swallowed her.

Oak Hill Assisted Living hunkered low on a wildly sloping, lush lawn, its dull grayness a contrast to the vibrancy of the grass that surrounded it. It wasn't so much that the apartments looked run-down or dirty, per se, but rather that something about the shadowed windows and the unsunned corners gave the viewer the impression of a furtive, almost awkward self-awareness of its own utterly bland appearance. It didn't have the impressive decay of a Danvers State Hospital or the pain-soaked hardness of an Eastern State Penitentiary, but it made Detective Sergeant Steven Corimar feel nettled in a way he couldn't quite explain. Like if the building complex were a person, he thought, it would have a drawn, haunted face, eyes flickering with suppressed anger, fists stuffed in baggy pockets, a lanky body clothed not for style but for function, for protection from judgment it felt coming from everywhere.

Steve had arrived at Oak Hill's side entrance at 8:13 A.M. A uniformed officer named Frank Kimner met him there. They'd been introduced sometime two weeks earlier during his first few days with the Lakehaven Police Department. The man, short and compact, dark-haired and dark-skinned, exuded warm politeness and a kind of confidence that Steve envied. He gave Steve's hand a firm shake and looked him square in the eye. Then Kimner led him through the employee complex and down a short hallway to a Plexiglas wall lined with security systems. He watched Kimner punch in a code that opened the door. They passed through another short hallway to an officer on guard by a steel door.

The officer smiled at him. He looked good, really good. Sunglasses lay folded against the breast pocket. Big, muscular arms lay folded over the broad chest. Buzz-cut dark hair gleamed with gel under the glaring lights. Steve had met this officer early on, too—Ritchie Gurban. Gurban loved being in law enforcement. Most of the men in his family were cops here and in Wexton and had been even out in Thrall before it withered away from the lifeblood of the county. But what made the biggest impression on Steve was the honesty in Ritchie Gurban's eyes and his warm grin. Ritchie took care to remember names, to remember mundane, pass-the-time conversations, and when he talked to someone, he always made eye contact. Steve liked that. He'd thought about what it would be like to grab a few beers after work at the Olde Mill Tavern with Ritchie, but he'd quickly squashed the notion. It was problematic enough that he even entertained thoughts about Ritchie in the first place. He definitely couldn't consider acting on them.

Besides, one afternoon he'd overheard Ritchie in the locker room talking about his girlfriend. He would not have admitted, even to himself, that it was a disappointment to hear, but some of the wind fell out of the day's sails for him.

He'd come to the conclusion that it was probably better that way, Ritchie being straight and all. No questions asked by the department, no complications between him and the other guys at the station. Even going out to the bar with them after shifts sometimes made him feel self-conscious, like every mannerism, every inflection of his words, every subtle context of their conversations was being scrutinized. It seemed like they talked about women and sex a lot. Nothing sacred or secret between brothers in blue, apparently. There were times when he heard them talk about the chicks they were banging or the stuff their wives and girlfriends (and sometimes mistresses) wanted them to try out in bed, and his mind raced for something to say, for the limited knowledge of women from his youth he could draw on should he be called to do so. They didn't ask him too much about his love life (he'd mumbled once that he was happily single and focused on his new job over any new relationships, and they'd left it alone), but Steve couldn't help but feel that they were waiting for him to contribute, that sooner or later one of them would ask if he ever got laid and what was wrong with him that he wasn't willing to give them the details?

Still, Steve couldn't help but return Ritchie's smile and the genuine amiability he found there.

"Hey, Steve. How's it going?"

"Not bad," Steve said. "Hope I didn't miss anything."

Ritchie ran a card key past the sensor, and the steel door opened with a groan. "No way, man. We saved all the good stuff for you, New Guy." He winked, and for just a moment, Steve felt a rush of warmth in his core . . . and then it was gone.

Steve followed Kimner inside. From there they passed into the recreation room and through another key-carded door to the outside. They crossed the quad to a paint-chipped door hanging slightly askew on rusted hinges.

"They found it open like that," Kimner told him in a low voice. "They always keep it locked, so it was sort of a heads-up. Her doctor—Italian guy, Fiorello or Fiorelli or something—is downstairs with the building manager, Henry Pollock."

Kimner pulled out a map of floor plans for the catacombs, frayed almost clear through where the folds lay. The ink that detailed the rough shapes and chambers was faded in places to an ugly brownish-pink.

"We're here," Kimner said, pointing to a spot on one of the bottom corners of the map. "We need to be here." He traced a path almost to the other side of the paper.

"She got pretty far."

Kimner nodded. "In the dark, in the damp, no less. Girl got herself all turned around in here."

Steve followed Kimner, who fell in line behind a few other officers with flashlights who seemed to know where they were going.

"Steve?"

"What?" Steve answered the voice before an eerie recognition sank in. The strange acoustics of the catacombs bounced a voice to him that had sounded an awful lot like his grandfather, rest the man's soul.

" 'What' what?" Kimner called over his shoulder.

"You call me?"

"No."

They traveled on, falling a little behind the officers they were following. Kimner panted a little. Steve guessed it was the hiking over fallen rocks and debris on the tunnel floor. That, and the weird air down there. The air inside the tunnel was thin and cold enough to make his toes chilly inside his boots, but occasionally a warm gust from origins unknown would blow across his face like a hot, wet breath. Otherwise, there was little circulation. Altogether, Steve found he either couldn't fill his lungs up, or the air just sat heavy in his chest when he did. Either way, he was looking forward to being in and out and done with this place.

"Steeeeve . . ."

This time, his cousin Charlie's voice rose from beneath the shrouds of childhood memory. Charlie had been hit by a train when he was nine. He'd been thrown all the way to the trestles behind Steve's aunt's house. Some of him, anyway.

Steve wiped his forehead with his arm and grunted. Very funny acoustics in this place. "You talking to me, Kimner?"

"What? No." Kimner had folded the map and tucked it in his back pocket, but he took it out again, along with a flashlight, when he noticed the growing distance between him and the other officers.

"I heard my name again. I heard it—someone calling me."

"Ain't me. Voices sound funny in here, though. They bounce down corridors, echo, that sort of shit. Maybe someone's talking about you and it's just carrying at all odd angles and shit."

"Yeah," said Steve, not entirely convinced that Kimner wasn't fucking with the new guy. "Yeah, maybe."

The Sussex County CSI team, careful, efficient, and fairly quiet, was nearly done collecting evidence along the hallways of the catacombs when they reached the site, but Eileen Vernon, the state medical examiner, was nowhere to be found.

Steve had met Eileen quite literally by accident. She'd bumped his car with her front bumper in the Lakehaven PD parking lot. He'd liked her right away—the way her gray-black hair frizzed out around her temples, the way she'd adjust her bra right in front of him if it so suited her. She had a flat-*A* Jersey accent that reminded him of a friend's big Italian uncle, both in cadence and just about in pitch. It made most of what she said sound like she was flipping off the subject as unimportant ("Fuggedaboutit, Steve"). He didn't think she was Italian, at least not mostly, but he imagined her with a bunch of cats at home and a saint statue in the front hall and something heavy and rich-smelling cooking on the stove on weekends.

In conversations, she had never asked him straight out

about being gay, nor did she ever mention it as a matter of fact, but he thought she knew. Her flirting was, at times, so direct that it might have appeared to border on sexual harassment were they any other two people with any less intuitive an understanding of each other's motives. But that was just it. He knew women who flirted like they were used to getting what they wanted. And he also knew women who flirted in a fairly harmless way, as if they'd never expect any serious reciprocation, and so felt safe but still giggled and blushed along with the flirting game. Eileen flirted with impunity not only because she didn't expect him to take her seriously, but because she knew somehow that there was no serious stock to be taken in his flirty responses. He thought it meant she knew. But she didn't seem to care. And more importantly still, she wouldn't tell.

"Where's Eileen?" Steve asked another detective, a tall, dark-haired, dark-eyed man named Bennie Mendez. Steve had also met Mendez early on; the position he'd taken over at LPD had belonged to Anita DeMarco, Mendez's girlfriend, before she went on maternity leave. Steve had inherited her desk, files, and all her open cases, as well as a slew of unfiled closed ones.

Mendez handed him a high-power flashlight and pointed to a collapsed area of the floor, which opened down into a shaft that fell to the subbasement. "She's down there with the body."

Steve gave him a nod of thanks, then walked to the edge of the shaft and peered down, shining the light. At the very bottom, some hundred or so feet, Eileen crouched, taking samples in the bright glow of hanging halogen lamps.

Steve craned to look around Eileen to the body. One of its legs twisted up under the hip. Blood stained the floor in a pool around it. A fan of blonde hair covered the face. He'd been told her name was Sally Kohlar and that she had been a resident of the assisted living facility who suffered from both auditory and visual hallucinations.

Steve called out Eileen's name, and she looked up from a pile of jagged tiles and waved. A flashlight of her own was hooked into the belt of her pants. Her rubber gloves shined in places with blood. "Hey, handsome," she called up to him as she stood.

"Hello, beautiful. What do you have for me?"

"Looks like our little lady banged herself up pretty good in the fall. Time of death, I'd place at three to five A.M. It's cold down here, though. May be earlier than that. I'll let you know once I get her back to my place."

"So did she fall? Jump?"

Eileen put one hand on her hip and used the other to shield her eyes from the light. Stepping away from the body, she said, "See, that's the thing. Like I said, I'll have more for ya later. But off the bat? I would've said suicide, except judging by the impact wounds, I don't see how the hell she wrote her note."

"Note?"

Eileen took down one of the halogen lamps and held it near a wall, hooking a free thumb at it. Steve looked in the direction of her finger, and what he saw on the wall flash-burned unease in his gut. He never could swallow suicides as easily as homicides. Catching a killer felt like standing up to the bully and winning, a public service, a balance of order. But suicides left him feeling like an invader. Who was the killer, the bully, in that scenario? And who was he righting a wrong for? It was the note, he thought, that got him—the ghost of words that meant something once to someone who didn't care about them anymore, that lasted longer than the person who wrote them. It always got a little under his skin.

On the wall, in the Kohlar woman's blood, in big, clear block print, someone had written one word: HOLLOW. Steve glanced back at Mendez, but the other detective looked down and away. Then he turned and walked toward some of the crime scene guys, flipping open his notebook and clicking the tip down on his pen.

After a moment of looking between the word and the body, Steve looked at Eileen and said, "She couldn't have written that herself."

"Ooh, brains and brawn. You excite me. Take me." She blew him a kiss, and without missing a beat, continued with, "But yeah, not likely she did it herself."

Eileen stripped off her bloody gloves and disposed of them in an envelope. "It would have been a bitch and a half for someone else to get down here, kill her, write on the wall in her blood, and climb up again, unless he or she had help. Just look over by Rubelli at that mess of cords and shit—that's what they're supposed to use to get me the hell outta here. And if you wanna know my opinion, any equipment that would get a killing type up and down this shaft would have probably attracted the attention of someone somewhere—ground patrol, security guys, what have you. From what I've overheard down here in the hole, no one saw nothing."

"Doesn't even look like there's much room down there for two and a struggle. Not likely someone was down there when she died, right? Sure she died of impact?"

"Pretty sure. And yeah, I think she hit bottom alone. No trace of anyone else here, except this note."

"Okay, thanks, Eileen. Thanks."

She nodded. "No problem, handsome. Stop by later for wine and cheese and lab results. It'll be a hoot." She winked at him in the semideflected glow of his flashlight and then added, "Do me a favor, sugar, and tell them to hoist this old whale up, eh?"

He smiled. "Wonder you can't float right up on your angel wings, beautiful."

She laughed, and he gestured to one of the officers that Eileen was ready. He walked off a ways, checking the route marked off in police tape that the officers thought might have been Sally's last hundred yards or so.

"No trace of anyone else here," Eileen had said. A locked room job . . . so to speak.

"But I am here," voices whispered close to his ear. His aunt, grandfather, Charlie, his old babysitter—a flood of voices that in an instant he both recognized and realized would be impossible. A fast shiver ran across his back. He turned sharply. No one stood close enough behind him to have said it.

Steve gazed around with deliberate, slow attentiveness,

looking for the smirking face, the chuckle stifled behind a hand, and saw nothing.

"And I still am." This time, the voices came like a cold breath on his neck. He jumped, turning again. No one was there.

CHAPTER TWO

Dave groaned when the phone rang, rolled over, and picked it up. He swore that whatever gods guided the hands of drinkers the night before slept on the job when it came to protecting said drinkers from early morning callers.

"Hello?"

"Hello, this is Detective Steve Corimar. I would like to speak to David Kohlar, please."

Dave passed a hand over his face and sighed. Early morning phone calls never meant anything good. And police phone calls usually meant some kind of trouble, either for him or for his sister Sally. "Yeah, this is Dave."

"Mr. Kohlar, we need you to come down to the station, please. It's about your sister."

Dave sat up in bed. The latter, then. "What—what about her? Is she missing?"

"We need you to come down to the station. Please."

"Oh God, is she hurt? What happened?"

"We're sending a police cruiser to pick you up. It should be there in a few minutes."

Also not good news. If they sent someone to get you so you wouldn't have to drive, that was like kicking off a conversation with, "Mr. Kohlar, are you sitting down? You should be sitting down for this."

"Yeah, okay. I'll be ready." Dave got out of bed, tugging jeans over his boxers as he balanced the phone between his ear and shoulder. He held the phone while he pulled a T-shirt down over his head. "Please, just tell me if she's okay."

The pause on the other end sat pregnant with discomfort. "We'll see you soon, Mr. Kohlar."

The policemen who arrived regarded his questioning expression with somber faces. There were two, an older man and a guy who looked a little younger than Dave. They introduced themselves as Jenkins and Pembrey. Neither knew anything about Sally, or else just told him that to shut him up. They spent most of the car ride in silence. Dave felt like a total wreck on the way to the police station. His head pounded, his stomach rumbled with acid, and his hands felt cold and slippery as he clenched nervous fists. It was something wrong this time, something really, really wrong. He cursed the cop for not just telling him over the phone, cursed Oak Hill for letting something horrible happen to Sally. He couldn't bring himself to curse Sally, but he felt angry toward whatever she had done to get herself in whatever trouble she was in.

And of course he cursed himself. The guilt, an ever-present albatross, never let him forget how pretty much everything to do with Sally was his fault one way or another.

He dove out of the car the minute the police pulled into a parking space at the Lakehaven police station and half ran into the building, where he pounced with frantic insistence on the officer at the front desk. She was a stout woman with wild puffs of blonde hair; the name on her uniform read Shirley Columsco.

"I'm Kohlar, Dave Kohlar. You called about my sister. Is she all right? Is she . . . ?"

"Excuse me, Mr. Kohlar. I'll find you a detective."

"Just tell me if she's all right. Please."

Shirley turned around, gave him a sympathetic look, and continued to a door over in the corner of the room.

Dave's thoughts tumbled all over each other, scrabbling for the forefront. The one that came most readily and painfully to the surface was of a little blonde girl lying on the ground, blood in her hair, little chest shuddering. Another thought repeatedly told him that calls about Sally meant trouble; they always had. And although no one ever wanted to tell him over the phone what the problem was, this time felt different. This time felt final. Permanent. This time, he was fairly sure that Sally was—

"Mr. Kohlar?" The detective that came out to see him had a kind face, a good-looking face, and short-cropped light brown hair. From the polo shirt and slacks, Dave could tell he worked out and evidently had better taste in clothing than Dave did. He was, Dave thought with a strange non sequitor twist of bitterness, the kind of guy he'd always pictured Cheryl leaving him for.

"Hello, I'm Detective Corimar. We spoke on the phone."

Dave nodded. "I'm Dave. Will you please tell me what's going on with my sister?"

He could see from Corimar's face that the news wasn't good. "Mr. Kohlar, please, this way." Corimar led Dave through a door and to a chair by a desk.

Dave frowned. "Isn't this . . . Anita DeMarco's desk?"

Corimar offered a warm smile. "Yes, actually. I'm covering her cases while she's on maternity leave. You know her?"

"Yeah, uh, yeah, you could say that. She investigated my sister's disappearance a while back." Dave took the chair offered.

Corimar wrote something down on a legal pad and then looked up at him. The smile was gone. "Mr. Kohlar. I am really very sorry to have to inform you of this."

Tears blurred Dave's vision. The rest of what the detective said and whatever he managed to respond sounded far away, like it was coming through a long tunnel. "There was an accident . . . She's gone, Mr. Kohlar . . ."

"How? . . . What happened?"

". . . She fell in the catacombs, beneath her living facility . . ."

". . . Suicide?"

"We're investigating . . ."

". . . You don't think it was a suicide?"

"We're looking into it . . ."

"Was there a note? Anything?"

"It was a word, Mr. Kohlar. HOLLOW. Does that mean anything to you? Anything significant about that word?"

That last part came clearly through the haze of grief. A word. A single word. An awful fucking string of letters that yes, actually, did mean something to him, but nothing he would ever admit to, not now, out loud to this pretty-boy detective, not even deep beneath the thoughts he could access and turn over in his head, because to think it was to give it a way to find him. And he wouldn't.

"No, nothing." He thought he'd said it out loud, but his lips felt numb, and his head, his hands, his legs in the chair didn't feel entirely there with him in the station.

"Can I get you something? Cup of coffee, maybe?"

Dave shook his head.

"Are you up to this right now? We can always—"

"No, if you've got questions, ask them. I'd rather do this now."

"Understood." The detective scribbled something else on the legal pad. "Mr. Kohlar, did Sally have any problems with anyone? Anyone she didn't like maybe or was afraid of? Anyone who gave her a hard time?"

Dave shook his head. "No, not one. People liked Sally. She was like a kitten. People thought she was helpless. Fragile. She was, I guess. People always wanted to take care of her." Dave had the strangest case of déjà vu, like he'd explained this to police before. He looked at the officer. "Someone killed her?"

"It's too early to say. I'm just trying to get a picture of her life. An idea of what she was like, who came in and out of her daily existence, that sort of thing."

"No one. She had her doctor and me. I don't think she even had a lot of friends at Oak Hill."

"So you aren't aware of any friends she might have had at the assisted living facility?"

Dave cringed a little, perhaps more sensitive than he should have been to undertones of accusation that he wasn't there enough for his sister to be aware of her friends. "No. No one that I've seen her with."

Corimar nodded. "Okay. I think that's it for now. Here's my card. If there's anything else you think of that might be of importance, no matter how small or unrelated it might seem, just give me a ring, okay? Again, I'm very sorry for your loss. Jenkins there will help you with arrangements and forms to sign."

"Thank you." Dave got up on shaky legs and followed Officer Jenkins. The rest of the afternoon blurred by. When he lay down later that afternoon in the dusky gloom of his apartment, he found the detective's business card, crumpled and worn from the sweat of his palm, still in his hand. He tossed it on the floor by the television and sank into exhausted sleep.

Jake Dylan sat on his couch, elbows on his knees and hands dangling between his legs, staring at the baggie of heroin on the coffee table. He suspected that it belonged to his sometimes-friend Scott, who, despite never having done drugs in his life, seemed bent on ruining Jake's sobriety lately. Maybe that sounded paranoid. Sure it did. And he couldn't be sure, of course, couldn't *prove* it, but there was no other explanation. Jake was very nearly sure that he did not buy the heroin himself or bring it into the house, so unless he was going crazy, someone was fucking with him.

He wanted it, though. He didn't much care whose heroin it was. He wanted to get high.

Jake stole a glance at his cell phone, which he'd taken out of his pocket and placed gingerly next to the bag of heroin. He could call Erik, his sponsor. Or he could just pick up the baggie by the ziplocked corner and throw it away. Flush it. Burn it. Snort it. Shoot it up. Get rid of it.

His hand reached for the cell and drew back.

He didn't need this shit. He'd been having some bad nightmares lately that had put him a little on edge—faceless parades of his aunt's boyfriends in fun house distortion, towering over him, smacking him into walls, shoving him into closets, stuffing him down, down into places that light and air couldn't reach. They didn't have faces. Or rather, they had a stream of faces, one bulky body passing from one hateful twist of mouth or blazing eye to another. In the dreams, his brother couldn't (wouldn't) protect him. He could sense Greg just outside the periphery of his dream-vision. There but not there. Aware that he was being hurt in an intellectual sense, but completely devoid of compassion or anger or fear or anything that had compelled him to protect Jake when they had been kids. It hadn't often come to physical confrontations in real life—maybe two that he could remember. But the things they said . . . God, the things they said drove Greg to mouth off with a quick tongue, while they drove Jake to drug-induced apathy.

The heroin on the table looked soft, inviting, not quite pure white but dazzling in his eyes just the same.

When the cell phone rang, he jumped and darted a hand out to grab it with a brief flicker of hope that it might be Greg that winked out, really, before his hand even closed around the phone. The incoming number registered only as "Unknown Name, Unknown Number." He pushed a button and said, "Hello?" His eyes never left the heroin.

There was a crackle of static. "Hello, Jake." The voices that spoke sounded choppy, overlaying each other like the signal came from some long tunnel, maybe, or under some heavily tree-shaded road that wreaked havoc on cell phone reception. *Greg sounded like that the last time I—*

"Who's this?"

"Don't you remember me, Jake?" The voices melded into one.

Jake felt cold across his back. It was his aunt's voice. His dead aunt's voice.

She made a clicking sound with her teeth that Jake loathed. It meant she was disappointed. Or angry. Or frustrated. Or too tense to have him around, messing up the vibes in the air that surrounded her already unsteady calm. "What's the matter with you, boy?"

"Who are you?" he repeated. "Who are you really?"

"You know who I am," she said, but the sound on the other end of the line wavered, and for a moment he heard that other voice, a threaded multi-voice of male and female timbres. The cold spread to his gut.

"Where are you calling from?"

"Look out back." The line went dead.

Jake pushed the hang up button and set the phone down next to the heroin. The sensation in his stomach was like taking a wrong step off a curb or sliding on ice—that slippery freezerburning feeling in the groin, like something awful was about to happen. Something he couldn't stop. Baaaaad high. Like the other times. Like the time he smoked that joint laced with PCP and all the people on the street started melting like wax . . .

He closed his eyes, covering his face with his hands for a moment, trying to settle his stomach and push away thoughts of that . . . whatever it was.

It couldn't have been his aunt on the phone. Maybe it was one of her old boyfriends calling to mess with him. Maybe it was Scott, or one of Scott's friends, whichever idiot left behind the baggie of heroin. He opened his eyes, dropping his hands to his knees.

The baggie on the table was gone.

Jake frowned. He peered under the table, then on the couch around and under him. He slipped off the couch and looked underneath it and underneath the cushions. The baggie was nowhere to be found.

He stood slowly, wary eyes on the empty space where the heroin had been, and crossed through the kitchen on the way to the back door. The kitchen was small, as the rest of the house he rented on Cerver Street was small. The windows boxed out most of the light. Usually he liked it, the cocooning dark. But there was something in it now, something thick and cold and coppery that he couldn't quite place. It felt wrong. Very wrong.

The back door, heavily painted wood that swung on uneasy hinges, groaned as he pulled it open. He squinted into the afternoon sun through the screen door. It took him a minute for his eyes to adjust enough to see the figure that stood at the far end of the yard by the tool-shed. Its head was bent, and the dyed blond hair, darker at the roots, covered some of the face. It wore a dark pink halter and capris that clung to the sizeable thighs. Strappy pink sandals showed off badly painted toenails.

Jake ran a hand through his dark, spiky hair, exhaled slowly, and opened the screen door. His eyes felt dry and heavy in their dark sockets as they kept up a steady stare. As he stepped outside, he pulled a pack of Marlboros and a lighter from his shirt pocket. He tapped one out and lit it, his eyes all the while on the dark roots of the head across the yard from him. The feeling had come back in his stomach, the sensation of falling and being unable to stop it. He sat down with a heavy thunk on the top porch step.

Keep it cool, brother. It's not her. Can't be her. Keep it cool and don't do anything stupid and this whole thing will pass. Even bad highs go away eventually.

But Jake's heart pounded in his ears.

The blond head picked up, and it took everything in Jake's power not to cry out, not to bolt from that step and back into the house. He couldn't do that; to do that would be to admit this was real or that he was crazy, bad-tripping on some kind of stress high or something. It would mean he'd lost control. If he stayed . . . it couldn't be real if he could stare it down, right?

The figure, seeming to sense his recognition, turned its head in his direction. The shriveled mouth, painted over in waxy pink lipstick, worked up a small smile. The eyes glazed over behind cloudy cataracts. The left hand made a fist, and then relaxed it into a little wave.

"Hey there, Jake," his Aunt Naomi said.

He took a long drag and let the smoke seep out of parted lips. His eyes narrowed. He felt the heartbeats in his neck, his wrists. His stomach swung out and away from him. The hand that held the cigarette shook.

"Wanna give your aunt a smoke, Jakey?"

Jake exhaled a stream of smoke but didn't move. The ingrained response to get up and do as he was told was overridden by an underlying fear that once he reached that thing that looked so much like his aunt it would wrap one of those clawlike hands around his wrist and tear both the cigarette and his hand away from him. Stress-trip hallucination or not, he didn't want it touching him.

"No, nothing like that," an alien voice in his head responded to his thoughts. "I won't touch you, Jakey. I won't have to. I can hurt you right from here." His aunt smiled at him, revealing rows of shark teeth.

Jake's fingers tightened around the cigarette, pinching the end of the filter. He tried to stand, found his legs wouldn't support the effort, and fell back onto the porch, scrabbling away from her until his back banged into the bottom of the screen door. Pain thumped across his spine.

"Who are you?" he asked.

"I think you know."

It wasn't her. Couldn't be. But Jake said, "You're dead."

The thing that looked like his aunt laughed; it was her smoke-crusted, throaty chuckle, just like he remembered.

"I'm ageless. I won't die. Come on. You *know*, don't you?"

Jake thought it might be right. He did know. Only the last time he'd seen it, in one of those awful newly sober dreams, it looked sort of like a man, with a man's long black trench and black hat. And it didn't have a face.

After a moment, it said, "You killed her, you know."

Jake felt weak and more than a little sick. He pressed his back against the door, hoping, he supposed, to pass right through it into the safety of his house.

"I didn't. It wasn't my fault. There wasn't anything I could—"

"You left her alone." His aunt took several rapid steps closer, and Jake cried out, his feet pushing uselessly against the porch floor. He dropped the cigarette, his hands smacking down against the wood to hoist himself up. He managed to get up off the floor, and then fell to sharp pain in his wrist. He reached up, grabbed the door handle, and pulled himself to his feet.

The Aunt Naomi–thing stopped when it got to the base of the steps. Its cloudy eyes caught fire, two tiny points of flame that burned out quickly into dark pits of ash. It leaned in with impossible balance, the top half of its body floating parallel to the porch floor, its legs keeping the angle of the stairs while its feet remained firmly planted on the ground at the base of the steps. It made his aunt's body look broken.

It coughed and spat a wad of something black and quivering just in front of his feet. "You should have killed yourself, you selfish brat. You should have died with her, instead of leaving her."

Jake felt tears burning his eyes. His tongue lay heavy in his mouth, too heavy to move. He shook his head emphatically, groaning a little.

Inside, the cell phone rang, and Jake jumped. He

chanced a quick glance over his shoulder. The phone rang again. He turned back to his aunt.

Whatever it had been was gone. Gone.

He'd stared it down. Not real. *Not* real. His lips formed the words, as if that would make them true, but no sound came out.

The phone rang again.

At his feet, the black phlegm dried and fell apart, no more than dirt, like the dirt around the shed. He kicked at it to get it away. His left wrist throbbed, and the palm of that hand burned. He turned it over and found the crushed remains of his cigarette there, gray-black ash around a tiny pit seared into his skin.

The phone rang a third time and kept ringing. He looked out over the yard.

He was alone. With his arm, he dabbed at his cheeks, which felt cold even in the late summer wind, and to his surprise, he wiped away tears.

It hadn't been his fault. He hadn't killed Chloe. He'd never made her do anything she didn't want to do—never.

Except . . .

"I don't know, Jake, I've never done heroin before. I'm scared, Jake. I'm really scared."

The new wave of tears felt hot on his skin.

He *hadn't* killed her. But he couldn't bring himself to mouth those words.

Jake pulled open the screen door and went inside, shaking his hand out as he crossed back through the kitchen to the den. The cell phone sat alone on the table, still ringing. No heroin baggie.

He noticed how pale his hand looked when he reached for the phone.

When he answered, dead air greeted him.

Dorothy "Dorrie" Weatherin knew every hateful inch of her own body. She knew how the inside curves of her thighs rubbed together when she walked and how they billowed out from the hems of her shorts when she sat. She felt the backs of her thighs curve around the edges of chairs, while the fronts of her thighs jiggled with every step she took. She saw how her skin folded on her back when she twisted to look at her view from behind in a mirror. Her hips made almost two curves between her waist and her legs, saddlebags that slid back to an ass like two large marshmallows. The skin under her arms jiggled when she waved. She saw double chins in every picture anyone took of her. Her large breasts drooped on the top of her gut. And her stomach—God, her stomach. When she wore low-rise jeans, she felt it hang over the belt line. When she wore waist-cut pants, it made a pregnant bulge beneath the fabric. When she stood naked, studying the ample curves, pressing into the skin to try to feel some muscle definition underneath, it made her want to cry. She imagined smoothing off the extra pounds as if they were clay and she a sculpture still in the making. She thought of the fat like cheese to be shaved off in layers with a grater. She thought of it like water balloons that she could prick a hole in, letting all the insecurity and extra baggage slowly leak out.

It wasn't just the aesthetic aspect that got to her, either. Her gynecologist and general practitioner both got on her case about her weight as a health issue. She had high blood pressure and high cholesterol. She got winded when she walked up stairs. Sometimes her chest hurt.

So at twenty-six, Dorrie decided it was time for a change. No more "but she has a beautiful face." No more being called "full-figured," "zaftig," "breeder-built," even "big-boned." No more well meaning (she supposed) advice that echoed condescension in her ears. She was tired of being in the "posey" category in women's clothing magazines, indicating a plump, round form. She wanted to be a daffodil. Even a tulip. She wanted to be thin. Fit. Healthy. Strong.

Today was day four of the new diet and exercise plan.

The actual lake in Lakehaven curved into inlets all along the shoreline, and in 1992 a track was paved around one of these inlets, with a quaint gray stone bridge stretching out over the lake itself. Inhabitants who lived close enough to the lake to pay the lake association fees used the track all spring, summer, and fall. They walked dogs and jogged and took romantic strolls. They played volleyball on the sandy shore just off the track. They pushed their babies in strollers and their elderly in wheelchairs. And many, like Dorrie, power walked around the lake.

Dorrie wore a T-shirt and sweat shorts. Self-consciously aware of the thin girls with their long streams of blonde hair tied up in ponytails, their muscles tightly propelling them laps ahead of her, Dorrie swung her arms and pumped her legs and felt her body groggily come to life. Her lungs burned, and her muscles started to hurt right away.

A couple of teenage boys with shaggy hair, dark T-shirts and jeans—bony and awkwardly tall—watched her round the first curve, and she felt her whole insides tighten. Teenage boys usually meant stares and snickers. They meant nasty muttered name-calling that she could just catch as she breezed by. These boys didn't say anything, but she felt heat in her cheeks all the same.

Day four was a bitch.

But once she was a good distance from the boys, she felt her breath loosen in her chest. A light breeze blew across the sweat that beaded on her skin and cooled her, and she had the notion that maybe she really could do it—lose the weight, tone up, slim down. She wanted to be faster. Sleeker. In control of her body as well as her mind. She wanted people to see the Dorrie she wanted to be. It just took time, was all. She'd known plenty of girls who lost a lot of weight right away, just to pack it back on a month or so later. She wanted it gone for good.

Dorrie reached the halfway mark—a metal bike rack at the dirt path entrance to bike trails through the nearby woods. She felt a little better. Only half a mile left to go. She focused her gaze on the road ahead and, taking deeper breaths, plunged a little faster forward.

Later, when she sat curled up under a blanket at home with a mug of hot tea, when she went over what happened in her head, she would think of that road before her, that stretch of path that mattered above all else. Her focus had been on the road. And she'd think that was why she didn't notice something wrong sooner.

She came out of that focus slowly, as she took in the last few landmarks indicating the home stretch—the fallen, twisted tree trunk, the stone park bench with "NIN" spray-painted in black letters. A gray cast of twilight had settled over everything, giving it a kind of pre-storm eeriness that in itself didn't quite unsettle her. But as she rounded the last curve and headed into the last eighth of a mile, Dorrie noticed the people were gone. The track around the lake was very popular; people dotted the path when she got there and remained when she left. However, as she took in the periphery of the path, she saw she was alone. She slowed to a stroll, glancing around her, behind her, trying to peer through the sporadic trees to see someone on the path or shore of the far side of the lake.

No one was there.

She picked up the pace again, suddenly very uncomfortable at the thought of being alone on the path. The woods, full and dark in some places, presented endless possible hiding places for rapists and muggers. The growing shadows threw a sinister quality over rough surfaces of wood and stone. Alone. She was alone and yet . . .

She wasn't. A figure leaned against a tree several hundred feet ahead of her, arms folded over the broad chest, black hat pulled down low over the face. She hadn't noticed him, maybe, because his clothes were so dark and parts of him blended with the pockets of oncoming night that had nestled into the spaces between trees. She frowned, slowing without really being aware of it, reluctant to get closer. Somehow, the figure's presence was worse than when she thought she was alone.

Because something . . . something wasn't right about it.

Dorrie was used to scanning faces, observing body language and expression for signs of derision, pity, even disgust, and she supposed her oversensitivity sometimes made her see those things even when they weren't there. But even from the corners of her eyes, she noticed faces. The head tilted up to her, and that's when it struck her what was wrong. The figure leaning against the tree seemed to have no face at all.

She came to a dead stop. It waved. She glanced behind her, just a quick look, to gauge whether she should turn and run the other way. She'd have to backtrack almost a mile if she did, and she was already tired and covered with a thin, clammy sheen of sweat. It could overtake her, if it tried. She had little doubt of that.

Day four was definitely turning out to be a bitch.

"Dorrie . . . ." The voice reminded her a little bit of wind chimes, many different timbres clinking together. It made goose bumps rise on her arms. The sound came from somewhere around the head, although she was sure now that the figure had no mouth. It was growing dark fast, and for every shade of night, the white head grew brighter. "Dorrie, you're so close . . . so close to the end."

"Who are you? How do you know my name?" Her voice sounded thin and strained in her own ears.

"I'm your new best friend, Dorrie. Where you go, I go. I want every inch of you. Dead. I want every inch of you dead."

Dorrie felt tears form in her eyes. "Please don't hurt me. Just . . . don't hurt me."

The head tilted thoughtfully as it stood straight. "But that's the fun part, Dorrie. And you and I, we're going to have a lot of fun."

It took a step toward her, and Dorrie cried out. She turned to run and tripped over a rock. She fell hard into the packed earth of the path, the impact forcing air from her lungs, her hands slamming painfully onto pebbles and sticks. She gasped for air, tears squeezed from her eyes as she blinked hard. She tried to crawl forward but found she couldn't. She rolled over, heaving breaths, and her eyes grew wide.

It was twilight, not dark, and two young men and a woman stood over her. She recognized them vaguely as other joggers she'd seen on the path before. She peered around their legs to the far tree where the faceless figure had been. It was gone.

She started to cry.

The bewildered joggers looked at each other and then back down at her.

"You okay, miss?" One man reached a hand down to pull her to her feet, and she grabbed it, cringing internally when a second hand reached down to help lift her.

She stood and dusted the dirt off her legs. Her face felt hot. Her breath came back slowly, and pain twinged in her chest.

"You okay?" the jogger repeated. "You, uh, you want us to call someone?"

Dorrie shook her head. "I'm okay. I'm . . . I'm okay. I'm just . . . I'm going home."

She gave the tree where she'd seen the faceless thing

wide berth when she came upon it, wary eyes darting around the area for signs of a black hat, a glowing head. She saw nothing, and as she got in her car, she let go of a long, shuddery breath.

And thought about day five.

CHAPTER THREE

With each ring of the telephone, Dave's chest tightened a little. Maybe she wouldn't be home. Maybe she was working. It was, after all, long past happy hour and well into any barfly's night of drinking, and he knew that nowadays she had a pretty good gig tending bar in California at a nightclub called Constellation. Part of him was glad she wasn't answering the phone. But another part of him, an achy part somewhere under his heart, just beneath where he was willing to admit he could feel, really missed the sound of her voice. The way her hair smelled. The softness of her shoulders. The shape of her mouth when she smiled. The way it felt when he slid into her.

The phone bleated again, and he felt a crick in his chest.

She answered on the seventh ring. Dave switched the receiver to his other ear to wipe the sweat off his palms.

"Hi, Dave. How you holding up?"

Dave shrugged, even though she couldn't see. "Hanging in there. I got your message—you know, returning my call."

"I'm so sorry, Dave, really I am." Her voice on the other end of the phone was so soft, so far away.

"Did . . . did the police tell you how it happened?"

"They told me what they knew."

"What did they say?"

Dave sat down on the sofa. What they'd said was just about too horrible to repeat. What they'd said was unthinkable. What they said without even knowing it was that he'd failed his sister. He'd let her die. That in spite of all his best efforts, in spite of all he'd done—all *they* had done, especially that night at Feinstein's house—it hadn't been enough. Her clock had been stopped for good.

"They said she left her room, wandered across the quad, and . . . you know that white door, the one with the rusty hinges that's always locked? Somehow she got it open and then got lost in the catacombs beneath Oak Hill. She fell through a part of the floor, I think. Broke her neck."

"Oh, Dave. God, I'm sorry," she repeated.

There was more—a word, smeared in her blood, a word that reminded him of a horrible monster in a black trench coat and a black hat. A single word: HOLLOW. But he wasn't going to tell her about that. He'd do something finally worthwhile for her and leave her out of that completely.

"Funeral's tomorrow," he said.

"Wish I could be there."

Dave couldn't tell if she genuinely meant it or if she was just being polite, and an ache in that place just beneath his heart made him close his eyes for a moment. "I wish you could, too, Cheryl." A pause. "I miss you."

Silence from her end of the phone.

"I'm sorry," he said.

"Don't be. I miss you, too, Dave. It's just—"

He knew what it was. His insecurities ignited broody bouts of jealousy. His fears made him quiet, cold, and distant. He'd thought he could be better, that he could shrug off the guys that hit on her constantly at the bar, that he could let her in and talk to her about Sally or about that night at the Feinstein house . . .

"Dave?"

"Sorry. Sorry, I was just . . . I didn't mean to make you uncomfortable."

"You didn't. Look, you know I'm here when you need me. Always. We've . . . been through a lot together. But . . ."

She didn't say it; he wanted to believe she didn't because she wanted to give him hope, but he didn't really dare think that. "*But you and I can't be together. I can't be doing all the reassuring, all the communicating, and all the things that make it a relationship.*" Fact was, whether she said it or not, it didn't change the reality of it—the finality of it.

Instead, she surprised him with, "It's . . . not like before, is it? Sally's death, I mean. It has nothing to do with . . . before, right?" The pleading in her voice, so earnest, so innocently hopeful, made him feel a little queasy.

"*It was a word, Mr. Kohlar. HOLLOW. Does that mean anything to you? Anything significant about that word?*"

"No," he tried, and then cleared the lump from his throat. "No, nothing like that. Just an accident. You know, just . . . bad luck. Bad locks on the door and bad luck all around."

"You sure?"

"Yes."

Although he couldn't see her, he could imagine from the relieved breath on the end of the line that she had worked up a small smile. He was glad for that, glad to set her mind at ease. He couldn't be what she deserved in a boyfriend, but he'd be damned if he couldn't at the very least keep her from reliving the nightmare of seven months prior.

"Cheryl, I should go." A pause. "It was good talking to you."

"You too, Dave. Take care of yourself, okay?" She sounded thoughtful. Sad, maybe. Just a little. Maybe.

"Will do."

"Call if you need me."

Dave stifled a long sigh. "I will. You take care of yourself out there, too, okay?"

"Sure, hon." Whether she'd slipped with the pet name or meant it with mild friendly affection, it still made him feel warm inside.

When she hung up, though, the cool rush of loneliness came back.

The scream from the jail cell jolted Steve from deep concentration. He looked up from the files he'd been studying and looked around the precinct. The busy chatter, the ringing of phones, the interrogation of witnesses continued as if no one had heard a thing. Steve frowned and turned back to his file. It was a missing persons case, a probable suicide by Steve's estimation. Based on the evidence found, the missing person in question, one John Peters, had gotten up and by appearances had gotten ready for work, just as he did every morning. He'd put on a suit, however. One was missing from the closet, and friends remarked at the oddity, as John's job at the warehouse was necessarily casual in dress. John had poured himself a bowl of Cheerios with milk and a cup of coffee, both of which he'd left unfinished on the kitchen table. And then he'd left the house in his red Toyota Celica and had never come back.

They found a patter of blood left on the floor, thinned to the occasional drop out in the hallway, and also a partial print in blood—his—on the wall at the base of the stairs.

Steve had noticed an uncanny parallel between that case and the death of Sally Kohlar. They'd found something on the second floor of the Peters residence. Spelled out with painstaking care on the bedroom carpet at the foot of the bed was part of a word: HOL. The tiny strips and chunks of flesh he'd used to spell it out in large Roman font were already dried and crusted to the carpet fibers.

The scream from downstairs came again, louder this time. It had the quality of someone being hurt, of someone, Steve thought, feeling the slow turn of the knife. He panned the room, looking for verification, looking for another startled face or disrupted phone call or anything. No one in the precinct reacted to it at all.

He rose slowly and headed for the door to the lower level, where the jail cells were. He passed Sharkey's desk, and the detective looked up.

"Told you Mendez's coffee would go right through you, New Guy."

Steve gave him a distracted nod. "Yeah." He continued on to the door, pulled it open, and slipped through. Pulling the door closed behind him cut off the sounds from the precinct. Cinder block walls sloped down to the basement. His feet slapped against the paint-chipped, pale green concrete stairs as he jogged down, the echoes bouncing all around him.

Lakehaven didn't have a high crime rate, and so Lakehaven Police Department's jails were neither as large nor as packed as someplace like Rahway. They remained cool and relatively quiet, and rarely contained anyone wildly crazy or dangerous. The lower level of the police station featured a narrow hallway of the same pale, chipped concrete and five cells lining the left-hand side.

There should have been prisoners in four of the cells: in cell one, a DUI sleeping it off, and cell two, a possession with intent to distribute. Cell three should have held two teenagers busted for boosting GPS systems and satellite radios from cars at the Lakehaven strip mall parking lot, and cell four should have contained a domestic battery.

There should have been prisoners.

But Steve's heart sank to his gut as he passed cell after cell. Every single one was empty. Evidence of their occupants remained, things like baseball hats, a flannel shirt, and a watch. But the drunk, the dealer, the crooks, and the batterer—they were all gone.

He tried rattling the cells and found them all locked. He gave one of the bars a good, sharp tug to see if it would open. It remained planted firmly in place. He peered in between the bars. The gloom inside was thick enough to shadow figures, but not so dark that they could hide. Steve could see without a doubt the cells were empty. On the floor by one of the cots, a shoe lay on its side in a sticky mess of something dark.

Where could they have gone, and how? Could they have been through booking already? Processed and sent on their way? Not likely. Not without their shoes or their watches. The crooks had only been arrested two hours prior, and the DUI had only landed in the cell twenty minutes before Steve had heard the first scream. No, no, something wasn't right, not at all.

"Shit. Shit!" Steve threw up his hands and headed back toward the stairs. He had no idea how to explain this to anyone. Five prisoners utterly vanished from four cells? He'd look like an idiot. Great first impression. LPD Funny Guys 1, New Guy 0.

He got as far as the bottom of the steps when he heard laughing, low, musical, soft, and terribly wrong in ways that made the hair stand up on the back of his neck.

He turned slowly and made his way back, his footsteps thundering with his heart in his ears, his chest tightening as he turned his head to look into each penned-in dark. He expected someone behind one of the sets of bars, someone with crazy eyes, a foaming mouth, maybe, and rotten teeth. Someone who smeared words into walls with blood or stripped flesh off bones to write sinister messages that stank and dried like beef jerky and stuck to the rug. Someone who whispered over shoulders then vanished from a room full of cops.

He found one cell after the other empty. Except cell five.

A figure in a black trench sat with legs tented up on one of the cots. Light from the window slanted in just across the peaks of the knees and the black gloves that rested on them. A black hat, pulled low over the head, obscured the face from view.

A chuckle came from beneath the hat, dripping menace.

Steve clicked the safety off his gun and took a cautious step toward the bars.

"You don't need to do that, Steve," the voice—voices, actually, woven together, male and female—told him. *Just like at Oak Hill, in the catacombs.*

"Who are you? And how the hell did you get in there?"

"I'm here to do horrible things, Steve. Unspeakable things. And I can be anywhere, any time."

"Do I know you?"

"You will."

Steve frowned. "I think you better identify yourself." His hand closed around the grip of the gun.

The legs swung over the side of the cot, and the head tilted up. It had no face. Steve recoiled back a step. "What the fu—What are you?"

Although it had no mouth, he was sure beyond doubt that it smiled.

"I'm your death, waiting to happen."

"Is that a threat?" Steve found he had trouble forming the words.

"I am threat, plain and simple."

50

His gun at the ready in his hand, he tried to peer into the other cells again, hoping, he supposed, that he wasn't alone. Even the company of drunks and disorderlies would provide some anchor to the real world, some reassurance that there had to be an explanation that made sense.

The cells so far as he could see were still empty. "Where are the others?"

"In some other place. Some otherness." It stood, and Steve raised his gun at it.

"What did you do to them? Did you let them go?" He chanced a quick glance at the stairs, hoping someone would assume New Guy was lost and come down looking for him.

"In a manner of speaking." The words seemed over his shoulder, around his head, clearly the will of the thing in the cell, although detached from it. He flinched away from them, his full attention again on the black figure.

"Where are they? For the last time, where are the others who were in these cells?"

"They've run off. Off to tell the world your secrets. Off to tell your police friends all about you. All kinds of interesting little things about you." It laughed.

Steve felt a rush of heat to his face. Sweat broke out under his arms. He tried to level the weapon at the thing in the cell, but the barrel shook slightly.

"You have secrets, don't you? Everyone does." It clapped its gloved hands together in delight, but they made no sound, not even the muffled slap of leather. "Ohhh, I know a lot of secrets about a lot of people. Things they think but don't say. Ways they act when

51

they think blind eyes will be turned. Do you know what Sharkey's friends did for him when he was fifteen? They beat the hell out of a fragile boy named Andy Franco with some sticks they found in the woods. They gave Andy two broken ribs, a black eye, a busted wrist, and a twisted ankle. He needed four stitches across his forehead and a new school when they were done with him. They did it for Sharkey, see, because he told them Andy was a 'faggot.' He never told them Andy liked him. And he never told them it made him feel kind of nice that someone—even Andy—thought so much of him as to write him a love letter."

"Why are you telling me this?" Steve suddenly felt light-headed. He slumped against the wall across from the monstrosity. It took a few steps closer, coming within breathing distance of the bars (if it breathed, and as it stood there, its chest still, its faceless composure sinister in its blankness, Steve got the further sickening notion that it didn't), but it didn't touch anything. It shoved its gloved hands in its pockets and tilted its head thoughtfully.

"You know what your boss says about 'those damn whining liberals and fucking queers' at any given Christmas party after a few rounds of eggnog? About what he thinks of gay marriage and about the time he let those kids go because after all, they were only kids, and all they'd done was 'rough up a queer a little, scare him a bit, no real harm done'?"

"Now look, I—"

"You look." It pointed at its feet, and Steve could see a gun—his gun. He looked down at his own hands and found them empty. "Know this, Steve. I can hurt you from right here, without ever touching you. But see, as you say, there is . . . more than one way to skin a cat. If your friends find out all those little secrets I know about you, I may not have to." It laughed again.

A metal groan ricocheted from the top of the stairs and Steve jumped, his eyes darting in the direction of the sound. Footsteps sounded on the stairs, feet that grew into legs that grew into Sharkey, who smiled, turning his hands palms-up, expecting an answer for Steve's disappearance. "Whatcha doing, New Guy?" Sharkey's eyes slid down to Steve's hands and the smile slipped off his face. "Seriously, Steve, whatcha doing?"

Steve looked down, saw the gun back in his hand, looked back up at cell five, and found it empty. He stalked back across the rows of cells and found them occupied as before—a pair of glassy eyes, two pairs of scared but rebellious ones, an angry glare, and a loud, drunken snore. Bodies, solid, really there, locked behind bars where they belonged.

"Steve? Man, you okay? You don't look so good."

Steve turned a bewildered face to the detective. "I . . . I'm fine . . . sure. Fine." He checked the bars again on one of the cells, rattling them to test their movement. The dealer behind them jumped and sat up, but the bars remained in place.

Steve brushed past Sharkey and the question on his face, went to the men's room, and promptly threw up in the first stall's toilet.

CHAPTER FOUR

On the afternoon of Sally's funeral, the sun was bright and cast a surreal shimmer on the hoods of cars that formed the cemetery procession. It was hotter than usual for June, and heat sank into Dave's black-suited back as he stood next to his friend, Erik McGavin, by the casket. Erik wore a black suit as well and a tie. He'd gained a little bit of weight since Dave had met him, and it looked good on him. The suit fit him. His brown hair, neatly combed away from his face, was bound in a rubber band at his neck, damp behind his ears and at his temples. Erik still wore sneakers. Vaguely, Dave wondered if Erik owned dress shoes and decided he didn't. The suit was probably borrowed, too.

The thoughts took him away from Sally for a moment, and he was grateful. He had almost worked up a smile over the simple fact that Erik came, that he cared. And then the oppressive reality crashed back behind his eyes, making him squint, drawing tears that he mashed away with a fist.

Sally was dead. And he hadn't done a damn thing to stop it. He hadn't protected her. He'd put her away someplace with pleasant-faced doctors who murmured soothing half words and administered medication when necessary but otherwise didn't register Sally's existence as significant. He'd put her away on a neat little shelf with a loose door and a weak floor, and she'd fallen through.

Dave felt his chest tighten. *After everything that happened . . .*

He felt Erik's hand on his shoulder and turned to his friend. There was a mist of sadness in Erik's eyes, and his expression of sympathy as his eyes searched Dave's face suggested understanding, even of Dave's thoughts.

After all they'd done to protect her . . .

Once, Erik had rescued her from the grass blades of a terrible lawn that existed in no place on this good Earth, while Dave scaled a fence to find a means of escape.

Once, Dave had stabbed a monster that had nearly torn his baby sister apart.

Once, Dave had felt Sally was safe, that she was in a place where she could get the help she needed and that nothing—no real or imagined haunters in the dark—could ever hurt her again.

But now she was gone. An idea came unbidden just beneath the surface of his thinking that maybe only *now* was Sally truly safe. He found it offered no comfort, because he didn't believe that death should be the only time a person could be free.

And also because, more insistently, he wondered what happened to the dead when the Hollower got to them. If it never touched bodies, then it stood to reason the meat it was after, so to speak, was something less tangible and more spiritual.

You're not sure about that, he told himself. *And besides, there's no reason to drudge up that old memory now.*

The mourners in the cemetery bowed their heads as the minister stood by the coffin and prayed for Sally's soul. Dave couldn't help but wonder what it was, where it was now. If the monster had left anything of it to go into the Great Beyond.

Don't be silly. You have no proof. No solid evidence at all that a Hollower had anything to do with Sally's death.

And yet, the idea persisted. The cop's words, *"It was a word, Mr. Kohlar. HOLLOW,"* echoed in his head. *"Does that mean anything to you? Anything significant about that word?"*

Once, that word would have made all the difference in the world.

But they'd killed it. They'd killed the Hollower, and there had been no more voices close to the ear, no faceless passersby on the street, no more walking into rooms and hallways that didn't exist anywhere on Earth. He and Erik and Cheryl and Sally and the boy, Sean, and the cop, DeMarco—one night, they'd cornered it in an unimpressive house on an unimpressive suburban street, and it had fought like hell, bending the world around them into unspeakable shapes and nightmarish landscapes. It nearly killed them, but in the end, the six of them had watched it die, its body deflating with a siren wail into the night sky that arced over a place that wasn't really there.

He looked at Sally's coffin, closed now, polished shine catching the sun. The air was thick with the flowers atop it, the kind of flowers you never gave a girl because the scent meant death and funerals and crying and failure.

Dave remembered Max Feinstein's funeral. Overcast day. Sally, her eyes worried and sad. She'd seen the Hollower for the first time that day. And that one time was all it took for the beast to target her. It was Max's videotape, the one he made the day he blew the back of his head off with a shotgun, that had given Dave the only real knowledge, apart from his experience, of what the Hollower was and why it did what it did. And it was Max Feinstein's house where they'd found it waiting for them. Where they'd killed it.

But there had been others.

There. He'd thought it, plain and simple, the true crux of his worry. Yes, they'd killed the Hollower. But there had been others at the end, others that had come out of the rip between their dimension (or world or whatever) and his. Three others. Two had taken the body of their fallen kin. And one—one had gazed without eyes, had sneered without a mouth, had scowled without a face, and Dave had been sure it promised revenge.

"How you holding up?" Erik's question broke through his thoughts. Dave squinted and looked around. Mourners were touching the coffin, tears streaking their faces, before making their way back across the soft ground to the trail of cars that lined the narrow road through the cemetery. His small family milled, talking in low voices.

"Not so good."

Sally's old doctor, Dr. Stevens, came up to shake his

hand and offer his condolences before leading other members of Sally's therapy group back to a dark green minivan. Her new doctor, accompanied by some of her neighbors from Oak Hill, approached him shortly thereafter. Dave felt numb as he shook hands, halfheartedly returned hugs, offered his face for cheek kisses. Crinch, his boss, and Georgia, one of his coworkers, swept him up in their sympathies—Crinch with his gruff shoulder pounding and handshaking and muttered words of strength, Georgia with her candy-sweet perfumed tight embraces and lipstick kisses and offers to be there if he needed anything, anything at all. Erik stood quietly by him through all of it, a background, a rock, an anchor amidst the tides of conversation that were stiff from discomfort and respect and sensitivity.

After a while, they stood relatively alone in the cemetery, aside from the gravediggers, who waited patiently in earth-toned clothes, set apart from the scene, and the funeral parlor men, looking neat and somewhat Mafioso in their crisp suits.

"I guess they want us to go," Dave said, eyeing the gravediggers. Out of respect, he supposed, they wouldn't lower the coffin until he'd gone.

"When you're ready, man. When you're ready."

Dave nodded. Erik stepped forward and touched Sally's coffin. He whispered something Dave couldn't quite catch. Then he stepped away.

Dave gazed down at the polished wood, and it blurred as tears rose in his eyes. "I'm sorry, Sals. I'm so sorry." He felt there ought to have been more to say, something about their childhood, her going off to their parents, something he could take away with him and think about while he was working on some kind of closure.

He found he really didn't have anything else beyond an overwhelming sense of failure. He turned and caught up to Erik.

They were almost to Erik's car when Dave cleared his throat. "I could really use a beer."

"Olde Mill Tavern?"

A familiar ache in his chest made him frown, but he nodded.

They took Erik's car. Cresting the road, Dave felt some of the weight lift just seeing the neon tubes, dark at the moment, which outlined "OLDE MILL TAVERN" against the soft blue of the sky. The building itself, long logwood stacked solid and assuring, promised sanctuary. The door stood slightly open, ostensibly to let in the summer breeze.

Erik pulled into the parking lot and parked the car. As they got out, Erik shook his head. "Been a long time since I've been here. I think the last time was the night DeMarco had her office baby shower. Remember? Last time I saw her."

Dave nodded. "Me, too. Funny, to see her pregnant. Tiny little thing, she is."

"Must be due soon, eh?"

"Any day now, I think."

There was a pause which bordered on uncomfortable. Erik broke it with, "Have you talked to her lately?"

Dave knew that Erik wasn't talking about DeMarco anymore. He meant Cheryl. Dave felt a heaviness pressing into his chest. "No, not really. I mean, she knows, you know, about Sally. I told her. We talked for a little bit, but . . ." He shrugged, pulling open the door to the bar.

The usual Sunday quiet greeted them—a few tinkling glasses, muttered conversation from the regulars, the jukebox playing old familiars like the Rolling Stones' "Wild Horses." The new guy—Cheryl's replacement—wiped down the bar. Behind him, liquor bottles neatly lined a shelf, their different colored liquids glinting in the light. A mirrored Jagermeister plaque above the bottles reflected the front window and the darkened "$1 DRAFTS FRI-DAY!" neon sign. In the corner, Dave remembered, there once had been a Carmen Electra poster. It had since disappeared, replaced by a pretty hot one of Pamela Anderson.

They sat down at the bar.

"I'll have a shot of tequila—Jose Cuervo—and a Killians, please," Dave told the bartender.

"Diet Coke," Erik said with a shrug and an almost apologetic smile.

The bartender, a college frat boy type with muscled, lightly tattooed arms and blue eyes, the kind of guy that girls gave big tips and real phone numbers to, smiled in such a way that Dave thought he probably practiced it and used it to serve a variety of purposes. "Sure thing, boss." He slid the shot glass neatly in front of Dave and poured the tequila in then popped off the top of a Killians and set that in front of Dave, too. "Tab?"

Dave nodded and downed the shot.

Clinking Diet Coke to Killians, Erik said, "A toast to Sally."

"To Sally," Dave echoed and then added "to all the ones we lost, one way or another," and took a swig.

On the jukebox, someone had programmed in "Angie." A Stones fan. A sad Stones fan.

"How are things with Casey?"

"Good. She's good. Busy, planning the wedding and all." He chuckled. "You know how they are, giggling with girlfriends, talking dresses and flowers and music. She basically told me to show up at the church in a black tux, clean and neat and on time, and to leave the rest to her."

Dave smiled. "Sounds like Casey. Glad to hear things are going well."

Casey was Erik's fiancée. They'd been having problems when Dave first met Erik, but things had gotten better, after. After the Hollower was dead. Erik had gotten better. He'd gotten a handle on his coke addiction and had even become a sponsor. Erik didn't talk about this young guy under his wing, not by name and not in detail, but Dave could tell Erik was proud to be able to sponsor the guy and proud of the guy's progress. Keeping him off drugs was intensely important to Erik, and few things made his eyes shine or his mouth settle into firm agreement like the brief mentions of this guy's successes—except maybe when Erik talked about Casey.

"And your sponsee?"

Erik surprised him with a frown. "Funny you mention him. Distracted lately. Won't open up to me."

"Oh. Something serious? Think he's using?" Dave gulped his beer.

Erik shook his head. "I don't think it's like that. It's . . . well, it's . . ." Erik's face flushed. "Actually, it's kind of like . . . ah, nevermind."

"What?"

Erik sighed. Looking away from Dave, he said quietly, "More like before. Like the way I was, nervous, looking over my shoulder, jumping at the slightest touch or noise. Like I was when I was seeing . . . you know. The Jones with the hat."

The Jones, as Erik called it, had been his name for the Hollower, before he'd known what he was up against, back when he, like Dave, thought it was all in his head. Dave shuddered inwardly. Outwardly, though, he shook his head firmly, took another gulp of beer, and said, "Can't be the same thing."

"I know, I know. It seems like such an impossibly long shot. It's just . . ."

"We killed it," Dave said in a low voice.

"I know."

He had told Erik once that he and Cheryl never talked about the Hollower. It was an unspoken belief that to think it, to talk about it, was to put into the air of the real world those vibes or thoughts or whatever psychic scent the Hollowers used to sniff them out. Irrational, maybe, but it had held true so far that not talking about them had coincided with a quiet in which the Hollowers didn't seem able to find them.

"It was a word, Mr. Kohlar . . ."

Dave debated telling him about what they found on the wall beside Sally's body but decided against it.

There had been others. Three others.

Dave finished off his beer.

Close to midnight, they paid the tab, left a tip that was not quite as generous as they would have left for Cheryl, and shuffled out into the night. Dave was "dulled fuzzy," as Cheryl used to say, with warm tequila in his gut and in his head. The breeze blew softly, rustling the trees overhead, cool on his face. It did little to penetrate the alcohol haze, though, which blurred the edges of his vision, giving everything a soft, diffused quality, so much so that it took his brain a moment to register the dark shape on the hood of Erik's car.

"No. No no no." Erik walked faster. Dave jogged to catch up, squinting ahead, trying to pull the black shape into focus. Was it a dead animal, curled up on the hood of the car? A piece of clothing? Why would someone—

It was a hat. Something in his brain turned over and clicked and he saw it clearly—a black fedora hat. And he didn't have to ask whose it was because at that moment, all his arguments and justifications to the contrary seemed flimsy and threadbare.

The two stood in front of the car, Dave slightly swaying in the breeze, gazes fixed on the black hat.

Finally, in a voice almost too soft to even hear himself, Dave said, "We killed it."

Erik didn't look at him, only shook his head and said in that same soft voice, "We killed one. But there were others. And the last one . . ." He didn't finish. He didn't have to.

The last of the Hollowers, before slipping back through the rip between their dimension and this one, had said, "Found you."

Erik reached a tentative hand out to touch the hat, to verify the reality of it, but the breeze suddenly gusted, lifting the hat into the air and shooting it into the street. They watched as it skittered and rolled into the woods on the far side and disappeared in the gloom between the trees.

Between them, in the air around their heads, Dave could have sworn he heard very faint laughter, the sound of its cache of voices. It could have been his imagination, most likely was because, goddammit, they'd *killed* the sonofabitch. But the tequila turned sour in his gut. The breeze had become very, very cold, and he shivered.

They got into the car and closed the doors without speaking. Then Dave opened the door, vomited the burning liquid from his stomach, wiped his mouth on the back of his hand, and closed the door.

"Some guy lost his hat," Erik mumbled. His tone was flat and lacked any real substance. Dave nodded anyway. Neither spoke for the rest of the ride home.

Dorrie's stomach went from mere rumbling to insistent growling and, in the last hour or so after midnight, had graduated to actual pangs. In the ranch she rented on Cerver Street, the kitchen was just three rooms and a hallway away. A quick snack would help settle her, physically and emotionally.

She lay in bed, debating whether she could sleep through the gnawing in her stomach. She thought of her thighs, her abs, her ass. She thought of the bag of

Tostitos on top of the fridge. She could walk the extra half mile to work it off.

But then Dorrie thought of how day four had gone and knew damned well that there would be no extra half mile and so no increased risk of running into . . . whatever the hell she'd run into that day. It had frightened her something awful, that thing leaning against the tree, but not so much because she believed it to be real. Rather, the thing she really feared seemed more tangible, closer to the possible truth than a faceless stranger making death threats.

She'd obviously passed out—hallucinated, maybe, and then passed out. Lack of food, overexertion. Maybe, just maybe, some tumorous thing brought on by bad eats and no physical activity, something newly burst or nearly grown to a grapefruit and pressing on her brain. More than anything, *that* was what she thought had happened. And she was worried. Scared to death, actually. And when she was nervous, she found comfort foods cleared her mind and enabled her to formulate a calm, logical plan of action.

It had looked real, sure. The darkness, the voice, the way it spiraled around her head and got under her clothes and sliced into the meat of her. But it wasn't. Couldn't be.

But she couldn't think rationally with that twisting ache in her gut, that hungry wrenching and the sloshing of stomach acid as she lay there. She was hungry. Day five be damned. She needed something to eat.

Tossing back the covers, she swung her feet onto the

floor and padded through the dark hallway, past the bathroom, through the living room, and into the kitchen. The low hum of the fridge and the occasional crackle of the ice machine on the freezer side gave her comfort. Reminded her, actually, of those nights as a little girl, with the yellow, lined-paper notes from her mom about working late and explaining what to do with the leftovers in the fridge.

"Help yourself to whatever you want to eat, baby," the notes had said. And Dorrie had done just that, alone in the dim light of the kitchen, most nights not even thinking too much about it. But that aching loneliness had been there all the same, chewing at her the way the hunger chewed at her stomach.

Her hand on the handle of the refrigerator, she frowned. She had trouble picturing her mother's face sometimes, except that it was lovely and it always wore makeup. She couldn't remember her father at all; she understood he'd been a mousy kind of guy that people walked all over in personal, social, and professional life, a smallish man with thinning hair and hopeless eyes and a light but rarely used laugh. He'd never stood up to anyone, including the beautiful, powerful, successful woman he'd married.

Instead, he'd simply shut off the TV one night, brought his beer can to the kitchen counter, and walked out the door. He hadn't even taken the car. He'd just walked out and kept on walking, and had never turned around once, not even to eye for one last time the bedroom window where his four-year-old daughter slept.

And Dorrie's mother had watched him go. She didn't

try to stop him or ask where he was going or why he was going out so late. She'd let him go. It might have been the only passive thing she'd ever done. She'd only mentioned it once to Dorrie, and never again.

It was as Dorrie was trying to call up her mother's face in her mind that she heard the giggling in the fridge.

The frown deepened. For a while, the hum of the refrigerator and nothing else filled the kitchen.

Then she heard the giggling again, coming from inside the fridge, followed by, "Dorrie? Dorrie, is that you, baby?" The hunger in her gut turned sour. It was her mother's voice, sharp and clear as it always had been.

"Dorrie, help me. Let me out of here, baby."

Her fingers tingled against the handle where they rested. She could almost feel the cold from inside on her face, her chest. "Mom?"

Until the voice coming from the other side of the refrigerator door answered her, she wasn't sure she'd even spoken out loud.

"Dorrie, open up. Let me out."

She took a deep breath and gave the door a yank.

Inside the fridge were the things she knew she'd bought: a gallon of milk, margarine, a liter of diet soda, a carton of eggs. She saw a jar of pickles she'd bought a few days ago, the ketchup, a jar of grape jelly, and a jar of mayonnaise, all as she remembered. But scattered on both the top and middle shelves were Tupperware containers she had never seen before. Inside them, something dark like raw meat pressed against the semiopaque tops and sides. And Dorrie couldn't be totally sure, but it seemed to her that the meatiness inside was quivering, moving by itself, humming and jiggling as if trying to wiggle itself free of the containers.

"Baby, let me out," her mother's voice said, echoing from the different containers.

Horrified, Dorrie backed away from the fridge. Whatever was inside the containers started to shake violently enough to cause the Tupperware to skitter and jump along the shelves. With a muted snap, one of the tops came loose along one side, and red-black ichor belched outward, followed by a thin bubble that looked to Dorrie like blood, which popped in a fine spray against the mayonnaise jar. The top flapped looser, and the containers picked up the giggling again, working themselves into a feverish high pitch. The other containers bucked and slid across the shelves, their tops straining as the shivering chunks inside pressed against them for escape. Blood—she could smell it now, feral and metallic like steak blood—splattered across the shelves, the carton of milk, and the eggs. The giggling dropped in tone so that strands of bass male laughter tangled with womanly peals. And soft, not scared but hurting, not weak but wounded, her mother's voice pleaded with her from the containers to be let out.

She bit her lip to keep from screaming, to keep the heat behind her eyes from exploding into tears. In one quick gesture, she slammed the refrigerator door, cutting off the laughter and the pleading and the awful bloody containers with their stench of dead meat and their splashing blood.

In the instant the door closed, all sound stopped.

Dorrie sank to the floor, her eyes all the while on her shopping list pinned to the refrigerator door by a Happy Bunny magnet. She listened to the low hum which now seemed to growl from under the fridge. The tile on the floor felt cool when she put her palms down. Dorrie didn't move. Shallow breaths caught in her chest.

She was losing her mind. Had to be. Chopped up remnants of (*God*, she could only guess who) something didn't just appear in refrigerators and hop around and speak with her mother's voice.

Her mother's voice. That was it. She'd call her mom and make sure everything was okay . . .

She rose slowly, keeping a level gaze on her shopping list, and made her way back across the kitchen to the phone.

Her mother answered on the sixth ring. She sounded drowsy but told her she was fine. During the course of conversation, Dorrie could hear muted voices from the fridge—no one she could identify—but voices vaguely familiar and insistent and anxious.

Dorrie hung up with her mom and slowly moved back to the fridge. Her stomach felt heavy and sick now, swinging uneasily with every step. She opened the door. No Tupperware containers at all. No traces of blood whatsoever. No smell of old meat.

No sound. She closed the door.

The voice of the stranger in the woods, the eerie wind chimes voice muffled by the door, said, "Found you, Dorrie."

For a moment, she thought she'd be sick. The world swam in front of her, and she took several deep breaths to pull things back into focus. Then she grabbed one of the kitchen chairs and pushed it up against the refrigerator door. It wasn't much, but it was something.

Dorrie grabbed her car keys, locked her front door on the way out, and drove to an all-night motel.

CHAPTER FIVE

The Primary Hollower had found them.

There had been many lightenings and darkenings of their world while it waited. It hated everything about their place, their noxious dampening of the air with their breaths, their assault of brightness and heat and noise. They used *words*, clumsy sound that fell with endless rapidity from the foul gaps of their heads. And they touched each other, actually pressed limbs to limbs, heads to heads, appendages to appendages.

They were weak and stupid casings unfit to carry the essences of their minds. It hated them. Found them, hated them, wanted them all dead and cracked open and sucked dry and left to wither, their hateful physicality to decay. It longed for the Convergence, the peace and quiet of the soft dark cushion between worlds where words went away—a place that was neither festering with blood and flesh nor barren like its own origin place, its . . . *home*.

The Intended meats had a word for it. Home. It remembered home. A desolate place now, vapid and crumbling, shifting, falling into itself, unfit even for those who straddled worlds by their nature.

It wasn't going home. The emptiness inside it pushed and pulled and stretched, a tumultuous hunger which compelled it to gather the small number of Intended meats to feed on.

It seethed with the rare emotions it had found occasion to feel in connection to perceiving the meats, emotion that alone eclipsed its hunger and made it demanding and specific. They, those loathsome shells in this place of bodies and sensations, called those emotions Hate and Anger. It understood little else of their feelings other than Fear and cared even less, except for what it could use to hurt them.

And it very much wanted to hurt them. Some, it discovered by rather delicious accident. Their Fear was new, born of confusion. But others it had watched and waited for. It remembered them from before.

There had been another, a Secondary, one who had made this dimension its hunting ground and who could abide the prey's physicality for a time and draw out sustenance from them. They called it a Hollower, gave it a word. And they were afraid, for a time. But then they had hurt it by yanking it into their world and making it like them, solid and clunky. The prey had reduced the great hunter to its base self and killed it.

The Likekind perceived its death siren and came for the body, and when they passed through from the Convergence to this dimension, the prey, dirty and triumphant, stood their ground while the Likekind claimed their Secondary. The thought even now made the Primary frost the air with Malice.

As Primary, it had confronted them itself. "Found

you." It formed words, which it took from their own minds, for the first time.

Found you.

They, the prey, the Intended meats it had sought out in this place, gave it back words, too—jumbled, panicky mindsounds that represented Fear, Uncertainty, Anxiety.

It would see them dead, every last one of them. The new ones, too. It would destroy every thread of their existence and see them reduced as its Likekind had been reduced. And it would feed until the voids were filled to bursting.

The idea satisfied it some, soothed it.

"Found you." It stole the female's voice, the one with the containers in the cold oblong.

It sensed another then and left the comfort of the in-between place to stalk its new hunting ground.

Jake found that more and more often lately the insomnia churned up his nights, leaving him tense and uncomfortable and sometimes restlessly horny, glaring at the clock, staring at the ceiling. Often his muscles would tighten, and he'd have to get up and walk around a bit, smoke a cigarette, stretch his legs, swing his arms. And he'd feel the tension behind the outer corners of his eyes, too—not quite a headache or even tightness in his face like wanting to cry, although it would be difficult to say that it wasn't that, either.

The symptoms weren't nearly as bad as when he'd gone through withdrawal—not even close—but they reminded him of those terrible shaking, sweat-soaked, nauseating nights all the same. Sometimes, jerking off to thoughts of the girl across the street relaxed him a little and he could clean up, go back to bed, and close his eyes. He could at least settle into some kind of half sleep. But then he'd dream.

He thought sometimes that maybe the answer lay in getting high again, but deep down, he didn't think a desire to get high was the only reason he couldn't sleep. He suspected it had something to do with the dreams. They were nearly the same, with little variation. In the dreams, he was in an alley with a thin blonde woman. She was fragile, very pale, with delicate, lightly veined hands and a curtain of blonde hair that hung in front of her bowed head. She wore a white dress with pink and orange flowers and she stood with her back to him amidst a scattering of garbage cans and chain link fences topped with razor wire, which seemed to crisscross along the length of the alley without keeping anything specific out or in.

He knew he was high in the dreams, and he'd sort of slump against the brick wall, staring at her back and not thinking too hard about any one thing. And then she'd laugh, the blonde girl. A deep rumbling, almost like thunder, would vibrate in her chest and spill out of her, and strange voices carried on its crest would tumble over each other in cascades of unstable laughter. Jake's high inevitably soured, and the former calm dissipated. He felt slowed down, weak, and vulnerable. It scared him. He'd try to stand up straight, move away from the wall and away from the girl and that hollow laughter echoing in the alleyway, but she'd turn around, and the curtain of yellow hair would fall away.

She never had a face . . .

He'd always wake up sweating, his stomach feeling tight and tortured and his heart painful in his chest.

The dreams had gotten worse since he'd seen that . . . whatever it was that had pretended to be his aunt . . . in the backyard. The alley had taken on a sickening Technicolor-bled aspect, fuzzy and dull and slightly skewed in angle and curve. And nowadays in the dreams, the blonde girl wore a long black trench coat and a Fedora hat tipped down low over the yellow hair. Sometimes, in the laughter he thought he heard words, terrible words like needles all across his skin, urging him to drown himself in a heroin high, urging him to die, die diediedieyoufuckingloserdie. And nothing, not even the subsequently feeble and half-hearted attempts at jerking off, could settle him down after that.

On the third night following the visit from the thing in the backyard pretending to be his aunt, Jake lay in bed, the sheets tangled around his waist. The digital clock on his night table read 3:14 A.M. His hand was still sore from the cigarette burn, and his wrist ached deep in his tendons. But those things were secondary. It was the TV that really bothered him.

Sometime while he slept, it had turned on. There'd been no sudden jolt of volume that woke him up. It was more sinister, more gradual than that. At first, the muffled commentator voices and the dull background noise of the spectators seemed a strange part of his dream, like sports fans watching from beyond the chain link fences surrounding the alley. He couldn't see them, but he could hear them, cheering, calling plays, blowing whistles. It passed vaguely through the dream-induced drug high.

But some back part of his mind broke through to the forefront of the dream, and it took form behind the faceless plane of the blonde's head. When the head picked up, he heard the voices over the laughter tell him, "Wake up, Jakey."

The music wasn't in his head but outside it, outside the bedroom, in the living room.

"Wake up. I'm waiting . . ."

In the dream, Jake shook his head, trying to clear it of the remnants of heroin, and in doing so, he found it—

"Waiting in the other room for you."

—difficult to breathe, and his body twitched in bed. Suddenly, he was awake. The sounds of some kind of sports still came from the living room. Jake looked at the clock. It had been 3:11.

By 3:14, he found that curiosity, mixed with an urgent need to see how the TV came to be on (he was sure he'd shut it off), drove him out of bed. He didn't quite want to believe the nagging certainty of there being someone else in the house, which dusted the crust of his thoughts; still, it was damned near impossible to get out of his head. And whoever that someone was, he or she was watching . . . baseball, it sounded like baseball in the living room.

He crossed the room and paused at the door to the hallway. He lived in a ranch—many of the houses on Cerver Street were built the same way, essentially, with the bedrooms on one end of the house, separated from the kitchen by a long hallway, and, beyond that, the living room. As he stood there, he listened for movement—the creaking of the floor, a soft groan from the couch springs, maybe even the clicking of the remote changing the channels.

He imagined his aunt in her sweat shorts and tank top, sitting on his couch with her bare feet tucked under her, a cloud of Marlboro smoke hovering above her head. He was sure, though, that the skin would be stained dark from her time spent in the ground. Milky film would cover the eyes, whose gaze would be fixed on the ball game. Her fingernails, long and painted, would look like claws.

And he would have bet money that when she turned to look at him, the features of her face would fall away, and she'd rumble deep in her chest and throw back her head to exhale the cigarette smoke and the erratic laughter of a hundred maniac voices would come tumbling out.

He moved into the hallway, taking care not to creak the floorboards himself. On the television, the commentators were discussing Yunel Escobar's RBI, how his season was going, how Pedro Martinez looked on the mound facing off against Escobar, and what Glenn Hubbard had to be thinking at that moment, whatever "that moment" was.

Jake inched around the corner into the living room, and, seeing the figure on the couch, sucked in a breath. A hot, unpleasant weight thudded in his stomach.

It was not his aunt, or anything remotely resembling his aunt. It was his older brother, Greg.

Jake came up from behind and so had a few moments to study the broad shoulders, the sandy blond hair, the barbed wire tattoo that ran around the thick left bicep. Greg wore a football jersey—his own from college, sporting his number across his back. Jake remembered with a twinge of sadness how that number—23—had always been a lucky number. Jake had been born on January 23. The 1987 Mets had scored a grand total of 823 runs, and on May 23 of that year, Greg had taken Jake out for the day to get away from their aunt. They'd gone to a baseball game, and it had been the best afternoon Jake could ever remember—hot dogs and soda and popcorn and baseball caps and cheering for the Mets as they took on the Los Angeles Dodgers. They'd lost, but really, it didn't matter. He'd been with his big brother, doing guy stuff, talking about girls and cars and sports and kick-ass video games like "Street Fighter" and "Double Dragon" and movies they'd seen like *Creepshow II* and *Ernest Goes to Camp*. On his twenty-third birthday, his aunt went to Vegas for the weekend, and he'd had the house to himself. He'd thrown a party that boasted four kegs, three pounds of marijuana, cocaine, heroin, and about fifty-seven people, including him and Greg. And his brother helmed the cleaning up of the mess the morning after, so his aunt would have less to bitch about. The twenty-third day of September 2006, he'd spent in court but had managed a probation and drug counseling in lieu of jail time. Greg sat there in the public section the whole time, grim expression betraying no disappointment or judgment. He'd hugged Jake after, then turned and walked out. It was the last time Jake had seen him.

He'd looked up to his big brother with the fierce, all-encompassing love and admiration that their personalities naturally seemed to allow. Greg was possessed of California looks, school smarts, and popularity that characterized the All-American Jock, and Jake was just young enough to be impressed by Greg's seemingly endless accomplishments, in that sweet and fleeting period before his own string of failures and insecurities both in school and in connecting with others made him the dark and reckless opposite of everything he'd ever been proud of in Greg.

Sitting on the couch in the living room, Greg leaned forward, elbows on his legs and a Corona bottle dangling from his hand between his knees. His attention was focused on the game. Jake followed his gaze. The Mets, hosting the Atlanta Braves, were up at bat at the bottom of the fourth. Atlanta, from the look of it, had been handing them their asses while Jake slept. The score stood at 9-3 Braves, with Buddy Carlyle pitching.

For a moment, it was like old times. Jake forgot the weirdness of Greg's presence in the living room. It felt right to have his brother there, watching the game.

Then his brother looked up at him, face empty, haunted eyes in purplish sockets. Greg didn't smile. For a moment, he seemed to look right through Jake, and Jake felt a pang of loss in his chest.

"Greg?"

His brother didn't answer at first. He turned back to the ball game, took a swig of his beer, and belched lightly. Jake crossed the room and sat in the big easy chair facing the couch. Greg's expression grew dark.

His facial expression never changed, not really, but something did. Something got cold and ugly, distorted under the skin.

He said, "So, I hear you killed her," without looking at Jake, without that somehow hard-to-pinpoint awfulness beneath his face ever changing. Jake felt all the air leak out of his lungs.

"What?"

"Chloe. I hear you killed her."

Jake's mouth dropped open, but there was only traitorous silence, so he closed it again.

"You never really were any good, Jake. Even Aunt Naomi, the old hag, even she knew you weren't ever any good. Just like all those asshole boyfriends she had. Just like Dad." This was followed by a healthy swig of beer.

Jake frowned. His brother never talked like that—not that he had kind things to say about the aunt that he made out to be little more than a necessary annoyance to him, or about any of the men she brought around, but he didn't talk about *him* like that. And their father was dead and therefore off-limits, the kind of sacred and untouchable concept that is reserved for living rooms where only grownups go, and for words and thoughts grown ups used to impress each other.

Jake swallowed hard and it seemed to return some stuttering semblance of speech to him. "I . . . I didn't . . . I s-swear I didn't k-kill her, Greg."

"Did she kill herself? Maybe she knew you weren't any good, either."

"Honest, it wasn't my—it wasn't me. I wouldn't . . . I

didn't—she just overdosed. Greg, ah . . . how'd you get in?"

"Yes, she overdosed, and you showed her how. You left her and you let her die. You might as well have shoved the needle in yourself."

"It's not," Jake pressed, unable and more than a little unwilling to hear what Greg was saying, "you know, not that I don't want you here. I'm glad to see you and all. It's just that I'm pretty sure I locked the door . . ."

Greg ran the free hand over his face, rubbing his eyes as if to wipe off the patina of stupid caused by Jake's presence. Then the hand fell away, and Greg looked up.

The head was pale, way too pale for the neck. Its eyes were rubbed out, the nose worn down to nothing, and smooth, unbroken white skin ran over the space where the mouth should have been.

Instinctively Jake pushed away from it, up and off the chair, away from the couch. "What the fuck!"

It raised an arm and waved a black-gloved hand at him, tilting that awful blank head. Its whole being radiated a cold kind of hate that gave Jake the sensation of sticking his hand in a freezer, pressing warm flesh against the ice crystals until they burned their own special super cold into him. It felt something like that—all over cold, all over hate. Jake shivered.

When it spoke, it had the girl's voice from the dream. "You're going to die, Jake, just like your aunt. Just like Chloe. Just like your brother."

Jake sank a little where he stood. His brother? His brother wasn't dead. Couldn't be . . . could he? The idea of it, even after all these years of estrangement, brought immediate tears to his eyes, hot, then cold beneath the gaze of the thing on the couch.

"Who are you?"

It made a fist. "Jake," it said with the mildest tone of impatience. "I am simply your death. I've come to make you nothing—unloved, unwanted, unremembered. I'll destroy everything you are, everything you might be, from the inside out, and then let you blow away like dust." It opened the fist, and an unfelt breeze carried white powder—heroin—off and away from its glove.

What if it was right about his brother? What if it had gotten to Greg first? His brother, his only family, his only—

His only anything. Besides the drugs.

And it occurred to him that maybe not all the effects of withdrawal were done with him. Suicidal, even homicidal, thoughts, hallucinations, that know-you're-caught sick feeling right in your intestines. Maybe this was some rare but powerful brain hiccup, like acid flashbacks or something.

Jake squeezed his eyes shut. He had never been so scared in his life. He thought briefly, just briefly, of calling Erik.

"You can try that," it said to him in many voices. "But I'll kill him, too. In fact, I will kill him anyway."

"Leave me alone," he whispered to it.

"Wanna get high, Jake?" The voices that responded were so close to his ear that he flinched, his eyes springing open.

It was gone. The TV stood silent and dark. The beer

bottle was gone. Jake searched the room with rabbit snaps of the head.

It took a long time for Jake to get the heat, the sensation back in his legs enough to walk. His hands shook as he lit each cigarette from the smoldering filter of the one before it. It took actual effort to lie down in bed. And the sky was taking on a pink dawn before his eyelids sank closed.

Across town, Dave, whose eyes were bleary and whose head was full of the roar of alcohol waves, flipped through the static channels of the TV and found a clear picture on channel 86 of 63 River Falls Road, just like it had been the night they'd killed the Hollower. He pulled back, shrinking away from the screen and against the cushions of the couch, his gaze riveted to what he was seeing. On the screen, the vast canopy of night had surged up from beyond the trees of Schooley's Mountain and swallowed up the whole neighborhood. Looking up into it as the camera panned up was dizzying, the fathoms of its endless depth rising above, its stars eaten by massive forms that passed like great ships across the sky, defying any real description or categorization. Some of the shapes groaned like old pipes, old houses, old bones. Some growled low from deep inside the core of them. Their gliding over the houses made little other noise, and they seemed, for the most part, oblivious to the little humans on the pseudo-suburban lawn below them.

Dave shuddered, sinking further into the couch. Those humans on the TV screen were him and his friends. He knew those big shapes above wouldn't touch them—they were not meant to be prey for ones so big and so old. He and his friends were, in that warped and dimension-dipped version of River Falls Road, expressly the meats of the Hollower.

On the television, Dave and the others stood on the front lawn, unmoving. The needlelike grass, a chilly tint of green, looked more frost than plant. He watched it wrap around their ankles, cutting into their skin. Blood welled up from the indents and soaked the cuffs of their pants, but no one moved or even acknowledged pain or discomfort. They simply stood there as the shadows of the great beasts floating above passed over them. Dave opened his mouth to speak to them—to speak to the screen version of himself—but no words, no sound came out. He closed it again. In those moments when the shades were cast over his friends, Dave lost sight of them and felt real, true panic, intense and physical. Then the shades would pass and the light, sourceless (as there was no moon above them) but possessing the moonlight quality of pervasiveness and clinical cold, would once again take hold of the scene. The grass no longer holding onto them glinted like shards of glass. The Feinstein house behind them sagged where it stood, and with each pass of shadow, it seemed to rot a little more, exposing framework or insulation like bone and muscle. The strange silver light on the faces of his friends as the camera passed in front of each gave them a gaunt, pale quality, making their cheekbones waxy and underscoring the haunted, grayish pockets beneath their eyes.

Dave was scared for them. He found the alcohol

made his limbs heavy. He couldn't get up and switch off the TV. He couldn't even raise his hand to change the channel. But his mind was getting clearer. He could feel it all—the chilly bite of the grass on his skin, the fear, the guilt, the regrets of that night. He could remember that sureness that he was going to die, that the Hollower was going to tear him up from the inside out. And he remembered the weird ripples of the air, the strangeness that signaled the approach of the beast.

He felt it now, there on the couch, the oncoming weird. It was coming. It was close; and there it was, a *wrongness* in everything. Sean, the boy, had described it as a likelihood of finding dead ends, daylight, or corners of the real world at the far end of the street, and Dave suspected he knew what Sean had meant. It was that influence of the Hollower, the slightly skewed, artificial quality, as if everything they knew belonged to it and not to them.

It had that night, as it seemed to now, on screen. The camera swung toward the trellis by the house between what would have been Sean's and the one next door. Black, pulsing, almost breathing, glistening in the silver light, the plant that snaked through the trellis was a grotesque, choking parasite of a thing. Four houses down from that, a blackened, burned-out stump of a trunk stood where there had been a large tree. Every house on the block, as far as Dave could see, had the same number—68, like Max Feinstein's house—and the scarce few cars parked in the street all had the same license plate. It read, "DieDieDie."

Like that night, there were six of them, watching and

waiting—Dave, Erik, Cheryl, DeMarco, who had been investigating both Sally's disappearance and Cheryl's work intruder, Sean, the little boy from across the street on River Falls Road, and Sally—

No, not Sally. That was the difference. She wasn't there with them now.

A scraping sound like metal skittering over metal filled the earspace around them. They looked up, to the source of the sound, and the camera panned up with them.

The Hollower stood on the roof. This time, though, it looked as it had first appeared to them—a faceless white orb beneath the brim of the fedora hat, a black trench coat and clothes beneath, a black glove raised in a wave.

Except that wasn't exactly right. Its hand was indeed held up, but it made sweeping passes over something in front of it that was just out of their line of view. The gesture was one that Dave had seen before, when the other Hollowers had come through the rip between their dimension and his. They'd made the same movements with gloved hands over the dead body of the Hollower that Dave and his friends had killed.

Silhouetted against a night sky that itself only existed between worlds, the Hollower giggled, high and hysterical, the voices of a hundred fragile minds breaking like glass. It made a dismissive gesture with the glove and, at once, heavy ash-colored bundles rolled off the roof. The thud they made hitting the edge of the driveway was jarring, an impact that Dave, watching from the couch, felt in his head, his jaws, and his feet. There were four bundles, huddled fetal forms that bled out crimson pools that crystallized upon contact with the grass blades. Dave knew with hazy certainty that they were victims, unfortunate folks whose insecurities the Hollower had fed until they'd oozed up and swallowed them. The bundled forms were turned toward Dave, and he could see that although humanoid, they were faceless, sexless, all of them featureless except for the last one. That one had a thin stream of blonde hair, matted pink with blood.

A deafening crack like lightning suddenly tore at the air over the driveway. The on-screen version of him and his friends turned their gazes toward a gaping black wound suspended in the air. It looked to Dave as if the canvas picture of River Falls Road before them had been ripped into with a knife, and from the frayed and displaced edges, gloved fingers curled into view.

Out stepped another Hollower. And another. And another. The first made a long, steady sound like a siren— not the death wail Dave remembered from the dying shell of the monster they'd taken down, but a low, strong, angry sound, a war cry, a cry to battle.

It stepped out of the way, and hundreds of Hollowers poured through the rip, stepping over the bundles, never touching each other and yet somehow seeming to flow around one another, vying for a good position to strike.

Their feet made no sound, but their voices were deafening. Thousands of stolen words and stolen timbres, the voices of family and friends and lovers, all saturated with hate, bombarded him and the other captives with human flaws, weaknesses, and fears until he thought the weight of them would bury him under.

Suddenly, the noises stopped. And Dave was aware of a buzz, a terrifying sense of utter vengeance, a collective thought coming straight through the television: this new one thought of itself as a Primary. And the other, the one they killed, had been a Secondary. And with that same alien invasive thought pattern in his head, radiating from the pictures on the television screen, he understood what that meant to them, the Hollowers. They would hurt him—even physically hurt him, without ever having to touch him. They could bend worlds. They could change things. But the Primaries could get inside you in new ways. The Secondaries were kings between dimensions, the thought pattern suggested, but the Primaries were damned near gods. They were deadly in ways he could only begin to imagine.

As one, they advanced, and Dave heard Cheryl utter a clipped scream off camera. The picture winked out and, within moments, was swallowed by static.

Dave immediately felt pain behind his eyes and an equally oppressive pain in his chest, which was made worse by the pounding of his heart. He clicked the television off with the remote and threw the remote across the room as if it were poisonous. It landed with a thud on the rug, buttons down. Dave wiped his hand on his pants, disgusted.

His head squeezed in on itself a little bit, and his mouth felt sticky and dry, but in spite of what was turning into the beginnings of a mild hangover, Dave's thoughts were very clear. He wasn't drunk anymore. And as if to rush and fill a vacuum, the seriousness of what had just happened, what had been happening for longer than he cared to see, really hit him.

Without the fumes of alcohol to cloud things, he could see a series of events whose import, if not entirely the fact of them, he had chosen to dismiss since Cheryl left. The hat on the hood of Erik's car that night hadn't been the first sign that a Hollower was back in their world. What had come back to him (assuming it had ever really left) was an intense insecurity, intense enough to frighten off Cheryl, to put her off. And there had been the dreams during those long nights when the empty bed made it hard to relax.

When he and Cheryl had been together, it had been easy to forget. But now . . .

"It was a word, Mr. Kohlar. HOLLOW. Does that mean anything to you? Anything significant about that word?"

And there was Erik's sponsee. And the television. And Lord knows who else, seeing what.

He went into the kitchen to the phone. He'd call Erik. It was true; there had been safety in numbers. And if Dave was seeing evidence of a Hollower, it stood to reason that Erik would be seeing it, too.

Plus, he didn't really want to be alone.

"Dave . . ."

He flinched.

The voice had come from upstairs. It sounded like Sally's voice.

"I am not hearing this." Dave ran a hand over his

eyes and wondered if maybe some of the alcohol still sloshed around in his head.

"Davey!" The word slid around the air above him, slipping under and over other sounds, other vague voices that were not hers. He followed the sound to the bottom of the stairs and peered up. Darkness obscured the second floor. No Sally-thing that he could see.

Still, he felt cold all over.

"Davey, help me. It's hurting me."

He took a step up. Another. His feet carried him up. He paused once, glancing down at where he'd been and beyond it to the front door.

He could leave, just get out now and—

"Davey, please."

He could hear crying now, muffled as if into a pillow, coming from the bedroom. His bedroom. It took all his willpower not to run—either to the crying or away from it.

Moving down the hallway, though, the crying got worse. To Dave, it sounded as if whoever was crying was being choked off at the throat by the tears, gurgling in phlegm and salt water, a wet, chunky sound that made his hands feel cold as he clenched and unclenched them. He came within view of the bedroom door threshold. The light was on. He peered in.

There, on the bed, lying face down, was Sally. He recognized the fragile form, the almost clear porcelain of the pale arms, the thin, limp blonde hair the color of yellow crayons.

A tight lump formed in his chest. It felt like a black

hole grew inside him, pulling his lungs, his heart, even his ribs toward it, crushing them.

"Sally." The word came out weak, brittle, and the form on the bed responded to it with a tiny shiver. Dave could still hear the sobbing, but the pillows and blankets, which were tangled haphazardly on the bed, muffled it.

Dave stepped into the room. Hot tears blurred her for a minute, and he blinked them away. "Sally?"

He got up close to the bed and looked down on her. Her arms were wrapped around her head, her legs sprawled out on the comforter. He reached out to her, his hand sinking slowly close to her as if through some thick liquid.

Sally's body suddenly jerked, and a loud crack, like the breaking of a chicken bone, made Dave flinch.

Her hip looked wrong, twisted in a terribly wrong way and separated from her body. Her arm flung out with another awful crack, the bottom half snapping so far the wrong way that her wrist touched the back of her shoulder. The bone that should have fit snugly and comfortably at her elbow protruded from the split skin, and blood so dark it was almost black dripped from the hole off the side of the bed, soaking a small puddle on the rug.

Dave recoiled in horror, squeezing his eyes shut and then opening them, hoping against all he knew and felt that this was some alcohol-induced hallucination, a delirium tremens, maybe, that had finally caught up with him.

She was still there. The other arm flung away from the face, and the fist opened, jetting teeth in a tinkling spray against the far wall of the room. Dave watched as her leg broke and twisted itself up in impossible contortions so that the side of her ankle touched one of her shoulder blades.

Dave thought for a moment he might be sick. He swallowed hard several times, sinking toward the floor.

Sally's neck cracked, and her head pushed up off the bed, off the pillow, until it almost touched her broken foot. Blood stained her hair a dark pink. The hair fell away from her face, but Dave couldn't bring himself to get up off the floor, to look at her.

The broken body that looked something like Sally twitched, and with jerking movements, turned on the bed to face Dave, the head righting itself to look at him, dangling awkwardly on the broken neck. Bloody pits watched him vacantly, any sense of eyes gouged out. Beneath that, a broken nose dribbled blackish blood, and lipless torn-up flesh where the mouth should have been twisted into a sneer.

"You're gonna die, Davey. Just like me. It's going to kill you, too, all of you. It wants you dead, dead, dead. Remember? It's ageless, and it won't die."

Dave tried to speak, but only air passed over dry lips. He swallowed and tried again. "It did die. We killed it."

The torn flesh pulled itself into a frown, and the brow crinkled. "No, Dave. It hurt me. You left me alone and it hurt me. Look what it did to me." It moved the stiff, broken arm with a grinding groan that Dave felt deep in the meat of him. Then it twisted the torn-up flesh of the mouth into a smile. Teeth like metal shavings filed to points glinted in the glow of the bedroom lamp on the night table. "The Secondary wasn't alone. And this one—this one—will see every one of you cracked open. Every one of you broken."

"You're not Sally." It was a lame thing to say, impotent and painfully obvious, but a part of Dave was already shutting down, already unable to swallow everything that was happening. Talking, saying anything, was allowing him to hold on, to focus on conscious functioning. Behind the empty words, behind his eyes, which blurred in and out of focus, his reason and security were crumbling.

Can't be, can't be, we killed it. We killed that one and the others left and we were done. We were safe. We were supposed to be free and this can't be, it couldn't have found us, it can't hurt us because we were supposed to be okay—

"You're not okay," the Sally-thing said, reading his thoughts. All the color bled from its face, and the blood of the wounds where the facial features should have been faded as well. The face itself, as if it were made of hot wax, melted off the head, dribbling in pale corpse-gray rivers down the neck and staining the nightgown with a kind of sallow stain. Dave turned his head away.

"Found you."

The horror of the words, the memories it brought back of that night at Feinstein's house, made him turn back to the figure on the bed.

It sat upright, restored and straightened out on the tangled covers, looking so much like the other Hollower that every nerve in Dave's body sang with fear. The black fedora hat, the long black trench coat, the black clothes beneath, devoid of marking or distinction, the black gloves, the black shoes that, although appearing to be planted firmly on the carpet, never actually touched any part of this world. And the bald white orb of the head, luminous, smooth and unbroken by anything even remotely resembling a face.

It leaned forward on its knees. "Found you."

Then it exploded in a cloud of dust and ash. Dave squinted, shielded his face from the spray, but the light snow of gray never touched him. He opened his eyes and surveyed the room.

The Hollower—this new Hollower—was gone.

Dave looked around the room. Everything seemed okay, except . . .

The hole. There was a hole in the wall, tilted slightly down, as if sinking into the depths of the house itself. He rose slowly, falling once on shaky legs, and crossed the room. Peering deep into the hole, he saw an endless darkness that reminded him vaguely of the night sky over Feinstein's house. And as he watched, there was a low rumbling. He had just enough time to throw up his arm to shield his face before a spray of pain knocked him on his back in the center of the room. When he looked down, he saw shards of the broken wall embedded in his arm. He looked up at the hole, and it was gone. The wall stood perfectly smooth. But there was a word there, carved into the drywall. And where the cuts in the wall appeared, a black ooze coagulated in the crevice.

DIE

Then that faded, too. Dave shut his eyes, sinking onto the carpet with the shards of wall still in his arm, possessed of a horrible idea. This one was different. It was stronger. It didn't have to touch him to hurt him, and . . . it knew tricks the other didn't. It knew different ways to use his own world against him. And it very much meant to see them all dead, perhaps with a drive and an ability even the other Hollower, in all its terrible power, didn't have.

Tomorrow he'd call Erik. But tonight, he was tired. Too tired. He fell asleep where he lay and didn't—couldn't—move a limb until morning.

CHAPTER SIX

It was downtime between shifts, and Shirley was out getting the morning guys' coffee. Sitting there at his desk, the light dawn casting shadow in the relatively quiet headquarters, Steve frowned over the files on his desk.

He would have thought, based on what he'd seen in the jails downstairs a few days ago, that the stress of being promoted to detective sergeant and the morbid strangeness of his most recent homicide case were affecting him mentally and emotionally, affecting his judgment. Maybe he wasn't cut out to be a police officer. Maybe he didn't have the intestinal fortitude for it. Maybe there was something unbalanced in his brain, something that ran in the family (*"Your father's right . . ."*) that made him prone to seeing things, to hearing things. Maybe (*"Boys . . . people like you, they can't be cops. It isn't right, son. They'd never accept . . ."*) his parents were right. Maybe guys like him (*"Son, if they found out . . ."*) really weren't cut out for police work.

That under-part of his thoughts was bullshit. He knew it—intellectually and in his heart, he knew it. Maybe thirty years ago, when his uncle worked for the

Bloomwood County Prosecutor's Office, maybe then people would have thought that his being gay would make him a bad police officer. Hell, maybe some people might think it now. But even at four years old Steve had been tottering after his speeding Tonka trucks, wearing his uncle's police hat, giving tickets to his teddy bears, and having shoot-outs behind the big easy chair, long before anything about sexuality mattered. Letting closed-minded homophobes hinder him from doing a job he thought he could do and do well just didn't seem like an option.

Especially if no one had to know. He was a cop before he was . . . anything else.

But his being stress-crazy . . . maybe that was bull-shit, too. Maybe. Sure it was. The files proved it. He'd found them shoved at the bottom of one of Detective DeMarco's desk drawers.

When he'd gotten to one labeled "Feinstein, Maxwell—Suicide," Bennie Mendez had swooped down out of nowhere, it seemed, and snatched the file out of his hand.

"Anita never was good about the filing," Mendez had said in an almost apologetic tone, and, not seeming to know what else to say—or maybe, afraid Steve would ask questions—he turned on his heel and walked back to his desk. Steve had seen that he locked the file in his own bottom desk drawer and pocketed the key, glancing up once to offer Steve what he seemed to hope was a nonchalant grin.

Steve didn't ask questions. He was new, but he was aware that some things were strictly need-to-know police matters. You had to earn your way into the information, if you ever got to have it at all.

But the other files, the ones that had been rubber-banded with the Feinstein file, Steve still had. Some instinct dictated that just for shits and giggles he ought to leave them be in the bottom drawer until Mendez and his partner, that Italian guy, left for the day. But now there was a lull, and no one was around, so he pulled them out to look at them.

The first was a homicide, a woman named Debbie Henshaw from Plainfield, who'd been killed up in Lake Hopatcong, house-sitting at her sister's place. She had been stabbed repeatedly in the chest and stomach, and most of the skin of her face had been removed. Someone had gouged out her eyes and filled the sockets with the ashes of burnt paper. She'd been a pretty young girl, freckled and blonde and small-boned.

The mess in the pictures barely looked human.

A neighbor had found her with half of her white blouse torn off. Someone carved a word into the pale skin beneath her breasts. Very much like the case of the missing guy and the strips of skin that spelled out HOL. And exactly like the Kohlar case, with the word HOLLOW written in blood . . . .

Good God. The hairs on the back of his neck stood up.

He flipped open another file. A woman named Savannah Carrington had been found dead on her back patio with several shards of glass in her neck, arms, torso, and legs. The impossible odd angles of some of the shards indicated a homicide rather than a suicide.

People didn't stab themselves in the back, down to the spinal cord. The report indicated the police searched both her front yard and back yard and the neighboring properties to either side but found nothing significant other than a cracked (but unbroken) glass table from one of the neighbors' patios. Yet there were huge pieces of glass in her face, chest, back, and abdomen. Glass glittered all over the lawn, glass glinted up from the bottom of the in-ground swimming pool. The photo in the file showed her slumped against the sliding glass door, her nightgown splattered with blood. Sticky puddles of blood—not quite foot- or handprints, but vaguely and eerily reminiscent of them—formed a haphazard halo around her. The door against which her bloody cheek was pressed was intact; smeared in blood on the large pane of glass above her head were two words.

"My face." It wasn't exactly the same kind of message as the others, but . . .

But wait. Something . . .

Steve frowned, spreading the photos of Carrington, Henshaw, Kohlar, and Peters. The photo of Peters' bedroom showed a mirror in the corner of the picture, just a sliver of it, reflecting the bed and a black fedora on it. Steve scanned the report again, but there was no mention of a hat on the bed or anywhere else in the room. He squinted at the picture of Carrington's back yard. Again, reflected in the glass of the sliding glass door, a blackish shape very much like a hat sat on the grass a few feet away from the body. And again, Steve searched the report for a mention of it in the scene and found nothing.

He let out a long, slow breath, and with the emptying of his lungs, there rushed in a horrible realization, a connection staggering in its implication.

The thing in the jail cell downstairs, that freakish faceless figure that had threatened him and stolen his gun, had worn a hat. A black fedora. Like in the pictures.

He closed the files slowly and looked up and around the office with a kind of new awareness and the half-formed idea that maybe he'd get caught.

Caught? Doing what, going over old cold cases? What's wrong with that? Nothing. Nothing at all.

But it felt wrong. It felt to Steve like the information contained in those files was a secret meant only for the cops from Lakehaven, the cops born and bred there.

Which was stupid. He was a part of the police force at Lakehaven. If he discovered something that might break a case, something like, say, a black fedora, then wasn't it his obligation to investigate?

And what are you going to tell them? the little voice in his head asked accusingly. *Gonna tell them that the boogeyman in the black hat made all your bad guys disappear from their jail cells, just so he could tease you about being gay? Gonna take that right to the chief, are you? How about telling him that after it threatened to see you dead, it just disappeared from a secure jail cell itself?*

Steve slid the files under a stack of papers on his desk, feeling a little sick. Just beneath the surface of fully formulated thoughts, he was only vaguely aware that it couldn't be work-stress hallucination if there really was a connection to these other cases. Not unless they all suffered from the same mental twitch.

It obviously hadn't worked out well for them. But Steve didn't think too hard about what that meant for him.

Shirley poked her head into the station room then and said, "Steve, hon? Someone here wants to report something. Intruder. I'm going to send her back to you. Cool?"

"Sure."

A minute or two after that, a woman came through the doors, clutching a purse. She had a smooth, soft face with large eyes and a pretty bow of a mouth, and she hovered just to the left of being a bit more than full-figured. Steve supposed she struck him so because of the way she moved—a practiced, almost stiff kind of gait that didn't bend too far in either direction, that was carefully reigned in to avoid jiggle. It reminded him so much of a girl he'd known in college, one who'd explained why she sat a certain way, or posed a certain way for pictures, how the tilt of a head could minimize the look of multiple chins and a turn of the hips deemphasize their wideness. That discomfort, that lack of freedom of movement, this woman possessed in every step.

Carefully, she sat down on the chair on the other side of Steve's desk.

"Hello, ma'am. My name is Detective Corimar. What can I do for you this morning?"

Her eyes swept the room before she settled on his face. "Well, I . . . I wanted to . . . okay, well my name is Dorothy Weatherin. Dorrie. And I . . . I guess I wanted to . . ." She stopped.

"Ms. Weatherin? Is everything okay?"

Her expression struck him as odd—soft, like her face, but running a series of thoughts. Finally she said, "I think it wants to hurt me."

"Who? Who wants to hurt you?"

"I don't know what it is. It isn't anyone I know. In fact, I'm not sure it's a person. I mean, it told me it wanted to kill me at the lake. And it kind of seemed like a person then. And then last night, in my fridge—" She studied his face for a minute, and her expression seemed to fall off her face. She looked utterly deflated. "Oh for chrissakes, I sound like a lunatic. I knew this wouldn't do any good."

"Ma'am, maybe you should start at the beginning. I'm a little confused. Now you say someone threatened you?"

"I don't know if it's someone or something. I see it sometimes. I hear it. It's cruel, and it knows about me."

"So . . . someone is stalking you?"

"I don't think—I don't know." She looked flustered, confused.

"But you're sure it wants to hurt you?"

She seemed to mistake his tone (and perhaps the expression on his face that his slow-dawning recognition formed) as doubt, maybe even derision. She got up. "I'm sorry for wasting your time. It—it was a mistake to come here. I'm sorry. Sorry."

"Wait, Ms. Weatherin," Steve said, rising. "If someone's trying to hurt you, you did the right thing in coming here, but I can't help you if you won't talk to me. Please—"

"You can't help me anyway," she said softly, and she moved with a quick grace across the room. He began to follow her.

"I can if you'll just wait a minute and explain this to me. What did this person look like? Can you describe height? Weight? Distinguishing features?"

At this she stopped without turning around and laughed. "Well," she said, and her voice sounded hysterically on the verge of tears. "It sounded like my mother."

And with that, she was out the door, leaving Steve dumbfounded in the middle of a just about empty station room, wondering what the hell her scant descriptions meant exactly. On the heels of that morning's file contents and his own unsettling experiences downstairs, he didn't like the sound of any of it.

When Erik saw Jake later that morning at the rec center, he was struck by how tired his sponsee looked. Bone tired, exhausted to the marrow. Erik remembered those days. He'd had many mornings where his whole body ached, even his scalp and fingertips, where his skin hurt to touch.

He'd wanted so badly to get high back then that the ache wore him out.

And that was before the Hollower . . .

Erik used to call it the Jones in a hat. He'd been convinced that seeing it was a bad trip, some weird side effect of his newfound sobriety. But then Cheryl had seen it, and Dave, and Sean and Max and DeMarco . . .

He worried about Jake. It had crossed his mind more

than once that if Hollowers could sense one's insecurities, one's fears about oneself, all the skewed perceptions and screwed up ways of thinking, then people like Jake (and people like him) were easy targets. Sitting ducks, really, bundled in jittery nerves and cluttered minds and weakened bodies.

But they'd killed it, like Dave said, and that was it. Out of sight, out of mind.

If he asked . . . if Jake mentioned a faceless figure in a black hat and coat . . .

He wouldn't. Couldn't. The chances had to be like getting hit with lightning. Of all the billions of fucked-up people in the world, there was no reason at all to think a Hollower would target the same fucked-up guy twice, or even any poor fool associated with him by common bond of sworn sobriety. It wouldn't get Jake through him. Couldn't. Erik was better. And Jake . . . well, he was getting there. Getting there slowly but surely.

Nevertheless, Erik frowned as Jake shuffled up to him with the last inch or so of a cigarette dangling between his fingers. He handed Jake a cup of straight black coffee, steaming hot and faintly metallic from overbrewing, in one of the cheap foam cups they had downstairs for refreshments. Jake took it gratefully and sipped at it through dry lips.

"You okay, J?" Erik asked him. "Everything going okay at home?"

Jake smiled, and the shadow of truth flickered in his eyes before he lied. "Sure, man. Everything's cool. Just not . . . sleeping well lately."

"Anything you want to talk about?"

Jake shook his head, looking down into his coffee. He dropped the butt of the smoke onto the ground and crushed it with small, thoughtful crescents beneath the toe of his boot. "Just bad dreams. Nothing. Nothing worth the effort."

Erik nodded, deciding not to press the issue. "Well, you know if you want someone to talk to . . ." As an afterthought he added on impulse, "Whatever you've got going on, I know I'd understand. I've been through a lot myself, J. Really, really strange shit."

The last part got a reaction, albeit subtle, from his sponsee. He raised an eyebrow at Erik and seemed about to ask something or say something, but then closed his mouth and offered a weak attempt at a grin. "Strange shit. Yeah."

Erik felt the beginnings of dread in his gut, lead-lining him and making him feel heavy, even poisoned. Jake knew. Something—something more was going on than Jake was telling him. And he hoped to God that whatever weird shit it was, it wasn't the Hollower.

Instead of asking, he said, "Part of recovery, man. The good, the bad, the strange, the dark, and the downright dirty, right?"

Jake seemed to let go of whatever guard had been up—just a little—and said, "Yeah, no kidding. It's been a long, strange trip every step of the way. Thanks for the coffee."

And with an uncomfortable side-step, he bypassed Erik and went inside for the meeting.

Erik kept an eye on him that morning, though,

through the prayer and the announcements and the accounts from veterans of the drug addiction wars. Jake seemed fidgety, distracted, unwilling to share.

At one point, he noticed a strange look on Jake's face. His sponsee had fixed a gaze on the door that was part confusion, part horror, and not a little bit of guilt. Jake glanced once back at Erik and the others in the rec hall and got up, making his way past crossed legs and folding chairs down the aisle to the doorway. Then he disappeared out into the hallway. With a nod from Terry, who was leading the meeting that morning, Erik got up and followed him.

Jake was nowhere in the hallway, nor was he in the men's room at its far end. He wasn't in any of the open adjacent rooms either. Erik made his way outside to see if maybe his sponsee had gone out for a smoke. No sign of Jake out there, either. He was about to turn around and go back in when he heard the crying.

Erik's heart sank. He knew the sound of the stuff inside a person, the stuff that keeps the person together and sane, breaking. He knew that kind of crying.

He followed the sound around the side of the building. In the narrow space between the rec center and the alley behind it, he found Jake crouched on the ground, hugging his knees and bawling. When he saw Erik, he toppled over, but quickly wiped his eyes and nose dry. Still, though, both were red.

Erik sat down on the ground in front of him. "Want to talk about it now?"

Jake shook his head, dazed. "I didn't do it, man. I didn't."

"I believe you," Erik said, not sure what Jake was talking about. "Tell me your side of it."

When Jake answered, his monotone was soft, almost soothing, except for the things it said. "I didn't kill her. It wasn't my fault. I just . . . I just left her. I went out that night without her, to get out, away from her. We were fighting about some girl that meant nothing. I needed time to think, to figure out how to make her understand. And she took the heroin and the pills and the booze. She shouldn't have taken it all at once. But I didn't put the needle in her arm. She only ever did it to keep up with me, but I never, never made her do it. Never even asked her to do it. I don't think. I don't remember. But I didn't kill her. She killed herself." The words came out on the crests of each wave of breaths, clumps of words at once that were hard to understand, nearly pulled under by the intensity in his voice and the tears in his eyes.

Erik knew a little about the girl he was talking about, an old girlfriend who Jake never mentioned without a dark flicker in his eyes. Carefully, so as not to break the thin strands of communication between them, Erik said, "You're right. Everyone needs to take responsibility for his or her own actions. You didn't kill anyone."

Jake finally looked at him. He looked haunted, red-eyed, his cheeks and the pale forehead sweating. "I saw her," he whispered.

The sinking feeling in Erik's chest and gut turned painful. "Who?"

"Chloe. I saw her, man. I followed her out here. I—" He stood up with a sudden, unstable jerk. "I've gotta go. I've got to—"

"Jake, wait. I—"

Jake held up a hand. "Sorry, but . . . I can't do this right now. I can't. I need . . . air, need fresh air and a walk and . . ." Whatever else he said was lost to a series of mumbles beneath his bowed head. He hurried away from Erik and fairly broke into a run once he hit the street. Erik watched until he was out of sight. Then he turned back to the alley. Beyond where he and Jake had been sitting, it continued and then veered to the right, around the back of the building. Erik concentrated on the space there, on the very air itself, searching it, waiting to see something materialize.

He saw nothing. He crept back there, every sense drawn tight and ready to spring if the bastard Jones in a hat made its appearance. But there was no upset of the world as he knew it, no turning the corner on some vivid scene of his past put before him to hurt him. There was nothing but the alley, the building, the cool air, the sound of the occasional passing car, and his own footsteps.

Whatever Jake had seen was gone now.

Erik got to the mouth of the alley, just about at the front of the building, when he heard the laughter, a twisted intertwined sound of many mocking voices. He spun around.

No one was there. The laughter faded, carried off on the cool breeze.

It took Dorrie most of the rest of the day to feel comfortable enough to go back to the house. By mid-afternoon, she grudgingly accepted the fact that she couldn't stay in the hotel room forever and that if she wasn't going to ask for help from the police, that she'd have to go back to her own place.

Besides, a nasty little voice in her head told her, *if you're crazy, that's going to follow you everywhere. You could just as easily see blood streaming out of the hotel shower head or open the minibar and see the severed head of the boy you had a crush on in the sixth grade telling you you're a fat-assed bitch who could just jump in front of a train and end it all, except you'd probably derail the train with all that blubber . . .*

The mean voice, and the sheer disgusted horror with which she now looked at the hotel room's plain black minibar by the television, made her want to cry again. Made her feel sick.

You cry a lot, the little voice said. *Big girls don't cry.*

"Fuck you," she whispered to the little voice and wiped away the wetness in her eyes.

It had a point, though. First in that crying wasn't going to solve anything. Second, if there was really something wrong with her, changing location wasn't going to help. If she were really sick in the head with a tumor, a brain lesion, whatever, then it wasn't the police she should have gone to that morning. She saw that now, that her choice to speak to the detective had been a last ditch effort to convince herself that it was really something external that was after her and not something in her head. But the responsible thing, the healthy thing (yeah, the sane thing) to do would be to go home, call a doctor, and schedule an appointment.

The house was quiet when she got back. No giggling coming from the kitchen—a good sign. She dropped her keys on the table by the front door and went into the kitchen anyway. The refrigerator stood closed and quiet. She spent several seconds just watching it, screwing up her courage to approach it and open the door.

She took the plunge and crossed the kitchen, grabbing the door handle and yanking it open.

All the contents were as they should be, as they had been before those containers jumped all over the place. There was no trace of any blood. She exhaled her relief and closed the door. Then she walked through each room, inspecting it, searching for any anomaly, even the slightest difference from the night before. Completing her inspection of the house, she went back to the front door and outside to the small front porch. Little sat out there besides a couple of chairs, a small table, a set of wind chimes that hung from a plant hook at the corner where the porch's roof met the end pillar, and a flower box that hung over the railing.

She'd call the doctor when she went back inside. A few more minutes to herself, believing that everything could be okay—that was all she needed.

A nice breeze picked up, lifting her hair as she stood there, leaning over the railing. It caught up the scent of the flowers and whirled them up to her face. It rustled the tops of the trees across the street. It blew low and soft through the suburban valley of Cerver Street. It was otherwise quiet. No people outside, watering or mowing or taking their afternoon constitutionals around the block.

She'd call the doctor, a general practitioner, she supposed, and tell him what she'd been seeing—what happened at the lake and what happened in her kitchen.

She'd explain about her exercise program and her diet. Maybe, yes, maybe that was it. Maybe she was working out in such a way as to cause some stressful side effect. Maybe she was dieting right out of her system some necessary food that kept her rational and calm. Maybe those diet pills . . . ooh, yes. The diet pills. Maybe there had been some chemical reaction she didn't know about, and those pills had given her some bad side effect. There were options, choices. She'd feel better, stronger, and more in control with a plan.

Unless . . . it wasn't her head that made up the figure without a face to hurt her. What if it was its own entity, using her mind to do the work for it?

Don't be silly, the nasty voice told her.

She looked at a house across the street and a few down from hers. There was a FOR SALE sign on it that had been there for months. Dorrie didn't talk to too many of her neighbors, but she knew that the house used to belong to a bartender, a nice girl. A very pretty girl, with a nice enough looking boyfriend (or, reasonably, Dorrie assumed he was her boyfriend, as he'd come to see her sometimes and stay the night). Dorrie had envied her, even knowing so little about her or her life. Girls like that, she had always thought, had everything. Looks, a nice body, a nice personality, and, therefore, a life she imagined was full of friends and dinners and parties and boyfriends.

More than the social aspects, though, Dorrie envied the confidence. The way the bartender moved, the way she held herself, the way she carried herself. All the rest could come in time, to anyone, she thought, if a person had the confidence to laugh easily, to move gracefully, to thrive in one's own skin. Girls like that didn't drive themselves nuts with hallucinations of monsters that thwarted every attempt to shed the weight that buried over her self-confidence.

Dorrie sighed, and then shivered, noticing the wind picking up. It made her skin tingle in little goose bumps all up and down her arms. It rustled the trees now so that they sounded like whispers of words. It tore a bit at the flowers in the flower box. By instinct, Dorrie looked up to the wind chimes, expecting to have to untangle them . . .

. . . and found them perfectly still. The wind blew all around them, but they didn't move at all. They made no sound. They seemed completely apart from the rest of the neighborhood, *like Colorforms or that transfer stuff you used to have to rub off with a plastic stick onto the background* . . .

She shook her head. Those were disjointed, weird record-skipping childhood thoughts. They didn't feel like her thoughts at all. And the wind chimes . . . well, maybe there was a current that was skittering around them, missing them. She reached a hand up and felt the cold air of the wind on the back of it. Her fingers trailed against the sides of the metal tubes and they dangled a bit where they hung and then stopped, hanging pin-straight as if another hand, invisible, had reached up next to Dorrie's to still them.

She drew her hand back and frowned.

Then she heard her name.

Only a tree-whisper at first. She wasn't sure she'd

heard it correctly, but then it came again, louder and clearer.

It was coming from across the street.

She turned and followed the direction of it, and there the figure stood. Her heart felt cold in her chest, each beat an icy stab.

It raised a gloved hand and waved at her, tilting its head as if watching her.

As if considering how to kill her.

The breath stuck in Dorrie's throat.

It took a few steps forward and began crossing the street. When it reached the middle of the road, it said, "I brought you some flowers, Dorrie."

Her brow furrowed in confusion. Flowers? She didn't see—

Then she realized and looked down at the flowers in the box below where she was leaning. The petals sparkled in the afternoon light, jagged shards of glass arranged on glass pipettes. They suddenly grew upward, shooting toward her fingers. She jumped, crying out, and tried to pull her hands away, but she wasn't fast enough. The petals sank into the flesh of her hands like thorns. The leaves curled around her wrists and cut into them. She screamed, shaking her hands until they were a blur in front of her. And when she stopped, she noticed the flowers were as they always had been in the box, not glass but organic petal and stem. Heavy breaths wracked her whole body. She looked down at her hands, turning them palms up. A dozen tiny cuts crisscrossed each palm, the thin lines of blood already coagulating. She watched them heal up and leave tiny white scars, which, within a few minutes, faded, too. The pain, however, still throbbed in her hands as if the wounds were still there, and Dorrie was gripped with the terrifying notion that the pain was the very intent, that the faceless figure in the street had specifically given her a preview of what it could do, what it would do. It didn't have to touch her, but it could hurt her. It could drive her crazy. It could make her head believe the whole rest of her was in pain. Maybe mortally wounded. Even dying.

It would kill her, when it was done toying with her.

She looked up. It was gone. This time she didn't cry.

Dorrie didn't call the doctor, either. She didn't need to.

CHAPTER SEVEN

"Wanna talk about it?" Casey asked Erik. The sun was going down, and Erik had come home from work early in a strange and pensive mood, one he figured Casey knew by instinct meant he needed her just to be there with him, close to him, real and solidly and safely there beside him, without question or comment. They lay on the bed, her arm and one of her long legs flung over him as if to protect him, the rising and falling of her chest pressing against his arm, her breath coming in soft tickles on his neck. However, one of the understandings they'd come to over the last few months of reconciliation was that sooner or later, Casey would need some indication of his mood's source, the seriousness of it, and the level of her participation in it. As his partner, she explained, she needed to know if it was something she should share the burden of worrying about, too. And if it was something that she was causing, she needed to know what steps to take to fix that. She'd give him space to brood if he needed it, so long as he gave her some gauge by which to involve herself or back away, in good conscience.

"Not really."

She made a little huffing noise that came out as warm air on his neck.

He considered it for a moment, and then said, "It's just my sponsee."

"Is he using again?"

"No." He rolled over to face her. "Do you remember, you know, back when things weren't going so well? Remember what I told you, about, well, what I was seeing at the time?"

The smallest trace of pain flashed in her eyes. "I remember."

"Well, I told you it wasn't just me, that other people could see it, too."

"You said that it looked like a man without a face, something like that? That it was . . . stalking you. Haunting you." Her voice came tight through her lips, controlled and careful. He'd asked her to believe something wild and impossible sounding during a time when she probably had wanted to simply forget he ever existed. But she'd risen to the occasion; she'd at least given him the benefit of the doubt that *he* believed he was seeing something, and that he believed others could see it, too. She'd never asked him what happened that night he spent with Dave and the others, and he'd never told her. She'd just taken him to the hospital to get his wounds looked at (she hadn't asked about those, either), and all she'd said about the whole thing on the way there was, "I hope that whatever happened last night means that this is over. I want us to start over, only better than last time."

He'd nodded slowly and, squeezing her knee as she drove, he told her, "It's done. No more, baby. I promise."

After that, no more on the subject came up. From time to time, though, he'd catch her giving Dave or Cheryl or even DeMarco a funny look, not quite jealousy over something shared that she was in no way a part of, but . . . a little like that. A little mistrust, maybe, too, of their common craziness that she couldn't—wouldn't—share.

Now she reminded him, almost too soft to hear, "You promised it was done."

"It is, for me," he said in an apologetic whisper. "But not for him. He sees it, too. I'm almost sure of it."

She turned over so that her back was to his chest and snuggled up against him. He slid an arm over her waist.

"I love you, Case."

She stroked the arm that was draped over her. "I love you, too. But you know that talk like this reminds me of the bad times. Scares me. I can't go through that again."

"I know. And I wouldn't expect you to."

"I almost lost you."

"I know."

She sighed. "So what did you tell him?"

Behind her head, Erik frowned. "Nothing."

She turned back to him, a surprised and not altogether approving look on her face. "What do you mean, nothing? Are you sure he's seeing this . . . this . . ."

"Hollower," Erik said.

She made a face like she was swallowing a bad taste. "This Hollower, you're sure he's seeing it?"

"Pretty close to absolutely." He tried to look unaffected, but it wouldn't stick.

"Then why would you leave him alone?"

"Huh?"

Casey shook her head. "Erik, I've always dreaded this topic ever coming up again. I hoped that . . . that night, whatever happened . . . I hoped you were done, even though from that very night on, there's always been a part of me that's been scared that you were going to slide back to that place, that dark place. And that the next time, I'd lose you forever. But, if it's really like you say, and this guy is where you were, and you . . . if you're in a position to help him—" Her eyes filled up with tears. "I don't know if he has family, a girlfriend or a wife, but I wouldn't wish those times we had on any couple. Erik, if you can help this guy . . . get past whatever it is you saw, then why wouldn't you? You told me that it was safer in numbers. You're his sponsor. How could you leave him alone?"

It was a good question, a noble one, and he had a whole bunch of answers to it, not a single one nearly as noble. He subscribed to Dave's and Cheryl's idea that to acknowledge the presence of the Hollower, to talk about it, think about it, remember it too much, would be to send up a red flare pinpointing his location and all the tasty insecurity it could eat. He also thought, as Dave had once, that the responsibility of having brought Jake into contact with the Hollower was too much a burden to accept. Sobriety, even now, was a struggle. A simpler struggle than it had been, maybe, but additional stresses made the rock you kicked in front of you more of a boulder you needed to roll up hill. And in spite of all the progress he'd made inside and out, that fear that the boulder would roll right back down on top of him and crush him never quite left him. He remembered the night he'd helped kill the first one, and the fight had nearly crippled him. When he'd talked to Dave on the phone, his friend had referred to this new Hollower as a Primary, that watcher from the rip, a higher breed of cruelty. The distasteful idea of fighting another one—a stronger one, according to Dave—made his entire body and soul groan inwardly. And if all that could be avoided by pretending nothing was going on . . .

. . . except he couldn't. Thus, the pensive mood, the worry about Jake, the nagging supposition that he should call Dave and give him a heads-up. What kind of a man was he that he could do to his own sponsee exactly what he'd convinced Dave and the others would mean sure death? He had, in a manner of speaking, Jake's life in his hands every time Jake was faced with temptation and called him, every time the resolve weakened and Jake needed a pep talk. The wrong word could send Jake back to using. And although Erik wasn't sure if he'd ever feel good enough or strong enough to speak to Jake without that fear hanging over his head, he still thought he'd done a passable job of keeping Jake straight, keeping him alive. Leaving him to fend off the Hollower on his own, though . . .

Erik stumbled through a long, uncomfortable silence before he swallowed the lump in his throat. "Because I'm scared," he answered finally. "Scared of going back to that dark place, too. Scared of dragging you down with me, or leaving you behind. Scared that even if I reach out to Jake, I won't be able to help him. I don't want to make it worse. I'm supposed to keep the guy off drugs, not off the radar."

She shook her head. "You don't believe that. I can hear it in your voice."

Erik settled back down on the bed and stared up at the ceiling. "I don't know what to do."

"Call him."

"And say what?"

"Whatever that guy Dave, who called you, said to you."

Erik thought about Dave and that phone call all those months back. *"I need to talk to you about the Hollower . . . I think you're right. About it being safer with all of us together, I mean."* It had been Erik's idea to fight together. Safety in numbers. No dividing and conquering on his watch.

"You really think I should call him?"

"I don't think you should let him handle this alone. No one," she said in that same tight voice, "should have to go through things like that alone." She put her head back down on his chest.

"And what about you, baby?" He reached out and stroked her hair.

"What about me?"

Erik didn't answer. He wasn't sure how to word what he wanted to ask. He needed to know if she'd bear with him, if he got involved. The truth was Erik was already thinking of how to kill the Hollower, where to find it, and whether Casey would still be there when and if he came back from another mysterious night out with Dave, bruised and cut and beat to hell.

That instinct for knowing him, he supposed, prompted her to say, "Do what you have to do. I love you. If this puts it to rest once and for all, forever and ever and ever

Amen, then do it. See him through this. But you come back to me, Erik McGavin, when this is finished. Don't come back until it's finished, because after it's done, I never want to talk about it again. I want you back. Do you understand?"

He did. He kissed the top of her head and murmured an acknowledgment.

This time, they'd finish it.

Over the course of his shift, Steve had gotten the idea in his head that Ms. Dorothy Weatherin had seen something very similar to what Ms. Duffy, Ms. Carrington, Ms. Henshaw, and Mr. Peters had seen. Something maybe exactly like what he'd seen in the cell. The idea took root and germinated. But it wasn't until he'd accidentally come across another missing persons file in doing a computer search that the idea became an imperative need to confirm.

Sally Kohlar, the dead woman from the assisted living place, had been missing for some time. There was a connection to Ms. Duffy, who, Steve discovered on his lunch hour, had moved to California. Evidently, Sally Kohlar's brother had dated Ms. Duffy for a time. But more interesting still, Ms. Kohlar had been a friend of Max Feinstein, the suicide whose file Mendez had snatched from him. That in and of itself wouldn't have really raised an eyebrow, as both Feinstein and Kohlar were in group therapy sessions together, except that when Kohlar went missing, Detective DeMarco had gone to the hospital to talk to a Mrs. Saltzman, a supposed witness. DeMarco had scribbled notes about a doctor all in black, who made it snow in the hallway of the hospital right before Kohlar disappeared. Real wacko stuff, most of it making no sense. But there had been a note appended to that, a Post-It afterthought, really, which read, "See Feinstein file—tape."

The Feinstein file. And there was mention of a tape, maybe a videotape?

Steve thought of the crime scene photos, of the black hat.

He needed that file. So he approached Bennie Mendez at the close of the shift.

"Mendez, I need to see the Feinstein file." Steve, standing next to Mendez's desk and trying to find a way to stand that was both casual and assertive, just came out and said it, and it sounded neither casual nor assertive to him. But after the visit from Dorothy Weatherin, kicking around the things she'd said, the little things, and looking over the files, Steve had to know. If he sounded desperate, fuck it. Any possibility that what he'd seen in the basement was some hiccup in nature, maybe an anomaly of some sort, or a hallucinatory effect of some shared bacterial infection or even some kind of mass hypnotic hysteria—if it was possible that the Feinstein file tied all the pieces together, including Ms. Weatherin's aborted attempt to explain her situation, Steve wanted to know.

He needed to know.

Mendez continued to ignore him, his back bent over some phone list. He was making little checks and cross-throughs next to various numbers on the list.

"Come on, man. It's important."

"Why?" Mendez didn't look up.

"Because," Steve said, thinking fast, "I know that De-Marco saw something. And I want to know how she put it in the file."

"You don't know jack shit about DeMarco."

But he had Mendez's attention now. The detective put down his pen and looked up at him.

"I know she made some important notes, pertaining to a videotape—"

"It's gone. Disappeared from evidence three months ago."

"Other notes, then, about what was on it," Steve persisted.

"Nothing you need to worry about, Corimar."

"Then there's no reason you can't give me Feinstein's file, right?"

"You're a pushy bastard, you know that?" Mendez turned around again, and Steve took the chair next to Mendez's desk. "You got no business poking around through that shit. We're behind with things as it is. We don't need no Columbo bullshit."

"Look, I may be new, but I'm not stupid. I'm not wasting time. I need to know how you guys handle the weird stuff. And not just for shits and giggles." He left it at that; let Mendez think whatever he wanted. Steve wasn't backing down.

"What do you mean, weird stuff?" Mendez finally closed the file he was working on. His eyes darkened for a moment, but the stubborn set of his mouth never faltered.

"I mean like, something you couldn't explain. Something you couldn't sign off on the line and file neatly in a folder and stamp 'Case Closed' because it just didn't tie up like that."

"Whaaat, you mean, like, a Kolchak kind of thing?"

Steve nodded slowly, vaguely aware of the reference, which was, if he recalled, a hell of a lot closer to what he meant than he'd intended to suggest. "I guess so. I mean, in the course of police business, things that you . . . maybe . . ."

"Reword for the report."

Steve couldn't tell anything from Mendez's expression, but from the tone, he clearly understood. Mendez sighed and leaned in with a conspiratorial glance around the room. To Steve, he said in a low voice, "Under any other circumstances, I'd tell you to go screw yourself. But you hit a nerve, either by happy accident on your part, or because—and I sure as hell hope this isn't the case—you've got a real reason for asking. And around here, sometimes that isn't out of the realm of possibility. So since I think I know where you're going with this, I'll tell you a story. You hear me out, and if you're still not convinced to give up on this useless shit, I'll give you the damn file, okay?"

Steve nodded. They did a subtle glance around the room. Shirley was up front, out of earshot. Some of the guys were in the locker room, a couple in the break room, and the rest out on patrol. The mostly quiet station afforded them some privacy.

Satisfied that no one else could listen in, Mendez continued. "Years ago, I was on patrol out in Wexton, filling in for a guy I knew whose kid's christening was that afternoon. I got a call to respond to a disturbance on one of the back roads that led out toward Serling Lake. You familiar with that area, up there?"

Steve shook his head.

Mendez frowned, that shade coming back into his eyes for a moment, then continued. "Apparently, from the report of one of the few folks who lives out on that road, an older man, kind of dirty and disheveled, was wandering the road, screaming out a girl's name and waving a gun. According to the report, he'd even fired the gun a few times into the woods. So, I and another officer, Jenkins—he got me the job over here, eventually—roll down this road, going slow, keeping an eye out for the man in question, and we find him sitting on the side of the road, crying, the gun right there next to his feet.

"So Jenks and I stop the car and get out real slow, guns drawn but down, and approach the man. He's a wreck; crazy gray hair sticking up all over, dirt worked into his skin. I remember he had his arms wrapped over his head. He was all bent over, crying into his knees. And his hands . . ." Mendez shook his head. "The old man's hands were shaking something awful. There was dirt beneath the fingernails, but there was something else. Raw meat, man. He had raw meat all over his fingers, like he'd just squished them all through hamburger patties. I don't know why it should have struck us as so . . ." Mendez seemed to search for the right word. ". . . unsettling. But it was. Unsettling. Very much. That's the thing we kept coming back to, in spite of every lunatic thing he said after—the raw meat on his hands, like it backed up every word he said. Like every word of it was true. Or at the very least, that he believed it so wholeheartedly to be the truth.

"He sat there just bawling, his hands shaking, his whole fucking body shaking, and he kept saying something we couldn't make out. So Jenks and I exchanged looks. We were thinking, likely the man's just distraught, maybe not even clinical crazy, just at the end of his rope. Didn't mean he wouldn't be dangerous, though, so we were careful. But I crouched down, all easy and slow, and I said, 'Sir? Excuse me sir, I—sir, my name is Officer Mendez, and Officer Jenkins here and I would like to help, if we could. Please—please, if you could tell us—'

"And he picked up his head, Steve, and the look in his eyes, Jesus. It was such a lost look, such a *haunted* look, like he'd lost everything that ever mattered. Which, according to what he told us, he had.

"He rambled a lot, so it was hard to catch everything. A lot of talk about wacky things, mostly. But we gathered that he'd been raising his granddaughter after the death of his son and daughter-in-law, and with his wife gone, the little girl was all he had. The night before, she'd run off into the fog, into the woods. He lost sight of her the minute she'd left the yard, and he'd been searching for her for hours, screaming her name until he'd gone hoarse. It was the first solid, real world kind of thing he said, so we jumped on this, helping him stand, explaining to him that we would bring him to the Wexton station to file a missing persons report. With kids, every minute of those first couple of days is absolutely critical, you know, so we didn't want to waste any more time. I assured him I'd recommend the case went to Avery in Special Victims, because Avery had probably the highest recovery rate in the county. And this guy sort of nodded at me, looking miserable, all hope gone from his eyes. He looked down at his hands, turning them over as if seeing the raw meat for the first time, and he said—I'll never forget this—he said to me, 'Officer, I'm afraid that when you find her, it won't really be her anymore. I don't know if the thing that ran off was her, even then.'

"So I asked him what he meant by that, and, Steve, he laid this crazy trip down on us again, about how the woods and the lake were packed with monsters that ate people. He talked about a whole town being cursed and people being poisoned. He said even the fog—he called it something else, and explained to us that it reminded him of a shredded stomach lining—that even the fog had secrets, and that those secrets had gotten into his little girl and eaten her from the inside out and made her a monster, too. He said that was what the raw meat was for, because 'they, the secrets inside her' liked it."

Mendez leaned back in his chair, the conspiratorial air between them not quite broken. From the look on his face, he seemed to need space between him and the memory to detach, to distance himself. "Jenks told me later that afternoon, when we'd gone back out on patrol, that once, in a grief-driven raving moment, he'd heard a scientist from around the same parts rant about alien creatures as big as whole places, and a language between them and other beings between worlds that was written only in three-dimensional symbols, that the 'letters' themselves actually had three dimensions, and their sound was something like the wind and everything it blows through. And I asked him then, like you asked me now, what went into the report if it ever turned out that these crazies knew what they were talking about. And he said that almost anything crazy could be made to sound sane, depending on how you spin it. It was all about spin. Nothing wrong with quoting lunatic rants verbatim, if it was all just a rant. But if there was ever any truth to it, you went with the spin, John-Hancocked the bottom, and closed the case."

Mendez searched Steve's face, shook his head, muttered something in Spanish, and then said, "Let it go. You don't have to spin or sign nothing if you don't take those old cases on."

"Did that old man ever find his little granddaughter?"

"No. Avery told me the search ran dead cold when they found out where the little girl disappeared. There are towns up past Wexton, almost off the Jersey map, where these things happen. Places where they say streets bleed and people disappear going down the block and the woods swallow up children and sometimes, just every once in a blue moon, you see something that maybe backs that shit up and you swear . . ."

Mendez shook his head, lost for a moment in another time and place. Then he said, "Places where even the cavalry won't come charging to the police's rescue. Places where you spin it, sign it, and close it, because if you don't, things have a funny way of getting worse, of devouring more people, their bodies and their obsessions, and the only thing that gives a guy peace at night is to accept the collateral damage, cut your losses, and go to bed knowing you won't lose any more. Avery tried, but that little girl was gone, and after the third bunch of search party cops disappeared, along with three of their best dogs, there wasn't nobody gonna find her up there, or hell, even help him look."

Steve took the information in. He'd grown up southeast of the area and although he'd heard a few stories, he had no idea as to the magnitude of them. He didn't press Mendez further about those. It was one case, one file he wanted. The one weird that he did need answers to.

He nodded at Mendez's desk drawer, the bottom one where he'd put Feinstein's file. "That what DeMarco did, spin it, sign it, and close it?"

Mendez followed his gaze to the drawer and returned a stiff smile and a tight nod to Steve. "That's what I told her to do when she asked me, too. I'm not saying DeMarco made all that up, or that she's crazy. She's pregnant, emotional, and hormonal, and she's damned good with a gun, so I'll tell you the truth. I wasn't about to argue. Still, she had that same look on her face that you have now. It's always been a sticking point, not that those people claimed what they did, but that she believes it entirely. But Lakehaven's had a couple of cases like that. Call it the fresh New Jersey air, call it something in the water. She told me about those cases you've been poking into on your off time, about what people thought they saw. And even if there's truth to what she believes, at best you're messing with people's fragile states here, and you'll do more harm than good by connecting the dots. Take my advice—don't expect to be a hero, upholding justice by bringing in a long-lost perp. Those cases, and whatever connects them, don't work that way."

"I know," Steve admitted truthfully. "I know that. I have more . . . personal reasons." Truth for truth, Steve supposed. Mendez had gone out on a limb telling him as much as he had. "I'm not in a position to let this go."

Mendez looked at him, seeming to accept this explanation. "Yeah, well, that maybe makes it worse."

"Mendez—"

The other officer held up a hand. "You can have the file, but I'm not going to tell DeMarco. She's got enough going on with the baby. I won't put her through more stress for nothing. And if you find whatever it is you're looking for," Mendez said, "and it hasn't found her yet, I won't give it any fucking reason to do so." He reached into the desk drawer and handed Steve the Feinstein file. Then he turned back to his work.

Steve got from his tone that the conversation was over, case, as they said, closed.

"And Steve," the other officer added over his shoulder as Steve made his way back to his own desk, "if you take it upon yourself to bring that mess down on her head, I'll make it miserable for you here. Threat, promise, I'll hold to it."

It found one at the airport.

That was the word the Intended meat used. It meant a place where great conveyances carried the meats from one place to another over a great distance. An airport was a hunting ground teeming with meats, their insecu-rities and fears and skewed perceptions screaming in glorious cacophony all around it. The airport was, per-haps, simultaneously the richest and most revolting spec-tacle it had ever seen.

However, it wasn't there for culling from an abun-dance of meats. An Intended, one called Cheryl, had flown in to see the others. It had been following that one for a while, although it had not given her any great thought, separated as she was in many ways from the one called Dave, separated from the herd that might have provided distraction, if not safety. Alone, it could get her at its leisure.

But she was startled—something inside that it could vaguely recognize as a sense or instinct, something which prompted her to find the one called Dave.

It would not have that.

She had thoughtprints—the meats called them "mem-ories," another *word*—and in them it found the images it wanted. She entered the chamber where the meats coordinated the flying of the conveyances and moved on and off them. With each step further into the cham-ber, the overhead buzz of sound and words slowed and deepened, grinding to a bass halt.

It perceived her rapid gait slow down, her small oblong ("suitcase," her mind read) containing outer skins rolling to a stop behind her. She looked up, frowning, and it reg-istered a sick and sinking feeling from her as she realized all the other meats in the airport were gone. Cups of cof-fee remained on tables. Suitcases lay strewn about the waiting area. The big boxes that showed them electronic

pictures of "tragedy" all over their dimensionworld flickered with static and then went out. The digital red numbers and letters (components, it had discovered, of the
things called words) that listed the arrivals and departures
of the airplanes—those it made into one repetitive scroll-
ing command, for her to DIE DIE DIE DIE DIE DIE.

It laid an outer skin (in her thoughtprint it was called a
"bathing suit"), still dripping with water, over the counter
of one of the desks, which it now made to look like a bar
counter at the place where she worked. It also dug up another image, a concept it found delightfully grotesque—
tiny hard-bodied, dead-shell versions of child-meats, with
unstaring eyes and unmoving chests. It understood that
these dead-shells, completely devoid of any sense of self
whatsoever, were given to other more vibrant child-
meats to play with. The word they used for the dead-
shells was "doll."

The doll meant to Cheryl what it perceived as Guilt
and Terror and Shame, and so it had propped the doll
up on the bar, next to the bathing suit. Then it pulled
back out of her view and waited.

When she saw the doll, the awful jelly orbs of her
face grew large and wet, and the wetness moistened her
cheeks in little streams. She left the suitcase and ran.

It bent up the foundations of the building, smearing
the outside beyond the doors so that there was only
blackness with stars behind the one she opened and a
horrible screaming and wailing behind another, which
deterred her from even trying it. She skidded to a stop
before falling into a huge chasm where the baggage

claim area had once been, and then flung herself headlong through a door over which a sign read "EXIT."

It made the outside into a dark alley, with garbage
cans that trembled in the wind, barbed wire fences, and
homeless, rotting, unsheltered things growling and hiss-
ing and limping in the shadows.

By now, the Intended meat was crying, a sound (one
of the only) that gave it comfort, which took the edge
off the terrible pulling and churning of the voids inside
it. She stumbled through the alley, groping blindly, and
her fingers closed over the metal chain links of a gate.
With some excitement, with some misplaced hope, she
pushed it open and stepped through . . .

. . . right into a lake, off the warm sand of the shore.

It felt her panic, intense and delicious, as she turned
around, splashing, making little kicking gestures with
her feet.

It stood there in front of her with the doll on the
sand at its feet.

Its aspect frightened her very much; the outer skins it
pretended with, the cast of obscurity beneath the hat,
the deep chuckling of its voices as it tilted its head to
regard her made her whimper. The water it made had
already solidified into ice around her feet, an arctic bitterness that bit into her skin, causing thin, watery trick-
les of blood to spill out onto the thick top layer.

Even the wetness on her face looked frosty, although
the rest of the simulated surroundings appeared warm,
even balmy, at least as far as it understood such tactile
things.

She didn't say anything at all. It could perceive a hundred different thoughts, most of them about the one called Dave and some of them about a man whose name she didn't know but who had done things to her once that made her feel more like one of the dead-shell child-meats than a living one.

It looked down at the doll. With stiff and jerking movements, the little dead-shell rose to its feet and looked up at the Primary, who gave it a little nod.

The doll looked at Cheryl. She began screaming and crying, bending down to tug at her feet frozen fast in the ice, clawing at her own skin with fingers raw from the frosty surface.

"No no no no no no," she kept whining over and over. The doll tottered closer. Each awkward step brought a fresh wave of screaming in higher pitch and more frantic pounding and scratching at the ice. The skin around her ankles bruised. Her nose bled. Her hair tangled itself over one eye as she shook her head against the approach of the doll.

When it reached her, it picked up its head. It had no face, no eyes, no ceramic smile. Cheryl wilted where she stood, the tears slowing to crystal on her face. The fight in her eyes went out. She looked up at the Primary, and it sensed Despair, the most sustaining quality any meat could produce.

The Primary drank it up.

The doll shattered beneath Cheryl's chin, just at her throat, and a thousand tiny shards of ice embedded themselves into her neck and chest. By the time her body hit the floor, the ice was gone and the beats of her cold-shocked heart were already quieted, while around her the airport bustled with meats and noise again. It watched a number of them rush over to her and signal at each other before it pulled back into the Convergence, the black holes inside it temporarily eased.

CHAPTER EIGHT

It had been her, in that alley. Chloe.

No, it hadn't. But it had looked so *much* like her, sounded like her, even smelled like her, for chrissakes. It had stood half-naked before him, wearing a ratty black broom skirt and no top at all. Then it stumbled toward him. Cuts haphazardly made up and down its arms and stomach bled a little when it moved. It stood barefoot, and its feet made little crunching sounds, like tiny bones breaking, as it walked over garbage in the alley, totally oblivious. It left white powder footprints in its wake that caught fire in blazes and then disappeared.

And yet, he wanted to hold it (her), to touch it (her), even ghost-pale and angry-eyed and very clearly not the real girl he'd fallen in love with. He wanted to pull it . . . her . . . close and tell her—tell it, he corrected with a grimace—everything was okay.

He wanted to say he was sorry, that he wished for all the world he'd never left the house that night, that if he could, he'd have taken death off her hands and the drugs from her system and made her free.

First, he'd seen something in the hallway of the rec center, a wave of hair, a flash of a long white arm, and they had seemed familiar to him. He even thought he could smell her perfume. He'd gotten up and followed the glimpses, always just enough steps ahead of him to make him unsure, outside and around the side of the building.

And when he'd turned the corner, he found Chloe standing there, bone-thin, oatmeal-pale, looking sad and needy at the same time.

His brain tried to lodge a complaint that, logically, what his eyes were seeing couldn't be possible. Chloe was dead. She had been for a while. He knew that. He *knew* it.

Then the thing that looked so much like her started collapsing from the inside out. Inky veins spidered outward from gaping, bruise-colored holes in the arms, giving the skin a kind of marblelike look. When the spidering reached the breasts, the nipples turned black and crumbled then blew away like ash. When the poison veins got to the face, the cheeks and forehead took on a drawn look, sadder and more sickly than when she'd been twitching and sweating and throwing up from withdrawal. It reached the eyes, and they turned a watery black, melting out of the head in sooty streams down the cheeks.

It hadn't spoken to him at all, only held out those broken arms with their collapsing veins working death through its system. But once, it parted the lips, just a little, and he'd seen what looked like heavy threads weaving in and out of the soft, wet inner flesh of the mouth, sewing it closed.

That, maybe, more than anything, scared the hell out

of him. That . . . thing wasn't a drugged out Chloe or even simply an overdosing Chloe. It was an already dead version of his ex-girlfriend, hopped up marionette-like on enough drugs to jolt a body into a grotesque parody of the movement of living things.

It made him sick. Scared. Disgusted that even then, *even then*, he still wanted to hold her (it) and tell it that he'd fix it, that he'd make up for everything, he promised, if she'd just promise to never go away again.

It was worse than seeing his dead aunt. Worse than seeing his brother, who he'd been trying unsuccessfully to get a hold of for days. Worse because of the things it said to him, the accusations and blame, worse because maybe, just maybe, it was right.

More than maybe.

"You let me die. You made me die, you bastard. You never were good for anything but ruining lives. It should have been you, you fucking junkie. It should have been you . . ."

It hadn't been hard to get the handgun. He knew a guy named Rick in Rockaway, way up Green Pond Road deep in the woods in a place they called Split Rock, who owed him money and was willing to loan out a gun to repay a debt and not ask any questions about it. They weren't Rick's guns; he thought of himself as a collector, in fact, for the very purposes of trade, and he collected from the teenaged hoods of Morris, Sussex, and Bloomwood counties—kids whose wildest crimes, at least the wildest they were ever caught doing, amounted to little more than bungling breaking and entering and boosting car stereos. If these hoods managed to come across any firearms, Rick was the guy to dump them off with.

Rick had been surprised but delighted to see Jake, and hugged him like a long-lost brother. He even seemed disappointed when Jake said he'd come to do business and couldn't stay long. But it was all business, in the end. Rick didn't care any more about Jake than whatever Jake could do for him. And at one time, Jake had done his fair share. He'd been a frequent visitor at Rick's place back when his habit had been manageable enough to work off in trade. And maybe as a nod of remembrance or fondness for those old times, Rick had handed him the gun upon request without so much as a raised eyebrow. More likely, his discretion was a result of not wanting to be involved—the less he knew, the less he'd be able to testify to in court, should the occasion ever arise.

In spite of his visits to Rick's and his full awareness of what was bought and sold there, Jake had never fired or even held a gun. The thought of actually pointing it and pulling the trigger absolutely terrified him. But he didn't see any other way.

He'd considered the possibility of keeping the gun on him as protection, until he'd managed to straighten the whole mess out, but the thought was short-lived. He knew better; guns didn't work on the dead. And in his gut, he knew that guns wouldn't work, either, on any kind of monsters that masqueraded around as the dead.

But they worked on people. They offered one bright

flash and deafening noise and then instant peace. He was afraid that he was left with little else as an alternative. He'd be damned if he'd fall apart and go crazy, and going back to getting high just flew in the face of everything he hated and resented about whatever these ghostly creatures were and what they were doing to him.

Slim pickings, optionwise, he thought, and uttered a short, bitter laugh as he held the gun in his hand. The cigarette clamped in his mouth sent up tendrils of smoke that got in his eyes and made them squint and tear. He sat in his bedroom, on the edge of his bed, feeling awkward and out of place. The air of the house felt different to him. He couldn't shake the sensation of unseen eyes following everything he did, criticizing, passing judgment, watching from the street straight through the walls.

The eyes of the dead, maybe.

There was, he thought as he held the gun, surrounded by the cottony, thick quiet, more than one way for someone to die on you, more than one way for someone to leave your life. People got mad or hurt and passed out of your life forever. People dumped you. People continued to forget to call back. They were all like little deaths. It hurt just as much to have people taken from you. Worse when they took themselves away from you on their own.

And if there was more than one way for someone to die on you, maybe that meant there was more than one way to kill someone. More than one way to lose someone forever.

The metal warmed slowly to his touch. It fit in his palm but didn't really feel comfortable there. It felt like having extra fingers. Deadly, cold fingers.

He thought of Chloe, and the fight.

The other woman had been a skinny-assed girl named Ali, with thin brown hair that was always in her eyes and pale, freckled skin, and tight T-shirts and jeans. She meant nothing more to Jake than the source of an occasional bag of smack; in fact, the longer he talked to her, the clearer he saw the stuck-groove loop of her words and the shallow repetitiveness of her thoughts. She possessed a kind of glassy calm, a sort of casual and accidental balance, like a sudden shock or a strong enough wind might blow her right over, but until then, she was just sort of hanging on.

There had been one night when Jake had no money, and Ali had drugs, and he'd been feeling sick and shaky and achy and sweating and all she'd wanted was a kiss. Just a kiss with a little tongue, and—

The memory made him feel sick, the heat of regret flushing his neck and cheeks.

It had only been a kiss, and kissing her had tasted like dry paper and cigarette smoke, but Jake's timing had always sucked, and Chloe always had a knack for catching him doing something wrong.

Chloe thought Jake kissing anyone but her was about as wrong as wrong got.

They fought for hours—Christ, *hours*—and he couldn't take it. The shakes, the ache, the awful alternate heat and chills. He'd simply lost patience. He'd given up hope trying to make them or anything else in his life work, and he'd gotten up and stormed out of the house.

He might have ended up exactly like Chloe, but his friend Joe down the street only had a few joints laced with heroin. Joe had handed them over willingly enough, and what there was in the joint calmed Jake down enough to sit there with his friend and watch the football game drinking beers until, as Joe put it, he could think of Chloe without wanting to punch a wall. That didn't take long. The heroin took most of the edge off, and the beer and football took off the rest. Jake and Joe didn't go back right away, though. They waited until they had a plan. Jake was to stop home, grab some stuff, and crash at Joe's. Joe even went with him back to the house.

The kind of dark that greeted them in the front hall was almost physically empty, as if some spark that normally made it a habitable dark had been snuffed out. It was the dark of warehouses, the dark of dead-end streets, a shade or dimension less than what he'd left.

Jake found Chloe in the bedroom. She looked pale and a little bluish around the closed eyes and the cheeks. She wore only her underwear, and the rest of her looked pale, thin, and kind of bluish, too. On the night table next to the bed, there were a few razor blades she'd used to cut up her arms, stomach, and thighs—something he'd never seen her do and hoped for all the rest of his life he never saw anyone do again. Her blood left little irregular spatters on the sheets. But there was also a needle—her needle (they always used their own, and never shared needles with anyone)—sticking half out of her arm, just below the rubber band where she'd tied off.

Jake thought he knew what she'd done right away. He tore through the room, looking in all the secret places where he suspected she stashed stuff to hide it from him. He found one empty heroin bag, a prescription bottle for Xanex with some woman's name he never heard of and only a few pills rattling around in the bottom in the first night table drawer, and on the floor just under the bed, an empty bottle of Rumplemintz, the kind she always complained tasted like mouthwash.

She'd been planning for this. She'd prepared for it. He couldn't imagine why, or for how long. There was more, he guessed, than just the thing with Ali, but . . . why couldn't he remember? What else had they been fighting about?

Jake thought about all that as he called 911 and managed to report the overdose in a fairly calm voice beneath the barrage of guilt. When he got off the phone, he broke down in tears, his whole body shaking from the inside. Joe stood behind him, uncomfortable, and patted his shoulder.

"I don't know, Jake, I've never done heroin before. I'm afraid, Jake. I'm afraid."

Years ago, that one time, the first time, had been the only time he'd even asked her to do it. At least, as far as he could remember. But she'd chosen to do heroin that time, and every time after that. He hadn't killed her. He hadn't even been home, and if he'd known, if he had any idea at all what she was planning to do . . .

Still, she'd only ever done heroin in the first place to be with him, to keep up with him. To connect. Like he'd told Erik. And he guessed she'd overdosed to get away from him.

Taking the cigarette from his mouth, he ashed it into the tray at his feet. He followed the pattern of the blanket, the one he'd taken from that apartment they'd shared, and his gaze fell to what would have been her side of the bed, to the pillow he'd also taken, the one she'd hugged and cried into on those nights he couldn't score them anything at all.

Yeah, there was more than one way to kill someone. With a final drag of the cigarette, he crushed it in the tray and straightened up. Jake's grip on the gun tightened.

He wondered if it would hurt. He hoped it would, just a little. It shouldn't be over without any sort of . . . exit moment. There should at least be a single moment of pain, of awareness, for someone like him. A moment to feel alive and aware, guilty and afraid of what would happen next. A moment to connect with the death that seemed to follow him everywhere he went. Jake raised the gun to his temple.

The phone rang, and he jumped, startled out of his thoughts, and pulled the trigger. Nothing happened. He took the gun away from his head and looked at it as the phone rang. The safety was still on, and for a moment he thought, *God, I can't do anything right*, and then pointed the gun at the telephone and made a gesture as if shooting it off the hook. It rang again. He sighed. A fourth ring. A fifth.

After the sixth ring, Jake put the gun down on the bed next to him and got up to answer it. His brother had told him once that maybe there was no such thing as fate, but there sure as hell were carefully placed coincidences. And even on the day you check out of life— those were his exact words, the "day you check out of life"—even then you shouldn't ignore those coincidences when they are laid right in your lap.

The phone rang again, and Jake picked up the receiver. "Hello?"

"Jake." It was Erik, his sponsor.

"Oh, hey, man. Look, I'm sorry for freaking out on you the other day. I just—I've been under a lot of pressure, and I just, I dunno. Had a little break with reality." He eyed the gun on the bed with impatience but kept that out of his voice. "Everything's okay now, though."

"No, it's not."

"No, really, I'm telling you the truth. I just . . . needed a few days to get my head together. You know, to think straight. I'll be back at Saturday's meeting, I just—"

"Jake," Erik said calmly, "please don't bullshit me. I know what's wrong. At least, I'm pretty sure I know. And I think we should talk about it."

Jake had never been able to lie to Erik, but he'd be damned if he could tell him about what was really going on. And even if he did, it wouldn't matter. Erik couldn't help him. The dead wanted to get him back, he supposed, and when that was the plain truth staring you in the face, what did you tell a guy who, but for the virtue of a few years' more sobriety, was really no better off in this miserable life than you? "There's nothing to talk about, man. I just saw—thought I saw—someone who looked like Chloe, and it bugged me out. I don't even think—"

"Jesus, man. I'm trying to tell you I understand." That calm rippled with annoyance. "I've been there, where you are. I've seen things, too. I . . . know what you're going through. It happened to me, too."

Jake frowned, offended by what he thought was Erik's implication. "I'm not using," he said in a defensive growl. "I swear on my life."

A sigh came from the other end of the phone. "Don't ever swear on your life. It's too easy to lose that. And besides, this has nothing to do with drugs."

Jake was momentarily taken aback by that. "Really? Then what does it have to do with?"

There was a long, thoughtful pause from the other end of the phone, and then, "It doesn't have a face."

For a moment, the world got fuzzy around the edges, and Jake slapped a hand against the wall to keep upright. "Huh?" No way, no way, no fucking *way* Erik could possibly be talking about the same thing.

But what he said made the hairs on Jake's arms and all along the back of his neck stand up. It made his skin tingle. He took a new cigarette from the pack on the dresser and lit it.

"You know what I'm talking about, don't you, Jake?"

Jake couldn't tell from his tone if he was coaxing an affirmation or looking for reassurance. "Yes." The word came out as little more than a hiss, so he tried again.

"Yes. I do. But I thought it was me. I didn't think—I mean, how do you—I, ah . . . I thought . . ."

He wasn't sure how to explain what he thought, exactly, because he'd never considered the possibility that it wasn't his punishment alone, whether in his head or outside of it. He'd always assumed that he'd done something wrong. That Erik knew exactly what it was he was seeing made him feel guilty, somehow. Exposed, like he'd been caught. He thought maybe a drug conversation might have been easier. "You know about it?"

"Yeah, I know about it. And we all thought we were the only ones, for what it's worth. That maybe we'd done something wrong, to deserve that. Yeah, I've seen it. It wears a black fedora hat and a long black trench coat. Black clothes underneath. Black gloves. Voice like a hundred people laughing at you, all at once." Erik cleared his throat as if dusting off a rusty old instrument and went on, his voice a little stronger. "That is, when it isn't pretending to be people you know, or . . . once knew. It doesn't have anything remotely like a face of its own because it steals the faces it needs. The bodies. The lives. It doesn't really touch anywhere when it walks, and it never touches you. But it knows things about you, knows about your family, your friends, your fears and insecurities and all your weaknesses. It wants to hurt you. It wants you to hurt yourself."

Jake cast another glance, this one steeped in guilt, at the gun on the bed. Erik knew. He knew, but how? How? He whispered, "What are they?"

"It. It may appear as many different people, but it's

only one—at least so far as it ever was in our experience."
Something about the way the words came out bothered
Jake, but he was too stunned to really think to question it.
Erik continued. "And we don't know exactly what it is,
except that we think it comes from another dimension
and can go between worlds. It can change and move the
world around you to confuse you and scare you. It uses
you against you, Jake. And it uses the people you love and
even the places where you feel safe."

"You're bullshitting me. Another dimension? You
know how absolutely, totally-not-funny-right-now, bat-
shit crazy that sounds?"

"Anyone else under any other circumstances would,
and rightfully so, hang up on me and write me off as a
fucking insensitive asshole at best, or a lunatic at the
worst. Except that you know I'm telling you the truth.
I wouldn't have called if I wasn't sure that you . . . that
I was right about this," Erik replied carefully. A pause.
"And this is the last conversation I'd ever want to have,
except that I can't avoid it. Not in good conscience, I
can't. It intends to kill you. But it isn't invincible. My
friends and I killed one once, together. We can kill this
one, too." At that last, his voice dipped into the tinny
quality of empty comfort words, but Jake nodded all
the same, right into the phone, still taking it all in. He
wasn't alone. He wasn't going crazy. And if he wasn't
the only one being haunted . . . maybe there was another way to end the bad stuff going on in his life.

Jake exhaled a slow stream of smoke. When he found
the words, he said, "We? Do other people see the—it,
too? Sober folks? Why does it want us dead?"

Erik replied, "I don't know why. We have something it needs, I guess, when we're at our weakest and most vulnerable. It feeds on that, gets off on it. And yeah, other people see it, too. Like I said, we—there were six of us—killed one a while ago that came after each of us. It tried to isolate us, make us give up on ourselves and each other. But we found we were safest when we were together. Jake, listen to me and listen carefully. You can't fight it alone. It destroys people from the inside out. But you don't have to do it alone, anyway. I guess that's why I called. I know someone who will understand. The three of us can stop it."

"This guy was one of the six?"

Erik laughed, a dry brittle sound that Jake didn't much like. "You could say, the first of the six."

Jake had no idea how to respond, so he muttered the first, most honest thing that came off his tongue. "I'm scared."

Erik was silent for several seconds. Finally he said, "You should be." As an afterthought, he added, "I'll pick you up in an hour. We'll go see Dave."

Jake didn't argue. He hung up the phone, finished the cigarette, and returned to the bed, picking up the gun. He looked at it, then at the phone, then at the gun again.

He thought, *Maybe there is more than one way to save a life, too* and slid the gun under the bed, before getting up to change his clothes.

Dave got out the bottle of tequila. Jose Cuervo. An old amigo.

149

He considered taking the phone off the hook, but Erik had gotten a hold of his sponsee and was supposed to call to let him know what time they'd be dropping by. Truth be told, although he didn't want to be around anyone just then, he thought Erik might be one of the few people who could appreciate his loss.

That is, aside from her brothers, he supposed. It was one of them who had called to tell him about Cheryl. She'd collapsed at Newark Airport. They'd rushed her to the hospital, but it had already been too late. In a strange turn of events, Cheryl's brother told him, the doctors were inclined to list her cause of death as hypothermia. Her heart had stopped, her limbs had evidence of frostbite, and even her body temperature was far lower than it should have been. The doctors had been baffled; she was young and otherwise healthy, and found in the middle of a bustling, climate-controlled airport. They suspected maybe it was some foreign substance, a drug or poison whose effects produced similar symptoms. They were waiting on the toxicology report, but the doctors had already gently prepped them that it was likely they might never know the true cause.

He'd called Dave because he knew that Dave would want to know. Cheryl, he said, had always cared for him. She would have wanted him to know.

Dave felt like all the wind had been knocked out of him. His legs felt weak and his chest felt heavy. He thought he might throw up. He muddled through the phone conversation in a haze, and when he hung up, he sank into a nearby chair and stayed there until the dizziness passed.

Two deaths. Two of the most important women in his life had been ripped away from him in horrible, painful ways. And he suspected the same fucking thing was responsible for both.

It was something her brother had said about cuts on her ankles and around her legs. It reminded him of the story she'd told him once about the man who had molested her as a girl at the beach. More so, it reminded him of the night the Hollower attacked her at the Tavern. She'd been alone, and he and Erik were on their way to pick her up, when it had found her. It reconstructed a whole shoreline, just like the day the man had touched her, and to keep her from running away, it had frozen the water around her ankles. The ice had cut into her legs, and when they found her, she was bleeding and didn't have the strength to stand. Cheryl had only ever told him once about what happened that night, and then she filed it away and never brought it up again. But there were nights he'd lain awake with the soft sounds of her breathing floating in the night air of the bedroom, and thought too much and too hard about what a failure he was for not having gotten there sooner to protect her.

But this account of her death (God, he had trouble even putting that concept together in his mind, *her death*)—the ice, the bruised, cut legs—sounded way too much like this new Hollower had gotten to her right through her memories. Right in a public place, in front of everybody. Like Sally, at the home. It was going after them, all of them who had been there that night, and some new folks, too, apparently, if Erik's sponsee was any indication. One at a time, it would kill them all. It would destroy the ones who had killed its kin. He wondered about DeMarco, about the baby growing inside her, and didn't envy what horrible things it could show her, if it found her. And poor little Sean . . . DeMarco had told him once that Sean's mom had moved him to PA, to a nice, quiet little place called Uniontown, about an hour outside of Pittsburgh. Too far for them to reach him, to protect him. It made Dave a little sick to his stomach.

It did not, however, keep him from opening the bottle of Jose Cuervo and taking a hearty gulp. It burned a little going down, but he didn't much care.

Cheryl was gone.

He loved her. He'd never quite told her in as many words how much she really meant, but he loved her. And the thought that he'd never see her again was like a heavy, black steel weight on his chest, on his back. It made him feel like he was being crushed beneath the sadness.

And the guilt.

She'd left because of him. And she'd been on her way back, he was sure, because of him. Because of Sally, maybe. Because of the Hollower. Maybe she sensed it. Maybe she knew. Or maybe she just missed him. But whatever the reason, she'd been alone because of him, and she'd been vulnerable because of him, and once again, he hadn't done a goddamned thing to save her.

Her or Sally.

He was useless and pathetic, and it should have been him. He'd gladly rather it had been, if he could bring them both back and make sure they were safe from it forever.

In that moment, his self-pity hardened into a black ball of self-hate. Somewhere beneath that, he was vaguely aware that it was exactly what the Hollower wanted, what it craved, but that didn't make the hate go away. If anything, it almost seemed an invitation for the Hollower to come get him, too.

She was gone. Both of them were gone. It was too much, too soon.

He'd let them die.

He drank more tequila, and taking the bottle, wandered over to the couch, fully intending to drink until blessed black oblivion swallowed him up.

The phone rang, and it made him jump, almost sending him flying off the couch. Regaining his bearings, he set the tequila bottle down on the coffee table. The phone rang again.

It was probably Erik. He groaned. He really didn't want to deal with Erik or the Hollower or anything else.

The phone rang again. He got up to answer it, swaying a little with the booze-induced vertigo. He steadied himself and made his way over to the phone, if for no other reason than because he'd promised Erik. Maybe he wasn't much good for anything, but at least he could try to keep his promises.

"Hello?" he said into the receiver. His own voice sounded funny in the gathering dusk, the empty, sad quiet of the house.

It wasn't Erik. The voice said, "Hello, Mr. Kohlar?

This is Detective Corimar. We spoke once before, when your sister passed. I'm one of the investigating officers."

Dave closed his eyes, opened them, reclaimed control. "Do you have any news for me on her case?" He wished DeMarco hadn't gone on maternity leave. He didn't feel up to playing the run-around game with an officer who wouldn't understand.

"I think so. Well, I have some theories, and I would really like to sit down and discuss them with you. Will you be free any time in the next few days?"

"I suppose there's tomorrow—"

"May I pay you a visit tonight?"

"Actually," Dave said, clutching at the oncoming headache in his forehead, "I'm not in the best shape right now. In addition to losing my sister, my ex-girlfriend just died—"

"Cheryl Duffy?" The recognition—the wonder—in his voice was evident. It made Dave feel nettled, maybe because Corimar was horning in on a private matter, because he wasn't DeMarco and couldn't possibly understand as much as he thought he did.

"Yes, that's her. Now if you'll excuse me, I've got a tall bottle of mourning to attend to and I—"

"Mr. Kohlar, I need to speak to you about a videotape."

Dave opened his eyes, focusing for the first time on the conversation. "I'm sorry?"

"A videotape. I understand you were sent a copy of a videotaped suicide note of one Maxwell Feinstein, as requested in his Last Will and Testament, is that correct? In his file, there is a note about the videotape, and your copy of it, but little else by way of explanation. Do you have the tape still?"

Dave didn't answer. Detective Corimar seemed to take this as an affirmation nonetheless and pressed on. "We had a copy here, of course, in evidence, but I was told it was lost, and when I did finally find it and attempt to play it, there was something wrong with the tape. Perhaps someone left it near a magnet or something, accidentally erased it, but like I said, all I got was static—" the detective's voice sounded funny, as if maybe that wasn't all he'd gotten off the tape "—and that was about it. But I've been reviewing some files that may or may not be connected to your sister's case, and I think there may be some important information on that tape. I'd like to see it, if I may."

Pushy sonuvabitch, Dave thought, the headache doubling its efforts. The detective had no idea how right he was—and how very unlikely it was that Dave would complicate things by showing him that damned tape.

"I don't have it," he said.

There was a pause, and then, "Mr. Kohlar, at risk of breaking our already tenuous rapport, I have to urge you to let me see the tape. I could go through the trouble of a subpoena and search warrants and all that crap, but I think we both know you don't want that. And I don't, either."

"Detective Corimar, I'm sorry, but I don't appreciate—"

"Look, I've seen it," the detective blurted out. It was the first thing the man said that didn't have that cop-confident authority, that practiced precision of words. It was the first genuine thing he'd said so far.

Dave sighed. "Seen the tape? I don't understand, then, why you need—"

"No, it. The thing without a face."

The words felt like a knife to Dave's stomach. The last thing, the very last thing he needed now was another person to feel responsible for.

The detective breathed for a second into the phone, excited, expecting argument, and getting none, continued. "There are several cases of Detective DeMarco's—I believe you're acquainted—that all seem connected, and you seem to be either peripherally or centrally involved in all of them. Feinstein's suicide, for one. A few unsolved homicides. Your ex-girlfriend—I am sorry for your loss, by the way—and her report of an intruder. Your sister going missing. Your sister's murder."

"Murder? I thought—"

"You know she was killed. And you know what killed her. I know it's going out on a limb to say that, but," he took a deep breath, "I'm not calling as a police officer. I'm calling as a guy who is being haunted by a creature that I'm willing to bet my career on your having seen before—all of you. A creature that has no face, no voice of its own, no remorse or conscience. It seems to know everything about me, and for that, it seems to want me dead." Softer, he added, "I just want answers. I need them. Please. Let me see the tape."

Dave sighed, defeated. "Where did you first see the Hollower?"

"The Hollower? Is that what it's called? What is it?"

"It's easier if you see the tape," Dave mumbled.

By the drawn-out pause on the other end of the line,

the detective seemed unsure how to proceed. Finally, he said, "I heard this Hollower first at your sister's crime scene. It talked to me. And then in the jails, down on the basement floor of the precinct. That was the first time I actually saw it."

"It knows things about you?"

Detective Corimar inhaled sharply. "It knows, yeah. It knows things about me, and it's threatened to use them against me. It's threatened to put that knowledge in the hands of people who could hurt me. Professionally. Possibly even physically."

"It won't leave hurting you to anyone else," Dave told him. "It will throw everything at you that you've ever been afraid of about others, about yourself. It'll use every dark and nasty little thing you're terrified to admit or to own. It'll kill you, if it can. Or get you to kill yourself."

"You saw it?"

Dave answered, "Me and about five others, including DeMarco. We all saw it. We . . . killed it. But now there seems to be another one."

"Can we kill this one?"

Dave noticed with grim amusement that the detective had already begun considering himself part of the hunting posse. "I don't know. I suppose it's possible."

"Are you seeing this one?"

Dave sighed. The phone felt very heavy in his hand.

"Will you let me see the tape? Tell me what you know?"

"Yeah. Yeah, okay. When can you get here?"

"In an hour."

"See you then, detective."

"Thank you, Mr. Kohlar."

Dave sighed. "Call me Dave. And don't thank me. You're not gonna like what you see."

CHAPTER NINE

Jake was waiting outside on the sidewalk by his house, smoking a cigarette while waiting for Erik to come pick him up, when he saw the girl from across the street have a meltdown.

He'd seen her before. To say his sentiments toward her amounted to a crush would have presupposed that he ever stood a chance at a relationship with her, which he didn't think was possible. He hadn't given that too much thought. Why dwell on something he could never have? But he did make sure he positioned himself by a window when it was time for her to set out on her afternoon power walks, and sometimes on his way to meetings he'd see her on the porch beneath her wind chimes, with her head tilted and her eyes closed and the sun on her face, and he'd just study the contours and curves of her. If she happened to open her eyes and look at him, he'd offer a wave, but most times he just shoved his hands in his pockets and trudged down to the end of the block, sullen, angry inner voices reminding him how humiliating it would be to have to explain where he went every Saturday morning, reminding him that someone like her would never have use for a loser like him.

He thought she was gorgeous, though. Her skin looked so soft and just sort of glowed, the way buttercups glowed under your chin. Her hair caught all the colors of a fire, golds and reds and soft browns. He didn't know what color her eyes were, as he'd never really gotten that close to her, but he always imagined them blue or green, some color that would catch the light and sparkle like gems in her face. And he liked her body, full, round curves that moved in sync with her movements. Some nights, when he had trouble sleeping, he thought of her as he touched himself, wondering what it would feel like to touch her, to hold her, for her to look at him with desire in those blue-green eyes.

She'd been standing on her porch when he came out, staring across the street as if shocked by some scene playing out there. He'd even followed her gaze to see what she was looking at, a vaguely unsettling sentiment of familiarity giving him pause to wonder if maybe she, too, could see it, whatever the hell Erik had called it.

But there had been nothing there. Jake had noticed that the flower box that usually hung from her railing was gone and that plastic containers were littered all over the grass beneath the porch.

She had opened her mouth, closed it, turned, and gone into her house. She returned a few minutes later with a knife. He frowned, unsure whether to turn politely away, but unable, really, to dismiss her completely.

She, on the other hand, seemed completely oblivious to him. She studied her arms, looking for something, waiting, the point of the knife trailing lightly over her skin. And then she plunged the point of the knife into the skin of the tricep, and with a grimace and a wail of pain, attempted to drag the blade through her flesh.

"Shit," Jake muttered, and dropping the cigarette, ran across the street. He could feel panic, a kind of protective nervous jitter in his gut. What the hell was she doing?

She hadn't managed to get the knife far when he leaped onto the porch and was on her, his hand closing over the handle of the knife. She put up some resistance to maintain control of it, but not enough, and with a jerky, awkward yank, he pulled the knife out of her in a small stream of blood. She looked up at him as if seeing him for the first time, and although her eyes were wet, she didn't cry.

She had aquamarine eyes. Blue and green.

"I . . . I'm sorry," was all he managed to say. He looked at the knife in his hand, and his fingers relaxed until it fell on the ground. He kicked it away from them, off the porch and into the grass. "I'm sorry, I just—I don't— what were you doing?" He took off the belt he wore and tied it tightly around her upper arm, like a tourniquet. "I'm Jake," he said.

"Dorrie." She tried to smile at him. He smiled back, looking more confident and, he hoped, more reassuring than he felt. He took her other arm and tried to steer her back to the house. She probably had antiseptic and bandages inside. She seemed to go willingly and then stopped short, a defeated look on her face.

"I can't go in there. It can get in there, too."

"What can?"

She shook her head. "I think I'm going crazy. Help

me. Please, help me. Call me an ambulance. I . . . I think I need a doctor." She looked up at him, then down at her arm.

"Why don't we go inside and call an ambulance, then? And maybe get you some bandages."

"I'm not meat. I don't go bad like that, with bugs eating all the fat, right? Tell me that can't happen."

Jake's eyebrows knitted in confusion. "I, uh, I don't think so. I mean, I've never heard of anything like—"

"It told me," she said in a voice almost too soft to hear, "that it could change the muscle to Eaters, to the things it put in the Tupperware containers. It said they would chew through all the fat in my body, right through my skin, through my bones and muscle. It said I could try to cut them out before they began to eat."

Jake eyed the plastic containers on the porch and had second thoughts about going inside alone with her. Hot or not, she sounded completely stark raving, knife-toting, someone-else-is-in-the-house kind of crazy.

"I know how this sounds. I couldn't tell the police. And normally I would never have believed something so nuts myself—I can't make you believe that, but it's true. That I've never been like this before—but I saw what it did in the fridge and with the flowers, and the things it knows, and . . . it told me it wanted to kill me."

Jake felt cold and stopped trying to tug her toward the house.

"What told you that?"

She hesitated, but only for a moment, assuming, he supposed, that he couldn't possibly think she was any crazier. "The man without the face. It—oh, God." And then she did cry, streams of tears spilling over her cheeks. "I'm going crazy. There's something wrong with me. There's something very wrong with me."

"No, no," he murmured, taking her arms, careful not to put too much pressure on her wound. "There's nothing wrong with you. You're okay. I'm here." That last bit sounded lame to him—like she could find any comfort in *him* coming to her rescue—but he meant it, for what it was worth. What had sounded crazy before suddenly sounded all-too-familiar.

She could see it, too. She and Erik and his friend. They could all see it.

"It wanted me to hurt myself. And God, I'm so pathetic, I almost did."

Jake thought of the gun under his bed and felt his neck grow hot. "Don't feel bad about that. That's what it does. That's its strength."

She looked at him, really looked at him as if seeing him for the first time. "What do you mean? Do you . . . know?" Her hand flew to her mouth, her wet eyes wide as she pulled a little away from him. "What do you mean by that? Can you see it?"

Jake nodded slowly. "And I'm not the only one. There are others."

Suddenly her face changed, and she looked suspicious. "Don't humor me just because you think I'm crazy. I won't have you making fun of me. Please." She tried to pull out of his grasp altogether and nurse her wounded arm. "Just let me go. I need to call a doctor."

"It wants me dead, too. I—I know what you're seeing.

163

It showed me my dead aunt. My brother. My ex-girlfriend, who died of a drug overdose." He winced at how easily that had come out of his mouth to her. "It showed me everyone I ever cared about, and it felt like my heart was getting ripped out. I don't know how to prove it to you, but I swear on my li— I swear on everything I have that I am not, absolutely not, humoring you, and I'm sure not making fun of you."

She searched his eyes again. She had an intense look, as if she were turning over rocks and beating bushes in his head to get at hidden truths and secrets beneath soft words. "Really?"

"Really." He crossed a finger over his heart.

The strength seemed to go out of her, and she sank a little where she stood. He caught her before she sank too far, and felt a thrill, in spite of the situation, in simply touching her.

"What is it? Where does it come from? Why is it doing this to us?"

Jake shrugged. "I don't know much more than you, but I'm waiting for someone to pick me up who's going to explain everything he knows." He paused. "You should come. I . . . ah, I insist. I can't leave you alone here, not now."

"Oh, I . . . I don't know, I—"

"I mean it. You shouldn't be alone. You shouldn't have to face this thing alone. Look what it almost made you do." He indicated her arm, and she blanched. Softer, he said, "I don't want to do it alone, either. We can help each other."

She seemed to consider this for a moment, and then

nodded. "Okay. I don't know why I feel like I can trust what you say, but . . . I don't know. I just do." She let him lead her inside the house to get bandages, and he gently rinsed her arm with warm water. She winced when the water touched the cut she'd made, but she didn't say anything. It didn't look to him like it was that deep a cut, so he bandaged it up and she followed him outside to wait for Erik.

They made little starts and stops of small talk; he asked about her job (she worked in the newsletters department of a medical equipment licensing company) and she asked about his (he'd recently gotten a raise at the Home Depot in the gardening department). She asked if he had family close by (he didn't, and kept his answer grimly short), and he asked her if she had a boyfriend. It just kind of came out, and when it hung there between them, he wished he could scoop it back up and chuck it over his shoulder. She blushed. It made her cheeks look pretty. But her eyes looked sad.

"No," she said, and offered no more explanation than he'd given about his family.

"I'm sorry if I made you uncomfortable."

She waved it away and put on a light, easy expression. "No, it's okay. No biggie."

He tried out a couple of different responses in his head and settled on, "Can't blame you for needing a break."

She looked confused.

"Pretty girl like you probably gets lots of guys hounding her."

She smiled a little and looked away.

A few minutes later, Erik rolled up to the curb. He wore jeans and a gray T-shirt with the logo of the landscaping company he worked for on the breast pocket. A baseball cap was pulled down backwards over his head. He cast a sidelong look at Dorrie and then raised an eyebrow at Jake.

Jake said, "She can see it, too. It attacked her." He nodded at Dorrie's arm.

Erik eyed her skeptically. "Are you sure?"

"It has no face," she said hollowly.

Erik looked at Jake. "How did it attack her? It didn't actually . . . ?"

"Touch her? No. But like you said, it doesn't really have to."

Dorrie's eyes looked wet. "Please, if you know what this thing is, then I need your help. Please." She paused, her expression betraying the discomfort of hearing her own desperation, and she added. "This . . . whole thing just seems so . . . crazy. But Jake says you know what's going on, and I . . . I'm so confused. I don't know what to do. It's getting worse, and I . . . I just don't know what else to do."

Erik paused for a moment, the wariness gradually changing, Jake thought, to a contemplative frown, sizing up Dorrie in her jeans and blouse, examining the bandage. Finally, he said, "I'm Erik. Pleased to meet you. Wish it could have been under better circumstances. Get in."

Dorrie got in the back seat and Jake in the front. Erik pulled away from the curb.

An uncomfortable silence settled over the car for a

few miles, until Erik cleared his throat and said, "My friend's name is Dave. He and I go to the same bar. The same monster that has been stalking both of you killed his sister."

Neither Jake nor Dorrie answered. After a moment, Erik continued. "We'll give you the details when we get to Dave's house, but the essential story is this: each of us was carrying around something inside, some guilt, some anger, some fear, some crooked view of the world." Jake could see Erik's grip on the wheel tighten and relax as he clenched and unclenched his fists, over and over. "It can sense those things, and that's how it finds you. Any time, anywhere. And, well you know what it can do."

The others nodded. Jake was afraid to speak, afraid of changing the dynamic of the car, he supposed—a dynamic that was already tenuous and awkward and heavy with fear and confusion. But Jake also felt a degree of hope. He found it surprisingly comforting to know that these ghosts he was seeing weren't really ghosts of people he'd hurt, but rather reflections of his own haunted thoughts. And more comforting still was the idea that he wasn't alone in seeing them, that . . . maybe he wasn't so much worse a human being than anyone else. Everyone carried around something, just like Erik said. And that made him feel closer to Erik—and to Dorrie—than he'd felt to anyone since his brother.

"What is it?" Dorrie asked. "Where does it come from? Does it have a weakness? I mean, can we stop it?"

Erik's face was hard to read. It seemed to Jake he was struggling with the answer he wanted to give. Finally he said, "We killed one once. This one is different. Stronger. But yeah. Yeah, I think we can stop this one, too." A pause. "I think it'll probably be easier when you see the tape—"

"The tape?"

Erik nodded at Jake. "A videotape Dave has. Everything we know about the Hollower we learned from that tape."

"The Hollower." Dorrie tried out the word quietly.

They fell into silence for the rest of the trip. Jake wondered what it had been like for Erik, confronting it that first time, attacking it head on. He wondered about other car rides, uncomfortable silences among people who felt closer than strangers should. And he thought about what it was like to think you'd put the worst of things behind you, only to find them looming over you again, faceless and thrumming with hate. It gave him a faint headache and a craving for nicotine.

Jake wasn't so sure he wanted to see what was on that tape.

Detective Steve Corimar arrived at Dave's house a few minutes after Erik and his passengers. Introductions were made all around, and while Dave went to grab beers from the refrigerator (for all but Jake and Erik, who politely declined anything to drink), the others chatted first of polite surface things, much as Jake and Dorrie had done. But by degrees—a joke cracked here, a witty response there—they eased into each other's company. Steve, although quiet, delivered well-timed comebacks in a mannered, articulate way, and Jake worked a room like a showman when he told a story, laughing and gesturing and doing impressions of voices. Erik grinned through one of Jake's stories, "calling bullshit" as he put it, and interjecting comments along the way. And when Dorrie laughed, it was like the clinking of crystal. It filled the room and made him want to laugh, too. He noticed that Jake seemed most pleased in amusing Dorrie, and she flushed warm and glowing when he paused to include attention to her in his narrative.

Dave smiled, too. He could remember that same feeling of connectedness, that same feeling of safety in numbers, when he and Erik and Cheryl had first gotten together. There was camaraderie there, a sense of having found people to believe in—and people who were willing to believe in you.

Dave thought maybe, just maybe, they had a fighting chance. And that possibility made him feel good. Better, he supposed, than the tequila made him feel. He held it together, intending to ride out the alcohol in his system, but Erik gave him a look that indicated concern (Are you okay, man?), and Dave nodded reassuringly that he was fine.

After a while, the chatter and the laughter died down a little, and the purpose for their meeting seemed to sink over the company like a heavy fog. Some of them still nursing their beers, they settled down around Dave's den. Steve and Erik took the couch, and Jake the easy chair. Dorrie sat on the arm, and Dave saw that Jake was holding her hand, squeezing it, he supposed, for comfort.

Dave himself stood by the television. He didn't feel

much like sitting, although the tequila made his head heavy and his limbs clumsy and oversized. He tried very hard not to sway where he stood and thought he managed tolerably well. Still, he could feel Erik's eyes on him, anxious, concerned. Dave imagined his friend felt that same anxious knot in the stomach that he felt. Erik had seen what was on the tape. He knew about Max Feinstein blowing the back of his head off in his upstairs bedroom because dealing with the Hollower had gotten to be too much. He remembered the night they set out with Cheryl and Sean and, later, DeMarco to kill the monster before it killed them. And whatever little answers they'd gotten from that tape, whatever little comfort their meager knowledge had provided, seemed to pale in comparison to the powerful, vindictive, savage thing they were up against now. He didn't much think that the tape would offer any new clues, or even anything this new crop of victims could take to sleep with them that night, and he suspected Erik felt very much the same way.

"You ready?"

They nodded at him, their faces solemn, their eyes expectant.

He pushed the PLAY button on the VCR and waited.

The blue screen was followed by a flash of static. Max's hand shadowed the screen for a moment, and then it pulled away. Max sat behind a desk, hands folded over a forest-green blotter amidst a tumultuous sea of curling Post-it notes. Max smiled.

"Who's that?" Dorrie asked. Her voice sounded loud among the held breaths. Dave paused the tape.

"Max Feinstein," Erik answered her. "He owned a

house on River Falls Road. It was his place where we found the first Hollower . . . its lair, I guess. We killed it there, on his front lawn." He barely glanced at her. Since all this business had started with the new Hollower, Erik had become quieter, more serious than he had been, and far less warm, less open. It was almost like he was constantly cringing from some phantom ache, ever tensing in his muscles to brace himself against pain. It made Dave despondent to see him like that, and it threatened to topple some of that newfound hope. Erik had always believed they could fight the Hollower. It was that unshakable belief that had encouraged them, united them. Without that . . .

Finally Jake asked, "Where is he now?"

"Dead," Dave answered flatly. "He shot himself in his bedroom right after making this tape."

Dave thought Jake's face drained of color at that, and the boy turned away from his gaze.

Dorrie shivered. "That's awful. That poor man."

Steve didn't look surprised, but Dave supposed he didn't expect the detective to. Steve had probably been putting scraps and bits of this story together long before this. The tape was probably the unifying element, the key to the code.

"It's not the half of it," Dave said, and pressed PLAY again.

"Uh, hi, David. Hi," Max's voice said on the tape. "Or maybe I should call you Dave. I hope you'll forgive me for taking the liberty of informality here, but I believe we share a common affliction." After straightening his tie, Max reached out a hand as if to adjust the camera angle then drew back, leaving the camera angle as it was.

Leaning into the lens, he said, "I hope you can see and hear me okay. I have so much to tell you. Sally tells me you've seen the Hollower. Worse, the Hollower has seen you." He chuckled. "I suppose 'seen' isn't the right word. It doesn't see you the way you or I might see each other. No," he said, and shook his finger in their direction. "Oh no. It's a different beast entirely."

He pulled a bottle of scotch and a glass of ice from some place behind the desk, poured some with badly shaking hands, and set the bottle down again off-camera. He raised the glass, and Dave noticed the tiniest tinkling of the cubes against the sides as Max held it up in a toasting gesture. Then Max took a gulp and swallowed. "I'd offer you some, but obviously, I'm not in a position to do that. I'm not a drinking man—never have been. But this is a special occasion. Today . . ." His voice trailed off and he took another smaller sip.

"Today is the last day."

There was an appreciative murmur from the new members of the audience. Erik said nothing. Dave glanced in his direction and saw the grim, set expression, the gaze fixed on the television.

"Dave," Max's voice was saying, "let me see if I can explain this thing as I have come to understand it. See, the Hollower is an intangible being. Where our senses stop, its senses start, and continue above and beyond the range of even the most psychic of our kind. The Hollower is not quite physical here, but it seems able to act on this world. As far out as all that sounds, I think you know this much. This . . . being, this monster—it feeds on its victims' sense of unreality. On their surreality, if you will. People's confusions. Their insecurities. I know that's vague, but it's the best way to put it, believe me. The Hollower is sustained by impressions and perceptions and points of view. Its greatest protection is its anonymity and androgyny. How does it find you on such vague terms, you ask? By 'smelling' "—Max made finger-quotes around the Hollower's concept of smell— "your most skewed thoughts. By smelling your irrational feelings. These evidently carry their own musk, their own meaty scent that clings to us. Think about it, about those wonderful, awful dating years and how you just got . . . vibes, I guess you'd call it. Feelings about people. The strongest scents set off red flags about their neediness, their stalker potential. So maybe we do possess a glimmer of that sense it uses to 'see' us or 'smell' us." He smiled, and Dave was once again struck by the fatigue in the man's face, the utter rubbing out of once clear features and sharp eyes. He had a dull, hazy look. He took another drink.

"It collects identities and voices at will and uses them against you. It's the perfect weapon—the perfect disguise. Few things can hurt us more than the way we can hurt ourselves, am I right? Little else shakes our faith in ourselves so much as self-doubt, however off-kilter or misplaced. And few things are more dangerous than misconceptions about the world around—"

On the videotape, Max drew in a sudden, sharp breath.

His eyes grew wide. In the background, the sound of a few footsteps drew closer to the camera and then receded. Dave felt his chest tighten in anticipation. God, he remembered this part. Hated it. He hadn't looked at the tape, not once, since the night he showed it to Cheryl and Erik. In truth, he hadn't even been sure he'd be able to find it to show to Steve. He'd gone to put the tequila bottle away, and when he'd come back, the tape was lying on the coffee table. Like someone had taken it out for him. Like something had wanted him to go ahead and have it at his disposal, by all means, for whatever little good he thought it would do. Like something was very much amused by the idea that Dave would show his weak and terrified little friends the last words of a dead man who hadn't been able to fend off even a Secondary.

That was the thought, almost verbatim, that had popped into his head. It wasn't his thought at all, not in even his own mind-words, but he'd understood it well enough, and where it came from. He'd been almost afraid to touch the tape (Hell, why not be honest? He'd been damned well afraid to even look at it too long), with the mental residue of the Hollower still in his head. So there it sat until the others arrived, and he'd pushed it into the VCR to give up its secrets.

All around the room, the others, including Erik, leaned in toward the television.

On the tape, a soft and sexless chuckling close to the mike caused Max to grow tense where he sat. The picture dissolved into static, and the chuckling broke up like cell reception in a tunnel. The static didn't clear, but every once in a while it would clear for just a second, just long enough for the eye to register Max's form, wide-eyed, leaning close to the camera.

"It knows. The Primary, it knows. It's here, I think. Outside," Max whispered. A flash of clear picture showed a trickle of blood from the corner of his mouth, and—

Shit . . . is that blood on the wall behind him? Dave felt a dreadful unease in his chest. The tequila, which had settled down to a manageable half-buzz, roiled angrily in his stomach, threatening nausea.

Something was wrong with the tape. Dave and Erik exchanged glances. This wasn't how it played out last time. The others, having no prior experience with the tape, kept watching.

"—always watching, waiting." Another pause, followed by his own laughter, tinny and forced, that was drowned out by a crescendoing wind-tunnel noise that roared over the static. Louder still than that came more laughter, the sadistic delight of many voices at once.

Another flash of clarity, and Max slumped over the desk, a rough exploded mess of red and gray and white replacing the visible back portion of his head. Jake squeezed Dorrie's hand. Erik shifted uncomfortably in his seat, and Dave shook his head, hoping to clear it, hoping to bring some sense back to what he was seeing. Steve, glancing up and seeing their reactions, gave them a quizzical look.

"What?"

Dave said, "It isn't supposed to show that. The tape is different. Different than last time. This"—he waved at the TV as the static took over again—"isn't supposed to be there."

In the next moment, Max, still slumped over the desk, no longer had a halo of blood on the wall behind him. Now it streaked the wall, forming crude letters:

HOLLOW

The frame of the camera only caught the side of a sleeve, a black glove, the flap of a trench coat that stood next to the blood letters behind Max. Most of the figure stood off-camera. But they recognized it; the collective gasp of the room confirmed that.

The wind-tunnel noise stopped dead, but the laughter didn't. And the black glove raised over Max's head and closed into a fist.

"Every one of you," it said, "will be killed."

Static erupted across the screen again.

Dave jabbed a finger out and pressed STOP on the VCR, but the tape kept running. The picture cleared, and Max's body was alone again. After a second or two, it picked its bloody head up.

There was a gaping hole where the mouth should have been, except that it was vertical, taking up the majority of the facial plane, its frayed edges of flesh singed black, swaying like cilia. Otherwise, the smooth, pale expanse of the head was blank.

"All of you will be killed, just like Sally, just like Cheryl, just like all the others. And I'll make it hurt so much that you'll trickle out all your pain and despair for me, just like they did. You will die, die, die, die, die." The voice that spoke didn't come from the mouth hole of the figure on the tape. In fact, it didn't seem to come from the tape at all. Each of them cringed when the sound got too close to his or her ear. Dave swore under his breath when the voice came close enough to make neck hairs stand on end.

The Max-thing on the tape rose and leaned in close to the lens, pointing a black-gloved finger. "Every one of you. You always were nothing but meat."

Then the gloved hand reached across the frame again and shut the camera off, and the screen went dark.

CHAPTER TEN

For several minutes, none of them spoke. Dave looked from face to face. All were washed out, with worry in the eyes, soft downturns of the mouth, all chests rising and falling with ragged breaths. All of them looked exhausted, unsure.

Seconds ticked by as they waited to see if they were alone in the house, or if the Hollower would make any other moves. They warily eyed the few paintings that Dave had hanging on the walls, mostly landscapes that they half-expected to become populated with distorted figures or horrific acts captured in the stark stillness of paint and ink. When, as a whole, they came to the conclusion it was gone, they began to relax a little and started moving around slowly, as if coming out of a deep sleep. But their few words were mumbled and sounded too loud, too stiff in the quiet of the house.

"Cheryl?" Erik looked pained and pale.

Dave nodded. "Her brother called today. It found her. Got her like the other one tried to do at the Tavern."

Erik passed a hand over his face, and in the breaks between the fingers, Dave caught a glimpse of wetness in his friend's eyes.

Jake hovered uncertainly by the door until Dave told him he could smoke in the house so he wouldn't have to go outside alone. The boy looked relieved. Granted the small comfort of a cigarette, he spoke what they were all thinking. "It knows we're here. You all saw it, on the tape? It knows we're together and that we know what it is, and . . . I think it's going to make things worse." Everyone nodded their confirmation at Jake, who lit a cigarette with trembling fingers and took several curt puffs from it before asking, "What are we going to do?"

Steve cleared his throat. "We're going to stop it. Kill it before it kills us. Question is: how do we do that?"

No one said anything. All eyes were on Dave and Erik. Erik shrugged and said, "Weapons don't really work. Dave and I—the whole lot of us—tried that. It didn't work."

"The mirror worked," Dave said, more to himself than them. But feeling their expectant stares, he said, "In the box that Max's tape came in, there was a mirror. At the end of the tape, the way it played when we first saw it, Max said we'd know what to do with it when the time came. Well, none of us did, but Sally, my sister, seemed to. She broke it and cut into the Hollower."

"Cut a big, gaping mouth across the bastard's face," Erik added, and grinned a little.

Dave nodded. "It changed after that. It became . . . I don't know, physical. Solid, somehow. And that made it weak and clumsy. We hurt it. Eventually, we killed it."

"You killed it. Remember, Dave?"

Dave nodded. He remembered. He'd charged that fucking thing with one of the sharp twisted-up objects he'd found in Feinstein's yard. He believed they had been keys to other places, other dimensions the Hollower hunted in. But they made fine weapons, too, he'd discovered. His whole hand had gone numb when he plunged the sharp end into what should have been a face. Contact had killed the first few layers of skin on his fist and split it where it was thinnest, like across his knuckles. But the Hollower's body had shaken all around his hand from what felt like a small implosion inside it. Immediately after, he felt a tugging against his fist, like a vacuum. He'd let go of the handle just as one of the Hollower's claws swung up and knocked him backward. Dave remembered watching the Hollower's whole body tremble in violent spasms, its head shaking back and forth until it was almost a blur. It tottered on the long, unstable legs of its physical form. Its whips had drawn away from Sally, and she sank to the grass. Still, it made no sound, except the spastic clicking of its claws as it crashed to the ground and stayed there, unable to rise.

The tequila lurched in his stomach when he thought of dragging Sally away from it, cut and bleeding, her eyes closed, whimpering softly. She'd said, "It hurt me. I'm scared of it, Davey. It hurt me."

He closed his eyes and opened them. "I remember."

"So, we need a mirror, then?" Jake looked around for a place to put out his cigarette and decided on the empty beer bottle with an apologetic glance at Dave. "We've got mirrors everywhere. We just have to cut this thing open, then? Let the bad juices out, so to speak?"

Erik shrugged. "Maybe. I'd always thought touching

it might upset whatever coat of indestructibility it seems to have, but Dave, I'm sure, can attest to the dangers of making physical contact with it."

Dave showed them the back of his hand. There was a little bit of scarring still; white lines over his knuckles, puckered white marks and fine lines all across the skin up to the wrist. It wasn't immediately visible and didn't ever bother him nowadays, but turning his hand in the den light, they saw what even brief physical contact left behind.

"Besides," Erik went on, "even if swiping at it with broken glass were the answer, it isn't as easy as it sounds to even get that close. And to tell you the truth, as much of a stubborn son of a bitch that first Hollower was, this one sounds leaner and meaner. I don't think it's going to go down the same way."

"What do we do, then?" Dorrie said. When none of the men answered, she said, "Look, this thing scares the hell out of me. I came very close"—she cradled her bandaged arm—"to doing something very dangerous and stupid, just to get that thing out of my head. I can't live like that, always on the edge of losing everything. I just can't. I may not have a terrible lot going for me, but . . . I like what I have enough to want to fight for it. We have to do something. Please."

Jake came up beside her and put an arm around her shoulders. "I don't know about you guys, but . . . this is the strongest I've felt in a long time. Since we first walked through that door, I felt like we could beat this, that we could take this Hollower down. I don't feel that way when I'm alone. Things come crashing back, and I can't think straight. Nothing to focus on, nothing to believe in. But this here, all of us here—I believe in that. Am I nuts for thinking that?"

Dave smiled and looked at Erik. "No, I don't think that's crazy. Safety in numbers, man."

"It's more than that," Steve said in a firm, quiet tone. "I don't feel so . . . wrong. I don't feel so unsure of me. Not here. Not since, like Jake said, since we got here."

Erik chuckled. "Maybe all our crazy brainwaves cancel each other out."

Steve rose from the couch. "It's not a bad theory." He began to pace Dave's den. "Okay, obviously it can still contact us, even if we're all together. The tape is proof of that. But for all we know, it could be throwing out a blind blanket threat. It didn't change the room, really, except to keep the tape rolling. It didn't reach out anything but its voice to us. Maybe it knows that our standing together gives us strength and makes us harder to find, harder to kill."

He looked to Dave for confirmation, but Dave's head ached and his stomach felt like a vat of acid, and he just shrugged.

They began talking at once: "Dave, what do you think?" "What should we do?" "How do we fight it?"

"I don't know!" Dave said, more impatiently than he'd intended. They paused in their chatter. Softer, he said, "I don't know. I always kind of thought that we killed the first one by sheer dumb luck. And it nearly killed us in the process. I want to help, folks, but I have to tell you, I don't have such a great track record with keeping anyone safe from one of these things." He sat down heavily. "I don't know how to kill it, and I don't know how to protect you from it any more than I knew how to protect my sister or my girlfriend or any of my friends. I honestly don't know what to tell you." He looked up at them all miserably, and the silence stretched out to the border of discomfort.

"Well," Steve said after a time, "it's a good thing you're not alone in fighting it, then."

Dave looked up and found him smiling. They all were. He gave in and smiled, too. "Yeah," he said. "Yeah, it is."

Dave went into the kitchen and got them all another round of beers. He also went upstairs and grabbed a hand mirror. After Cheryl had left him, he'd been in a CVS one day, cutting across the hair care aisle, and he'd spied it. It was an impulse buy, an instinct buy, maybe, but he'd kept it close to the bed ever since, the unrealized and certainly unarticulated thought being *just in case*. Also, he supposed, on impulse, he grabbed a printout of an article he'd found online from the drawer of his night table.

He came back downstairs and found them settled back down on the couch and chairs.

Erik clapped his hands together. "So what's our plan?"

He sat down on the chair next to Erik and put both the mirror and the printout on the coffee table.

"You never know. Better to have it if we need it."

"What's this?" Dorrie picked up the paper.

"It's something I came across on the Internet," Dave explained, "while looking for ways to keep busy after Cheryl left. I wasn't looking for stuff about the Hollower—well, not intentionally—but I found that from an accidental click-through on one of the sites about ghost sightings in New Jersey. You all know what they say about some of the places up in Bloomwood County, right? Just weird things that happen, people disappearing, doing crazy things? Very Lovecraft kind of stuff sometimes."

"Sure," Steve said. "Since LPD went electronic, we have a whole case file directory unofficially known as the Weird New Jersey files. You know, like the magazine."

"Well," Dave said, "this is probably one of those things that would end up in those files. Basically—you can pass it around if you want—to sum it up, it's a brief mention of a teenager from Wexton, recently transplanted to Lakehaven. The teenager keeps an online journal—a blog, they call it. It's anonymous, but her visible user information identifies her as a girl, and as being about fifteen.

"Anyway, this blog entry is dated, what was it, the sixth of January or thereabouts? Some time after we killed the first Hollower and before there were any real signs of the second. Now, I guess because it's anonymous she feels free to discuss anything and everything. There is entry after entry of angsty rebellious ranting, secret worries about boys and friends and sex and even how her underwear fits. You know, teenaged girl stuff. You've got all the usual things she sees at school, at home, at the mall with friends. But she also talks about a stalker, with alternately melodramatic and unaffected tones, that follows her and some of her classmates around. She calls him 'the man in the mask,' and she makes him sound almost ghostlike. That he can walk through walls and disappear, that he leaves her 'presents' in her locker like dead mice (she's afraid of rodents) and lunch bags full of spiders. That he cut the face of the pot-head four lockers down from her.

"The part I thought was interesting is near the end, there. See? Where she mentions how she intends to make the man go away.

"She says 'we plan to blind its eyeless sight, and then push it back into the Abyss of Hell.' I think that was how she put it. I scanned a bunch of the other blog entries before and after to see how, exactly, she did it or how it turned out, but I couldn't find anything. Her entries after January sixth make no mention of the stalker at all, or any resolution regarding the problem. I went through them pretty thoroughly. Even for an anonymous blog, she speaks a lot in code, and I wrote all kinds of quirky little phrases down, did Google searches, looked them up in slang dictionaries. I came up with nothing. But the point is, she does describe her stalker man as someone very much like our Hollower. And whatever she did to make him—or it—go away, it seemed to work. The reason I printed it out is because, well . . . Erik and I can tell you, this Hollower is different. Meaner. Stronger. It's called a Primary. It's . . . a different species, maybe, or a different class. I don't know. And there is one throw-away reference in there, if you skim down, where she calls her stalker a Primary. See? What I'm saying is, even the Primaries, the tough ones like we have now, even they aren't invincible."

Dave looked to each of their faces, taking some comfort in the glimmers of hope their eyes reflected back at him. He didn't have the answers, but he thought that at least the potential for victory was something to go on. Back when they'd fought the first Hollower, the boy they were with, Sean, had believed wholeheartedly that all monsters had an Achilles' heel, that nothing, natural or supernatural, was completely invincible.

"Everything has a weakness," little Sean had said. And he'd been right. Sure, he and Dave and Erik and Sally and Cheryl and DeMarco had all dodged its attacks, had all overcome its temptation to lie down and die, but they hadn't held much hope that they could actually hurt it, let alone kill it. But it did have a weakness, and they had managed to destroy it. Even if this new Hollower was a different class or even a slightly different species, that didn't mean it couldn't be killed, too.

"Best as I can figure," Dave said, "we can beat this thing. If we can find it, that is."

"Well," Dorrie said, "I was thinking a lot about what you said about Max, that you found it . . . its lair, I guess . . . where Max died. Where it drove Max to suicide, I mean. So maybe, and, Dave, I hope you'll forgive me if it sounds insensitive, but maybe we should start looking for it where it caused its first death here. That we know of, I mean. Maybe we should look where Sally died."

It made sense. The catacombs beneath Oak Hill Assisted Living offered potentially endless possibilities for the Hollower to hide. *Well, maybe not hide, exactly*, he thought. It didn't seem to be hiding from anyone.

"It won't be easy getting in there," Steve said, but Dave

could tell from his tone that he was already working out a plan in his head for getting them all into the catacombs.

"At the risk of sounding all Late Night Horror Show," Jake said, "we could go at night. I've uh . . . had some experience with getting into places where I wasn't supposed to be." He offered a sheepish look to Steve, who replied, "Good. It's a crime scene, after all. I can go in as part of the ongoing investigation, but it's a whole other kettle of fish getting you in there. Maybe you all can meet me somewhere . . ."

Jake looked solemn. "You get in, get the key, whatever we need. I'll get the rest of us in."

"We'll need flashlights," Erik said. "Casey bought a new pack of double A batteries. I'll grab them and the flashlights I have. After last time . . ." He looked at them with a kind of embarrassed shrug. "It was an impulse buy at Wal-Mart. I guess I figured, you know . . . just in case."

Dorrie sipped at her beer. "It's a good thing you did. Now, how will we find it once we get in there?"

Jake squeezed Dorrie's hand. "I think it'll find us."

"When do we go?"

The warmth between them and the sense of accomplishment in coming up with a plan cooled. It was one thing to talk in theories and generalities about how to fight the Hollower, but it was another thing entirely to set a date and time.

"I say the sooner, the better," Steve said. "I don't want this dragging out any more. Tomorrow night sounds good to me."

"Me too," Jake said, and Dorrie nodded next to him. She gently nudged Erik. "What do you guys think?"

Erik and Dave exchanged glances. Erik ran a hand through his hair. "Can we do this again, big D?"

Dave replied, "Well, I don't have any other plans for tomorrow. I think I can squeeze you all in for one last hurrah and a quick brush with death, so long as I'm home by a reasonable hour."

The dry chuckles that followed did not obscure the fear beneath them, not completely.

"Let's say we meet at ten o'clock tomorrow night, at the door to the catacombs. I'll go in first and secure the area, and then you slip in and we'll head down into the catacombs and see if we can find the bastard."

"Works for me," Dave said to Steve.

"I feel better knowing we're going to do something about it," Dorrie said, and Dave and Erik nodded without much enthusiasm. A plan, they knew, didn't guarantee anything.

"How are we going to kill it?"

They all looked at Jake. Dave finally said, "We can try to kill it like we did the first one, but . . . well, I guess we should all think it over for the night, see if we can come up with some backup plans, too. Just in case. The more options we have, the better."

The others murmured their agreement, each lost in thoughts of ways to take the monster down.

"This one gets inside you somehow," Erik said in a faraway voice.

"I know what you mean," Dorrie said. "Sometimes I'll have thoughts in my head that don't sound anything like me. They're things I wouldn't know, framed in a way I don't usually think."

"That's part of it. But this one does more. It's hard to explain. It's not just that it puts its own thoughts into your head. It confuses things. It's almost like if you let it take hold, it makes you feel . . ." His voice trailed off.

"High?" Jake asked softly.

Erik sighed. "Yeah. Just remember, tomorrow night it'll throw everything it's got at you. It'll change the floor under your feet, even. You've got to keep it together and keep the Hollower out of your head. This one is a hell of a lot tougher than the last one."

Still, with a plan in place, their spirits all seemed lifted. The night wore on, and no one made any move to part company until Erik announced that he needed to get home to Casey. He was afraid to leave her alone. With warnings all around to be careful, they made their way to the door. Erik left with Jake and Dorrie in tow, and Steve picked up his things to leave as well.

Dave walked them out. He took hold of Steve's arm and stopped him. "Listen, man. Be careful, being in there alone tomorrow night, even if it's for the short time until we get there. We're more vulnerable when we're alone. And this one, it doesn't just show you things. It changes things. That kind of power . . . well hell, our first Hollower seemed to have to work up to those things."

"Okay, man. Sure." Steve didn't look as confident as his tone suggested. He got about halfway across the lawn, stopped, and turned back to Dave.

"Do you think we can kill this? Do you, I mean, personally believe it?"

Dave thought to all the times Cheryl had asked, to when Sean and Erik had asked, to DeMarco's face when she asked if he was up for getting them out of that mess.

He watched Erik's car drive away. He had trouble looking Steve in the eye when he said, "No. But I'll be damned if I won't put everything I have into trying."

Steve considered that for a moment, nodded, and made his way back to his car.

Dave turned back to his dark, quiet house to face the next twenty-four hours alone.

While Dave and the others discussed where to find the Hollower and how to kill it, it busied itself with tormenting the strangest and possibly the most grotesque of all the meats. This one, a woman who called herself Anita, but who the others thought of as DeMarco, was the most difficult to find. She did not produce the same kind of Hate or Fear or Doubt that the others did, and so it was little more than vaguely aware of a somehow round impression of her, and a sense inside a sense, a fullness inside her solid shell.

Her Worry seemed, by all accounts, to be focused on the consciousness inside her. She used the word "baby" for it. It could not sense this baby, not fully, but it knew the baby was there. Anita worried when it moved too much inside her, or not enough. She worried about the liquids and solids she sent splashing and sliding down inside her, whether they were enough or too much, whether there were (she called them "chemicals" in her thoughts but it read her impression as "poisons") in the liquids and solids, and how they would affect the way the consciousness, the baby, grew its shell and all its internal physical things. Her Concern for the baby outweighed and eclipsed all other Concerns, and a part of that Concern, Anita knew, was unfounded. This made it very difficult to find her.

When it did, though, it considered showing her terrible things—bullets tearing through stomachs, distended flesh bursting open and spilling its contents. But it searched her mindprints and found that she compartmentalized such things, that she put them in a different, distant place in her mind that seemed unconnected to the concept of the "baby." Those thoughts were "work" thoughts, and the baby was a "home" thought, at least so long as she carried its shell inside her.

It didn't matter. The Hollower discovered that those "work" thoughts did not have nearly so much an effect on her as simple puddles of blood in the small outer shell she called "underwear." It told her that she was not strong enough to hold the baby, that the baby was not strong enough to be born. It couldn't find the baby to quiet it, but it didn't have to. She had seen the blood, and that was enough. She called her male to come get her right away.

When the male ("Bennie") found her, she was curled up in a corner of the room, crying in the dark. She showed him the blood on her hands, the blood in a small pool on the floor.

It felt sharp waves of Fear from the male, then, too.

Although the blood had disappeared by the time the ground conveyance got them to the hospital (it remembered this word from the one called Sally's thoughts), Anita remained tense and inconsolable throughout the darkening. It was the clearest the Hollower had ever seen her.

When it came back for her, it would know how to crush her.

It was late when Erik dropped them off on Cerver Street. Stars twinkled here and there in the sky, and a mild breeze lifted Dorrie's hair. She was relieved to hear her wind chimes tinkling softly against the wooden post of her porch. Still, the street was much too quiet otherwise, and when she looked up at the moon, a full round white head without a face, she felt cold all over.

She glanced at her house, willing her feet to move across the street. They wouldn't. It was dark, and her house hulked, unfamiliar and unwelcoming, on her lawn like an animal waiting for sudden movement to spring.

She felt Jake's hand on her shoulder. "You okay, Dorrie?"

"I'm afraid to go back in there," she said plainly. "After feeling so safe with you guys, I just . . . I don't know if I can go back in there."

Jake squeezed her shoulder lightly and blurted in a breath, "Look, I don't mean this to come out all shady and wrong, and you can totally tell me to go to hell for even asking, and I swear I'm only asking because I know what you mean about feeling safer before, but . . . I don't want to stay in my house alone, either. So if you wanted to, I mean, if it wouldn't be too weird or uncomfortable, well, you're definitely more than welcome to stay at my house tonight."

Dorrie felt a flood of relief. "Really? It's cool if I stay?"

Jake smiled. "Of course." He led her to the front door, unlocked it, and let them inside. He gave her a tour of the house, and they chatted, that familiar, comfortable sense of security returning now that they were off the street. It didn't feel like they had just met, but, rather, that they had run into each other again and had a chance to reconnect.

"So how about Cheryl living on this street, too?" Dorrie asked as they detoured through the kitchen. "I thought I recognized Dave from his visits to her, when we first walked in."

"Crazy small town, small world stuff right there." Jake opened the fridge, oblivious to her flinching at the motion, and grabbed a bottle of soda. He offered it to her, but she shook her head. He put it back in the fridge. "And what's up with Cerver Street? This has gotta be the most cursed neighborhood in Lakehaven."

"Yeah, tell me about it. I remember Cheryl, though. I can't believe she's dead. It's so sad. I'd see her on her way to work sometimes, or coming home. She always seemed like she had it all going on, you know? I always admired her. Envied her. She was so beautiful, so well put together. I always thought nothing bad could happen to a woman like that, and if it did, there would be nothing that she didn't have the resourcefulness to handle. I guess—it's stupid, but it's true—that I made her something of goal to reach for."

"I think you've done just fine being you." He winked at her. "Cheryl never really did anything for me. I mean, she was really pretty and all—I see why Dave liked her—but I thought she always looked kind of nervous, like she figured no matter where she was going, she was going to be late and get in trouble. Plus, she was, I guess, too skinny for me."

"Don't you like skinny girls?" Dorrie crossed her arms over her breasts and her stomach with sudden shyness.

Jake looked pained. "Nah, I don't like girls who are too skinny," he answered, looking away. He absently rubbed the crook of his elbow. She thought he might have been thinking about that girl, his ex-girlfriend, who he'd told her about on the porch, the one who died of the drug overdose. Maybe he was done with bony hips and hollow eyes and arms weak and bruised and too thin. She suspected that maybe it was very much true, what he'd said, that maybe his taste for skinny girls was long gone.

"Well, what do you like?" she asked, timid. She'd never been much of a flirt, but she found she genuinely wanted to know what kind of girls Jake did like nowadays.

He looked up at her, seeming to remember himself again, and offered a smile. "I like women, with real curves. Breasts. Hips. Thighs."

As he mentioned each, his eyes traveled over those parts of her. It didn't feel dirty or disrespectful to have him look at her like that, even though his gaze was so intense, and the thoughts behind his eyes so startling and unbelievable to her in their clarity. Instead, it was with such an earnest longing, such an honest appreciation of her as he looked at her body that it made her feel good. Sexy. Even a little bit adventurous.

His eyes returned to hers and with them, nervousness in his expression. "I think you're beautiful."

She felt heat in her cheeks. It was her turn to look away. "I . . . I'm not that . . . ehh, I don't think so."

"You should know so." His voice was low, soft, as if the moment were encased in a bubble he was afraid of popping. "I wish you saw what I see."

Her gaze returned to his. "What do you see?"

"Someone who's never looked at herself long enough to see the beauty in her eyes or her smile, or the grace in the way she moves. The way she lights up a room."

Dorrie looked away again, embarrassed. Guys didn't say things like that to her often. She didn't think Jake was a player type, the kind of guy to wax poetic at a girl who looked vulnerable, easy to lay, and so incredibly grateful for the compliments as to do anything to please him. But the insecurities flared like flames, hot in her cheeks, hot down her neck and across her chest. Hot everywhere. The feelings inside her confused her, made her feel light-headed. She wanted to believe him, but she couldn't wrap her brain around his being attracted to her, to his wanting to grab rolls of flesh, to sink into the fat of her when he touched her.

But he stood so close to her, his breathing different now, the scent of him in her nose, in her lungs, inside her, and she wanted him. A part of her didn't much care if he fed her lies right up until he kicked her out the door, so long as, for at least a little while, for a time, she could have an experience to take out to remember when she felt like it. He made her feel special and desirable and wanted, even needed.

"Why me?" Her voice sounded almost too quiet for her to hear herself. "Why do you like me?"

Jake flinched, but never broke his gaze. "For lots of reasons. I know you don't know me that well, and, under the circumstances, you haven't seen much to want to get to know. I know I'm probably the last guy you'd want attention from. But I do like you, Dorrie, for lots of reasons. I've always thought you were great looking and funny, and today I saw how cool you are to talk to. When I first saw you, I was just wowed by you. But it's more now. When I'm around you, I don't feel stupid or useless. Maybe I am, but . . . look, I'm not good at this. It's been a long time since . . . since anyone has mattered. I don't think I've ever had anyone in my life that I didn't cause pain. After a while, you just push people away to keep them safe . . ." His eyes, glassy, almost wet, continued to look at her with that honest longing, so full of genuine feeling that Dorrie felt her own chest tighten.

"Maybe I'm just selfish, but I'll tell you the truth, Dorrie. Since I first saw you, I've thought about you—where you go when you take walks, what you think about when you stand on your front porch. I never dreamed I'd be spending time with you. Or be alone with you." He tilted his head, taking an awkward step closer to her. "But I've thought about kissing you. Touching you. Does that make me sound like an asshole? I'll just—"

"No," she said hastily. "Not really. I think it's sweet."

He managed a small smile. "Good."

In that moment, nothing else mattered. Dorrie wanted to be close to him and to kiss him, too, to feel the weight of him on top of her, to feel him pressing inside her. Surprising herself, she wrapped her arms around his neck and kissed him. He seemed startled but returned the kiss fiercely, slipping his own arms around her waist. She cringed in that first second that he'd feel her and think her fat, but the way he kissed her melted those worries away. When they parted, panting heavily, he took her hand and led her without a sound to his bedroom and eased her down onto the bed, kissing her again. Just the contact of his skin felt good. The scent of him was intoxicating.

"I want you," he whispered. She wasn't sure if it was meant as a request, whether he was looking for permission to take her, or whether he was simply stating an intention. She responded by kissing him and reaching for him. He was already hard, and this, more than anything else, convinced her that whatever happened after didn't matter, because for this moment, he did want her, and she felt gloriously attractive.

For a good two hours, neither of them thought of the Hollower, of getting high or losing weight or flashing cop lights or cruel teasing teenage boys and unkind names, or of anything else except being with each other, close to each other, in each other's arms. They touched and kissed, delighting in discovering those places that made the other gasp or breathe heavily, and later, in discovering each other's rhythms and feeling like they belonged to each other. They felt alive, protected from the Hollower so long as that connection between them remained unbroken. And when they were done, Jake held on to her like he would never let go. They fell asleep like that, tangled arms and legs and wet skin drying pleasantly cool.

It was the first night in a while that Dorrie felt safe and maybe the first night ever that she felt good enough for someone else. And although she didn't know it then, it was the first night in longer than Jake could remember that he slept easily and soundly, without bad dreams.

It took many lightenings and darkenings of their world before it had found the child-meat they called Sean. He lived outside of the Secondary's hunting ground, and the Primary had found that child-meats were far more resilient in some ways than those who had marinated in their Fears and Insecurities well into adulthood. Therefore, he appeared blurred in its perception, much like the oddity called "baby" inside the meat called DeMarco's shell.

This did not mean it couldn't hurt him. It could get to him, given time.

But that would have to come later. The other meats had plans that demanded its immediate attention.

Still, it would make the child-meat feel its presence.

It gave him a terrible nightmare about big red bug-filled shells that floated on strings, a whole roomful of them, and a decaying figure known to Sean as "Dad." It rubbed out the dad's face, as a reminder.

Sean remembered. He awoke and spent the rest of the darkening with his room filled with light.

Satisfied, it pulled back and waited for the next darkening. When the others were destroyed, it would come back for the child-meat and kill him, too.

CHAPTER ELEVEN

Early the next day, Steve had brunch with Eileen, who was up from Trenton on another case and had stopped in to say hello. She didn't have much to add to Sally Kohlar's case except that she'd died from a severed spinal cord and head and neck injuries. She confirmed that the blood that formed the word on the wall was in fact Sally's, and that given the nature of her injuries, she could not have smeared it herself. This was confirmed by the fact that there was no trace of blood on Sally's fingertips and no skin or anything else to indicate a finger had smeared the word onto the wall.

"Meaning what?" Steve stirred Splenda into his coffee.

Eileen shrugged. "Glove, maybe, although the blood layer is thin and there just isn't a seam mark, a brush stroke, a stray fiber, a layer of epithelials, or a fingerprint anywhere. Not a breath of a clue as to who made those marks, or how. It's almost like the blood just flew up onto the wall and flowed into a pattern of letters." She laughed and sipped her coffee.

He couldn't quite return a laugh with ease. But he wasn't really surprised. He figured the Hollower hadn't really touched Sally's blood at all—couldn't, maybe. But it could have made the blood move. The thought made him feel a little sick around the edges.

Eileen handed the Kohlar file to him. Sally Kohlar had been a delicate little woman, and even minor stresses on her system had effects that wouldn't have registered with a normal body. Steve looked at the pictures, seeing the family resemblance between her and her brother in the blonde hair, the gray-blue eyes, the haunting shadow that never quite left the cheeks. But Dave was sturdier, hearty in spite of his evident drinking problem. Sally had been a wisp, a fragment of that health.

After lunch, he'd thanked Eileen and gone back to the station. That's when Bennie found him.

Bennie looked tired and angry. But when he saw Steve in the locker room, he lunged at him, pushing him up against a locker.

"Man, I told you to leave it alone. I told you."

Steve tried to loosen Bennie's grip on his neck. He managed to splutter a choked, "Wha-whaha?"

"She says you woke it up." Bennie eased up on his neck. When he spoke again, the faint Hispanic accent and the utter exhaustion tinted his words. "Some kind of . . . I don't know, some kind of monster, a *monstruo* that eats souls or something. She thinks it came after her. It's crazy talk, the same fucking crazy talk in the files you asked me about the other day. I told you she was excitable. Impressionable."

Steve gave Bennie a little shove, not hard enough to elicit fresh anger, but hard enough to put some space between them. Mendez's implication was clear. "Bennie, I swear I didn't talk to her. I know she's got enough going on. I wouldn't involve her in any of this. Is she . . . okay? What happened?"

Bennie pressed his palms to his temples, as if trying to wait out the pain of a headache. Still, though, his eyes remained fixed on Steve. "I just got back from the hospital. I came home last night, and she was bleeding. Crying. Thought she'd lost the baby."

"How—"

Bennie held out a hand for him to shut up. "There was blood on the floor, Corimar. I saw it. Blood all over her sweat pants. Blood on her hands. But it was gone when we got to the hospital. All of it. Like it had never been there. And she kept mumbling about it, about the voices in her head telling her it had killed the baby, that her body wasn't strong enough to hold it, that the baby wasn't strong enough to live. It was dead inside her, dissolving into poison right inside her. That it was gone, stolen. All night long like that. All night, man." And Mendez mumbled a word.

"Bennie, I'm sorry, I—" Then it sank in, what Mendez had called him. He pulled away from the angry officer, hands outstretched in a "hold up there and just wait a sec" kind of way, and inched out from between Mendez and the locker. "W-What did you call me?" A distinct unease made his heart beat faster, and he felt heat creeping up his neck to his cheeks.

Bennie glared at him. "What are you, deaf, too? I said, 'all night, man.' I didn't call you anything." From his expression, he honestly didn't seem to know what Steve had meant. He didn't pause long on the subject; instead, he launched into a monologue of half English, half Spanish about how he didn't know what, exactly, was going on, but pregnant-lady rantings about boogeymen that ate babies right out from between their mother's legs and babysitting new detectives who wanted to go play ghost hunter amounted to too much crazy talk on top of twelve-hour shifts. He slammed his locker closed and stormed out of the locker room.

Steve just stood there, shaken up and a little scared.

Maricón. He'd been sure Bennie had called him that. And he was pretty sure it meant something like "faggot." Still, there had been a different quality to his voice when he'd said it, something musical but off-key, something disturbingly multiple. Real or imagined, Steve didn't like that numbing chill and that helpless shock that followed in the wake of Bennie Mendez's departure. He looked after the empty door through which Bennie had exited.

If he said anything to the other guys—

If they heard . . .

Steve kept his head down the rest of the day.

They were coming.

In the collected expanses of what they called time, it had seen its world shrivel and dry up, crack open and bleed out all life and vibrancy, just as it had seen the shells and the minds of countless weak and wounded do the same. It had filled the air of a darkening with the wails of the dying, like a canopy blocking out the beyondlights. It had invaded subsewer holes and deep wells and boxy chambers without cutouts or portals, and it drew all the oppressive Panic and Pain in and out of the cowering shells that occupied them until they exploded in a showy display of Insanity.

Never before, though, had the prospect of devouring the Despair of meats ever excited it so much. Its arrival in this dimension had been shrouded in disgust, but it had come to find what it was about these meats that made its Secondary stake out their world as its hunting ground.

They were capable of more complex thought than some of those in other dimensions, but not so complex as to present impervious mindshells. They were succulent in their misplaced emotions, skewed thoughts, and slanted perceptions. Their insecurities came in such abundance and variety. And their shells were easy to punch through. Theirs was a world of possibility.

But that was not for now. For now was simply to destroy the foremost meats, the Intended. It would have them all in one place, one captive place, and it would do things to them. Delicious things.

In the Convergence, where the nothingness ate all lower senses, it pulsed *zshsian*. It the world of the Intended meats, that would have translated into *sound*, a crude and base approximation for the capability of a Self to express. The Secondary had called out to the Likekind as it lay dying, and the meats had thought of the *zshsian* as a "siren." A sound.

It pulsed *zshsian* again. The voids churned inside it, but the discomfort was eclipsed by its excitement.

They were coming. And it would be ready for them.

Standing in the quad of Oak Hill Assisted Living made Steve feel nettled all over again. The anxious lean of the buildings pressing in what should have felt like open air and space, the self-conscious gray stone, everything. He couldn't imagine how anyone felt safe and happy there. Every time he took in the height of the rough gray walls, the sharp corners of the boxy buildings, and the sea-sickening undulation of the hills, he felt ill and a little dizzy. It seemed as perfect a place as any for a monster to live.

In doing a perimeter of the place, he had discovered a back entrance to the quad where two wings of the buildings met perpendicularly, a chain-link gate to enter through, or more likely, to exit from in case of emergency or fire. The quad itself was quiet. He couldn't shake the feeling that like the inhabitants, even the buildings and benches and the grass itself were sleeping and oblivious to his presence. So oblivious, maybe, that no amount of banging on doors or screaming up at the buildings would bring any kind of help running . . .

It was a stupid, paranoid thought. He checked the time on his watch (it was just about 10 p.m.) and then crossed the quad to the catacomb door, aware of the rustle of his footsteps in the grass and the feel of the night wind blowing past his bare arms. He repressed a shiver.

Since the scene had already been processed, he'd

made a quick phone call to Henry Pollock, the administrator of Oak Hill Assisted Living, who had been accommodating enough (*"Sure, officer, feel free to drop by any time. Tonight, if you're so inclined. Whatever you need to resolve this tragedy . . ."*), whether to avoid the trouble of a warrant or the extra publicity of police activity. He'd given Steve full rein to look around.

One problem solved, at least.

Although Pollock told him he'd wait around to let him in, Steve didn't want to encourage him hanging around. The supervising officer of the Kohlar investigation had been given a key to and a map of the catacombs. In the event that Pollock couldn't stick around, having the police copy of the key and that map would mean one less obstacle to overcome. Steve hadn't asked for either or signed them out. He'd found them in their respective envelopes in the board room, where the detectives met to go over charts and graphs and photo displays pertaining to cases, and he'd just slipped the key and the folded map into his pockets right after his shift. He was fairly sure no one saw, and that mattered to him. He wasn't one to go against rules; he never had been. He thrived on structure and the sense of security derived from order. He'd felt like the key was burning a hole right through his pants the whole way out of the station, and on the drive over to Oak Hill, he kept expecting Shirley's voice to break in over the radio and ask him to return what he'd taken.

But standing there in front of the catacomb door, his hand in the pocket with the key, feeling the smooth brass neck of it, he felt like he'd done something good—or at the very least inevitable. Sometimes sacrifices had to be made, he told himself, so that others could be saved. If bending the rules meant he could uphold a greater good, he was willing to accept that.

He checked his watch again. They were late. He hoped nothing was wrong.

"Excuse me, uh . . . excuse me there. Hi, there. Yes, I see you've made it."

Steve turned at the sound of the voice. A dark-haired man in glasses and a neatly pressed suit and white coat had closed most of the distance of the quad between him and the main doors of the building. He recognized the man as Henry Pollock, the administrator at Oak Hill. When Steve first had gone down into the catacombs to investigate Sally Kohlar's crime scene, Pollock had been there, a small man in smart clothes, explaining liability and accessibility to the supervising officer with careful, quiet, even-toned speech.

Nothing about Pollock initially struck Steve as threatening, or even easily excitable, but an air of confrontation preceded Pollock as his purposeful strides brought him to the catacomb door.

"I see you've made it back," he repeated with the slightest tinny twinge of annoyance.

"Yes, and thank you for allowing me to poke around, Mr. Pollock. I'm just here to give the Kohlar crime scene another once over, to look into a few things down there that may help me put some of these pieces together. I apologize for not stopping in the office first. It didn't seem worth disturbing you, since we had a key and all." He produced the brass item from his pocket and offered the doctor a smile that he thought reflected unquestionable authority as well as amiable confidence. *No questions need to be asked and no paperwork needs to be done, thank you. Just take a hike.* He chanced a quick look down at his watch and hoped Dave and the others would have enough common sense to lay low until Pollock disappeared.

"Well, thank you for the phone call. I have to say, though, that I expected you earlier. I was just about to leave for the evening, when I got a call from Sherman, my security man on nights. We have a camera that surveys the grounds here, and you almost gave poor old Sherman in the security room a heart attack. Things are usually quiet here, and I suppose it slipped my mind, letting him know to be on the lookout for you." The doctor chuckled, and Steve tried to volley back a light laugh, too, but he was worried about the others. The security camera might cause a problem for them to get in unseen. He hoped Jake would think enough to check for one.

"Oh, allow me at least to open up for you. And then, please do take your time and feel free to roam about. Sally was like family to us, so we want done everything that needs to be done." The mild, modulated tone of his speaking voice was there, and the expression on his face placid. Maybe Steve had imagined the confrontational air about him. He seemed fine now. "I do hope you find everything you've coming looking for."

"Well, thanks. I'm hoping it will be a productive evening."

As he drew close, Pollock slowed before a big red

rubber ball on the grass, which Steve assumed had been left over from some recreational game of kickball or something. Instead of sidestepping it, though, the doctor gave it a savage kick out of the way that launched it against the wall near the door. It popped when it hit the gray stone near Steve's feet. It left a black starburst pattern down near the ground, a sticky sort of stuff that quivered when it hit and then stayed put.

Steve frowned. The doctor was speaking to him, but he hadn't been listening, something about his work on the force—

"—as strong looking as you. It's amazing how far we've come in even say, the last fifteen, twenty years. I guess that's maybe why they overlooked you being a queer, is that it?"

Steve's head snapped back to the doctor. "Excuse me?"

The doctor, facing the door, had his back to Steve, but he reached into his pocket to produce a key to the lock. Steve didn't know how he'd missed Pollock's black gloves.

Pollock said, "The other detectives. They know, I'm sure."

Steve was about to answer when there was a click and a groan and the door flew open. Pollock turned around, and Steve felt his stomach bottom out.

The doctor had no face. What had been neatly-combed black hair formed a hat. The white coat disintegrated into ash that blew off toward the center of the quad. The Hollower tilted its head to the side, and even without a mouth, it seemed to smile at him.

"You don't really think you can kill me, do you Steve?"

By reflex, Steve clicked the safety off his gun and rested his hand on it in one motion. "We intend to, or die trying."

The Hollower's laughter engulfed him, swimming in and out of his ears. Then it snapped off suddenly. "Then," it said with ecstatic glee, "you'll all die. Starting with you, Steve."

It backed through the open doorway into the gloom of the catacombs' interior.

At a quarter after nine that night, Erik pulled into the parking lot of Dave's apartment building. In the back seat, Jake sat with Dorrie. All of them wore black. The two in the back fidgeted with the flashlights in their laps. As Dave got in the passenger side, he scooped up the flashlights meant for him and Erik.

"Ready to go get us a monster?" He tried to sound light, but it fell flat in the tense air of the car. Erik gave him a weak smile.

"How did Casey take it?"

Erik looked pained. "She won't talk to me about any of it—or anything else, really—until I come back." It looked as if he were going to add "if I come back," but he didn't. Instead, he added, "She kissed me good-bye, though."

"Good luck, you mean."

Erik shrugged. "Maybe."

"I called my brother," Jake said from the backseat. "He wasn't . . . that's not his number anymore. He was the only one I would need to say good-bye to." Then, realizing the implication in what he said, he hastily added, "Not that it's good-bye. But it would have been nice to hear from him anyway, ya know?"

"I called my mom." Dorrie looked out the window. "She sounded so happy to hear from me, I thought at first. Mostly, though, she kept rattling on about her job, her friends, her ladies' group." Dorrie wiped at her eyes, her head still turned away from them. "I had this friend Nela in college. She and her mom were best friends, and she always used to say how she could hiccup and her mom would know her well enough to know what she'd drunk too fast. I talked to my mother for a little over an hour, and she never once asked me what was wrong. And I never told her."

Jake put his hand over hers and squeezed.

Dave wanted to be able to tell them that they'd talk to their family again, that Erik would be home and helping Casey pick out napkin colors for the tables at the wedding reception, and Jake would find his brother and maybe they could grab a beer, and that Dorrie could call her mom tomorrow and try to work a word in edgewise. But he found the words wouldn't come. He couldn't make them surface.

"So where do we go first?" Erik turned left at the corner onto the main road, toward the turnoff for the highway. Like Cheryl, he'd been with Dave to see Sally a few times, so he knew how to get to Oak Hill.

"I don't know. When Steve first told me, he just said they'd found her down in the catacombs. He didn't say where. But I'm sure he could find the way back to the . . . place where she was. The crime scene."

"*It was a word, Mr. Kohlar. HOLLOW. Does that mean*

anything to you? Anything significant about that word?"
Dave didn't think he had the stomach to see that.

"I hope he'll be okay there by himself, until we get there," Dorrie said.

No one answered, lost each in his own thoughts. Dave was worried, frankly. And not just for Steve. He remembered what happened last time, when they'd gone into Feinstein's house.

As they approached the turnoff, Oak Hill Assisted Living loomed gray and sad against the night sky. Dave shook his head, wondering how it was that he ever could have found that place a comforting and inviting home to leave his sister. Looking at it now, it filled him with such a distinct sense of unease.

It will swallow everyone whole.

It was a sudden thought, and he was fairly sure it wasn't his. It had a mocking quality to it that he associated with the Hollower, reminding him it was never too far away.

Erik pulled the car around back, and they parked toward the edge of the lot, near a dense line of trees and out of the pale, tan glow of the arc-sodium lights.

Gripping their flashlights, they sat for several silent seconds in the car, their breathing falling in sync, their gazes drifting out over the property in front of them.

Dave could see a side gate between two of the buildings, one of the metal link kinds with the U-shaped piece of metal that wraps around a solid bar to keep it closed. It mildly surprised him that there was no other lock on the gate and no other visible means of securing the facility.

And then, of course, it dawned on him that easy access was probably exactly what the Hollower wanted.

Come to me.

Dave got out of the car. The others followed.

And that's when they heard noises in the quad.

Steve remained stone still, waiting, counting off the seconds in his head, feeling each breath, *in, out, in, out*, and yet, the quad remained quiet. Confused, Steve peered into the doorway. He could see no trace of the Hollower in the inky interior, even when he shined the police-issued flashlight he'd brought into its depth. No sign of life in the windows above, he noticed as he turned around. He surveyed the quad in the moon- and starlight. Nothing in the grass, either. The benches squatted silent and empty. Not so much as a cricket or a tree frog.

The Hollower was gone. He chanced one more sweep of the flashlight, keeping it low as it glided over one empty bench after—

Wait. That one's not empty.

Someone sat on one of the far benches, down at the bottom of the sloping grass. Whoever it was sat facing away from him, unmoving. Maybe waiting for someone. It occurred to Steve that maybe the others had come separately, moving in at different times so as not to draw attention. Maybe that was Dave down there, or Erik.

Either one of them would have come up to the catacomb door first, to look for me.

He checked his watch again, pushing the button to make the numbers and hands glow. 10:30 P.M. already.

They were late. Very late. He looked up at the figure on the bench, who did not turn to scan for him across the quad, or even shift to a more comfortable position.

Steve started toward the bench. When he got within ten feet or so, his heart jumped a little in his chest, and he slowed down.

It was Ritchie Gurban. The hair, gelled sharp in the moonlight, the back of his neck, the sprawl of his shoulders were all familiar.

But what was Ritchie doing there?

The answer came to him, plain and simple. It wasn't Ritchie. It couldn't be. It flew in the face of logic.

And if it wasn't Ritchie—

A brilliant, blazing pain in the back of his head made the quad swim like white smoke in front of him for a moment. Drawing his gun, he spun around and aimed it about where the blow had come from. But seeing what had hit him, he lowered the gun, stunned.

A humanoid form, made entirely, it seemed, of ash and strips of paper and torn up manila bits of tightly packed file folders glued together with the same black jelly that had splattered the wall from the burst kickball, raised a fist. A light wind blew, and fragments from the arm blew away from the main bulk. The wisps and scraps paused in midair and reformed into something that looked to Steve very much like a sledgehammer. The paper form swung this and connected with Steve's wrist. He heard a crack on the heels of which followed a sharp pain, and he dropped the gun. Steve backed away from the paper thing in horror. From one of the buildings near where they stood, a window opened, and sheets of what maybe were medical forms or patient records followed by folders and interoffice envelopes streamed like confetti out into the quad. These tore themselves into tiny pieces amidst a swirling wind that seemed to move nothing else. The bits quickly reformed themselves into other paper creatures like the one who had hit him. One of them had simulated a tire iron. He could tell by the shape. Another had a bat.

Steve ducked down to pick up his gun as the one closest to him raised the paper sledgehammer again, and he raised it to shoot a hole clean through the bastard. The paper creature leaned over and made a motion like it was blowing on him, and the gun disintegrated in his hand. He shook off the black dust, horrified.

Then the paper creature kicked him hard in the ribs, and he felt all the air being knocked out of him. He rolled over and tried to stand, but the other ones closed in around him and rained down blows with their weapons. They were the paper-trail anger and fear of hundreds of patients' case files, the torn up resentment, reassembled and refocused. He heard snaps and cracks all over as explosions of pain went off like fireworks across his back, through his ribs, along his arms and legs. He kept trying to stand, his mind a whirling mess of panic and fury, but he couldn't seem to get his footing before the next wave of blows from above. He managed to pull himself closer to the bench where he'd seen the likeness of Ritchie Gurban, and as he did, this seemed to spur it into motion.

Ritchie got up and turned around. He did indeed have a face, but all the warmth and honesty had been drained out of it. Slack-jawed, dull-eyed indifference met Steve as the thing pretending to be Ritchie took a few steps back. From the shadows stepped other figures, nonpaper types. Steve recognized each with an internal twinge of pain in his chest. His brothers in blue, his fellow officers, formed a semicircle around him as he got the shit kicked out of him, and not one moved to do a damn thing to stop it.

Their faces, passive, disinterested, watched as a thick paper bottle exploded against his nose and blood spilled out and into his mouth. He spit. His angry eyes searched the faces of the other cops, but they made no move to help, no move to extend a hand. They didn't look guilty or helpless, nor did they look pleased. They didn't seem to think anything of it at all.

Except maybe the world was better off with one less gay guy.

He covered his head with his hands, unable now to catch his breath or to manage to even pull himself up on his hands and knees, and that was the thought, whether from his own insecure mind or from the seething hate of the paper monsters, that echoed in his head.

One less, one less, one less . . .

The sound of stacks of paper falling hard slapped down all around him, but it was starting to sound far away, like he was under the waves of the ocean and they were crashing over his head, pounding and tossing him against rocks and stones and surf.

Through a small space between his forearms, he could see their black shoes lined up in a row in front of him. He thought he heard one say his name, but it sounded very far away.

"Steve!"

That sounded like Dave. He peeked through his arms. The black shoes were gone. They'd left him. But he heard a little thunder in the ground beneath his cheek.

"Steve! Get the fuck off him, you bastards!"

He rolled a little and felt a sharp pain that made the air leak out of his body. Throbs of pain went off sporadically all over. He couldn't seem to figure out where his legs were or where they belonged on the ground. Then the night sky swallowed up all sight and sound.

CHAPTER TWELVE

It was dark when they passed through the gate, and when Dave saw the weird paper people beating the hell out of Steve, he looked around for something, anything to fend them off with. Finding nothing, he charged them anyway, swinging his flashlight. The others followed close behind. They connected plastic to paper and sent bits of printed forms and folders and envelopes scurrying into the wind. The paper people broke up easily enough, a flutter of papers dervishing up into the air above Erik's head. Dave suspected it was an empty victory. The Hollower had eased up on trying to kill Steve because it knew it would have another chance. A chance, now, to kill all of them.

Steve didn't look too good. Aside from a hundred little paper cuts all across his exposed skin, there were blotchy bruises on his face and arms, bloody patches on his back, little splatters of blood on the grass around him. He was breathing, but it came in hitching, irregular shudders that worried Dave for more reasons than those in the here and now. They crouched down around him, trying to get him to speak. Dave and Erik turned him over fully on his back. His left wrist was swollen and ruddy

218

with the blood pooling beneath the skin, which had taken on a waxy shine. One of his eyes looked puffy and red. Blood darkened his chin and lips and spattered the light brown fuzz of five o'clock shadow on his jaw and beneath his nose.

"Oh my God," Dorrie muttered, and started pulling out the handkerchiefs she'd brought. She tied the long one into a sling and, with Jake and Erik's help, slipped it over Steve's head and got his arm through it. Dave kept trying to talk to him, to get him to wake up.

After several long minutes, Steve groaned and opened his eyes. The others breathed a collective sigh of relief. Steve said something which came out cracked and smoky. He spit blood onto the grass and with another groan, sat up, and tried again. "Door's open. It knows we're here."

"I see that," Dave said, and offered him a hand to help him up. "Are you okay?"

Steve wobbled a little when he got up but righted himself and stood on his own, even if he did slump a little. He nodded at Dave but winced as he tried to rotate his wrist. "This is busted, though. Not that it much matters. Firing a gun at it is useless, and I'm sure as hell not going to swing at the fucker." Then to Dorrie, "pardon my English."

Dorrie waved it off. "I don't intend to swing at the fucker, either."

"Are you going to be okay to do this?" Jake glanced at the open doorway to the catacombs. "Devil only knows what it's going to throw at us in there. Are you okay to get around?"

Steve regarded him with solemn eyes. "Doesn't matter either way. There is no way in hell I'm letting you all go in without me."

"Safety in numbers," Erik muttered.

"And it's too late to turn back now, anyway." Dorrie wrapped her arms around her body as if to shelter it from cold. "Can't you feel it? Something's different. It's already changed things around us. No one's going to come if we call. No one's going to hear a damn thing. Because they're in their world and we're in the Hollower's version of it. There is no place to leave Steve that the Hollower can't make rise up and tear into him."

"I think Dorrie's right," Jake said. "I feel it, too." He shined his flashlight up at the windows, waving the light wildly. Dark forms moved across their field of view but didn't seem to notice them at all. "See? Wherever they are, it's like there's a one-way mirror between us. We can see out to them, but they can't see—"

One of the figures passing the window stopped and turned to look out at them.

Dave felt his heart jump in his chest. Jake slowed the movement of the light and retrained it on the window. Whoever the person in the window was—and Dave was pretty sure that "person" wouldn't cover the half of it—waved at them. Then it darted away from the window.

Like it's coming down here to meet us.

"Run," Dave said.

"Huh?"

Dave tugged at Steve. "Run! It's coming!"

"What is it?" Steve limped alongside Dave while the

others, confused, hurried forward toward the catacomb doorway.

"I don't know. Let's not find out." Dave pulled him through into the darkness behind the others. From the mouth of the catacombs, they peered out, tense, ready to spring forth into the dark if necessary. Several seconds passed in silence with no sign of any figure emerging from the building.

"What do you think it was?" Jake rubbed hands against his thighs and exhaled a shaky breath.

"I think it was a nudge to get a move on, frankly." Dave turned toward a long cement staircase leading down into the earth. He shined his flashlight down into the darkness, and they could see a gray door at the bottom, half-open, the rust from its hinges bleeding out on the cement walls. "Guess we should get going."

Steve limped in front of him. "We're heading toward where they found Sally, right? Let me go first."

They followed Steve down the stairs, their footsteps echoing against the walls. When they reached the bottom, Steve moved to open the door. "Guys, help me. I can't do it with one hand."

Dave and Erik pulled at the door while Jake slid partly through and helped Steve push. The door moaned grudgingly and gave them a few inches, enough for them to slip through to the other side.

They congregated in a cavernous room that formed the mouth of a long tunnel. Their flashlights reached only so far into the blackness beyond their collective glow. Their tentative arms of light faded without really showing them much of anything beyond cracked slabs of thick, uneven concrete that made up the walls, floor, and ceiling, and faded paint, like old scars, which might have once labeled the tunnels and where they went. The air in the tunnel smelled stale and vaguely of ammonia, and it sat heavier in the lungs than the air outside.

"So," Dorrie gazed up and around the chamber, "where to, Steve?"

Steve frowned. "Looks different. This . . . room, I don't remember . . . it wasn't like this." The stiff, minimal movements of his lips revealed his pain. With a wince that came out as a flat whistle, he pulled the map out of his pocket and unfolded it. It had gray lines delineating the faint pink tunnels that ran under Oak Hill and indications of occasional rooms at the ends of smaller branches leading off from the main lines. Squiggly lines, inked over the map in pen, illustrated obstacles and blocks from caved in walls, weak ceilings, and weaker floors that made tunnels impassable or rooms inaccessible. Color coding marked off pipes and old electrical lines, which, Steve informed them, Pollock had said were dead now.

Steve pointed to a large irregular shape at the bottom left corner of the map. "We're here. I . . . I don't know. I mean, it's on the map, but . . . there's something different about this room."

Erik frowned. "Maybe it's already started changing things. Do we trust the map?"

"We don't have much choice." Steve pointed to a small tributary tunnel running almost vertical on the map to a side branch off one of the main tunnels, about two-thirds of the way across. Someone, ostensibly one of the officers, had marked a grayish spot with a large red ball-point circle. "That's where we found your sister, Dave. Shaft was right there."

Dave nodded. Something about even just the circle marking off the place where Sally died gave him the chills and soured the taste in his mouth. "We should go that way."

Steve indicated the middle-most tunnel of the four ahead of them. "We should take that one. That, at least, looks kind of familiar. I remember we took a tunnel that went that way."

Jake shined his flashlight at the head of the tunnel. The light spilled only so far as to illuminate a huge gray spider with very long legs scurrying away from the brightness. "Let's do it."

They moved as a cautious whole in the direction Steve indicated, crossing the large cavern, flinching at the echo of their own footsteps.

They stepped into the tunnel.

"I probably don't need to suggest that we ought to all stay together, huh?" Steve looked down at his swollen wrist. Dave thought he could detect fear in his voice—fear of being alone and even more vulnerable in his present state. Dave was pretty sure that Steve believed one more round with the Hollower would be the end of him.

Dave knew the feeling.

Erik chuckled, a sound as dry as the air around them. "Yeah, we thought so last time, too."

"What happened last time?" Dorrie asked.

Before Erik could answer, a low rumble from behind them drew their attention back to the open chamber.

"Oh my God."

It was standing in the center of the room, and it looked very, very tall to Dave, taller than the last one, taller at that moment than anything Dave had ever seen.

The Hollower tilted its head as if studying them. The subtle ripples of its head suggested amusement.

Jake raised his flashlight and shined it in the Hollower's blank countenance. The ripples of the surface pinched in anger, and the black glove flicked in Jake's direction. The light died. From the light of the others' flashlights, though, they could see the one that Jake held shake in his hand.

"Oh, shit!" He dropped it, and it rolled toward the Hollower's feet and came to a stop an inch or so before the toe.

One by one, the flashlights in each person's hand winked out, and the chamber got darker and darker. Dave felt the flashlight in his hand vibrate, and then struggle violently in his hand. It began to buzz, and he felt something serrated scraping into his palm. He dropped his, too, and from the clatter of plastic that followed, he figured the others had followed suit.

For a moment, silence reigned, and only the heavy, ragged breathing of the others verified that they were still there. Dave opened his mouth to ask if everyone was okay, and—

A roaring, bestial face flew out at them from the darkness, glowing silver, hungry, hateful—an awful thing that morphed from one atrocity to another. They screamed and fled blindly into the tunnel. For a long time, the pounding of feet against concrete drowned out all other sound. Dave was afraid to look back for fear of tripping and maybe being trampled in the panic, or worse, being left behind. He felt occasionally for the wall to his right, its rough surface slicing into his hand as he grazed along its length. He cringed against the pain, drew his hand away, and kept up with the breathing and the slapping of feet and the crying which didn't seem to be coming from anyone immediately around him but from some nebulous place in front of him.

Crying? He didn't understand how it was possible, but it sounded—it was crazy—like Sally . . .

"I . . . I think . . ." Erik managed through breaths, "think it's gone." They skidded to a stop—that's how it sounded to Dave. But something was wrong. The air was different. The feeling of space being occupied next to him was gone.

The crying in the distance became laughing.

"Okay, now what? The flashlights are gone, and we can't see the map. I don't think I can find this place on feeling my way alone. I think we should go back, see if we can find the flashlights and proceed from there." Steve waited for an answer . . . a mutter . . . a mumble. No one answered.

"Dave? Erik? Dorrie? Jake, come on, man. Somebody? Anybody?"

No one answered. Steve was alone in the tunnel, in the dark. His wrist pounded out pain up his arm and down into his hand. Although he couldn't see anything anyway, he felt one of his eyes was nearly swollen shut.

It was tender and painful when he touched it with his good hand.

Steve was in trouble. "Shit," he muttered. "Fucking great."

He reached for his gun in the dark but remembered it had been reduced to powder. He couldn't remember if he'd brought the hunting knife or the mace . . . he didn't think so. No matter; weapons probably wouldn't do him any good anyway, even if he did have them.

He limped back in the direction from which he'd come. Even if he was alone, it didn't mean he shouldn't try to go ahead with what he'd said about finding the flashlights. He wouldn't be able to find jack shit without a light—tunnel sites or people. The pain in his body made him want to just sit and let the darkness bury him over, but he kept on.

When he'd gone what he thought was just about the distance they'd run away from the initial chamber, he felt around the walls for the mouth of the tunnel and an opening out into a larger space. His hand turned a corner, and he breathed a sigh of relief. He slid down slowly to the ground, feeling along for the dropped flashlights. As each minute passed where his hands turned up nothing but rough rock, that relief slipped further and further away.

He was about to give up when his hand closed on something cylindrical and ridged, reminiscent of a flashlight handle. He slid his finger along to find the button to turn it on. It took a few seconds, but when he found it, it exploded in light. He blinked a few times and, standing with a groan, shined the light around the room.

It was not the room they'd first found upon entering the catacombs. It was a locker room. Recognition dawned in degrees as he looked around. A row of lockers ran down the center of the room, as well as along the sides and back wall. Behind where he stood, three sinks lined a short wall, and beyond that, around the corner, was the shower.

"Boys say things, sometimes. They don't mean it."

Steve crossed his good arm beneath his bad one, over his chest. That had been a long time ago.

"Boys say things, but that doesn't give you the right—"

It didn't. He knew that. He'd put that kind of hair-trigger impulsiveness behind him. But the feeling was there, all the same. He remembered.

He was a grown man, for God's sake. A police officer. He'd passed the Academy at the top of his class. He was one of the youngest officers to make detective in the whole county.

And just the sight of those lockers frightened him. It wasn't about the Big Bad Gayness magnified by being a teenager. It wasn't being unable to control his erection around other boys or being unable to listen to them talking about jerking off or screwing some girl in the back of their dad's car without being distinctly uncomfortable. It was that terror, that anger when Robbie McCormick called him a homo and his thoughtless swing that sent Robbie flying into those tiles. His head cracked like a melon, and his blood gave those pale blue tiles a funny tint. Steve was fourteen.

It had never been the fear or confusion of being gay. It had been the fear of getting caught.

That, and the guilt of knowing he'd do just about anything, even hurt someone else, to make sure he didn't get caught, bothered him.

He crossed the locker room and moved around to the showers. The tiles where he'd knocked Robbie down still had a dark brownish stain.

He blinked, shaking his head. This couldn't be happening. Shouldn't be happening. He was in a tunnel somewhere underground, under the Oak Hill Assisted Living facility. He was not, *could* not be in the locker rooms of Bloomwood High School.

He reached out a finger to touch the tiles. They felt cool and smooth. The room smelled faintly like sweat socks and sprays of deodorant—smells he associated with gym class.

A sharp whistle made him jump. His gym teacher had a whistle like that. He turned around. All the locker doors were open. Every single one, as far as he could see. He made his way back through the locker room and down the aisles. Locker after locker contained bloody clothes, bloody sneakers, gym uniforms soaked so dark Steve couldn't read the logos.

As he turned the corner, he saw one of the lockers wasn't open. A combination lock hung from the door. Smeared in something black and goopy on the door were three numbers: 18-9-13.

With his good hand, Steve tried the combination and pulled on the lock. It opened. He eased open the locker door. There was a folded note inside and his gun. He took the note and unfolded it. It simply said, "Shoot yourself. Make it stop. Shoot them. Make it all stop."

He dropped the note, kicking it aside. But he took the gun anyway. He had no intention of shooting anyone, but . . . it felt better to have his gun back on him. Just in case.

Just in case of what? He didn't know. *Just . . . just in case, dammit.*

A school bell rang, the kind indicating class changes, and it made him flinch. At that moment, the lights blew out in a fizzle and light spray of sparks. A door opened somewhere, and a low growling entered the room, followed by a shuffling, lumbering sound. Steve hid behind one of the lockers and peered out. Things were filing into the room; things that moved on appendages that dragged and slithered and undulated over the floor. By shapes in the dimness more so than in any detail, Steve picked out their grotesque forms. One looked eerily reminiscent of a decapitated head (*Robbie's head. Oh my God, it is! It's Robbie's head.*), its vacant, dazed expression rocking back and forth on what looked like an over-sized hand with too many fingers. Another looked a little like an angler fish hoisted on long stiltlike legs. The last two of them came in dragging something that looked like a gnawed part of a torso, stringy flesh hanging from stumps where the legs and waist would be.

Steve groaned. He crept around the side of the row of lockers, doing his best to keep the metal between him and the indescribable things on the other side. He glanced at the door and then back at them, judging distances, wondering how fast they could move if they saw him.

They were spreading out along the row of lockers, slapping at each other, making gurgling and warbling sounds among them. The only place out of the line of view of the lockers was in the shower, and he'd be damned if he'd back himself into that particular corner.

The end cap of the locker would be too narrow to hide him for long. They were going to see him, and if they caught him—

A long, high-pitched scream speared the air over his head, and he looked back. One of the monsters, a creature with a bulbous body that seemed to fill and shrink, waved a long black tentacle lined with spikes in his direction. He dove for the door, feeling the heat of acrid breaths and the smack of something wet and scaly on his back. He cried out when it hit him but pushed through the open door anyway and tumbled out next to Ritchie Gurban's bench outside in the quad.

Confused, he collapsed on it, feeling its solid cool surface beneath him, and dragged in full lungfuls of outside air. The place where the thing had touched him burned on his back.

Dave spun around to see an empty black tunnel. He waited a moment, his heart knocking on his chest. A cold, panicked sweat formed under his arms.

"Erik? Steve?" No one answered, but his voice bounced lightly against the catacomb walls, taking on a ghostly thinness that Dave couldn't help but feel was mocking him, moving away from him into the darkness and changing into the sound of many odd voices.

He almost called out Cheryl's name but stopped himself, remembering this was a different time, a different place. He felt a twinge of sadness. The last time, he'd been fighting for women he cared about—a sister that he felt he owed a better life, and a woman that he very much thought he could marry someday. Who was he fighting for now? And what difference did it make if the Hollower got to him, too?

The difference, said a voice in his head, *is that if you don't fight, it gets away with killing the people you loved most in the world. Vengeance can work two ways, Dave. It may have its facelessness in a twist because you killed its Secondary. But then it went and killed people that mattered to you, too. It comes down to you or the Primary, one way or another.* The voice had a Cherylish aspect to it, and Dave supposed that was because he wanted to hear those words in her voice. He wanted to believe she could still be with him, at least in some small way, even here and now.

He wished for the flashlight as he took a few steps forward. The mustiness of the air, the faint smell of ammonia and dust, got caught up in his nose and made him sneeze. The sound reverberated into the black.

He hadn't gotten that far when he noticed the outline of something in the distance lit by a faint aerial glow. As he got closer, it became clearer, and at five feet away, it was very nearly spotlit from the sourceless light above.

A small table (*like the one in Feinstein's upstairs hallway*, he thought) stood in front of him, made of polished wood with thin, slightly curving legs. On the table sat a black toy telephone, an old-fashioned rotary type with a wheel that spun out dialed numbers in a series of clicks. Dave scowled at it. His whole life phones meant doctors calling with bad news, police calling with worse news, Cheryl calling to say she was leaving; Georgia calling to tell him his boss was angry again.

He hated them. Them, and big grandfather clocks.

Still, when it began to ring, he closed the remaining distance between him and the phone on numb legs and answered it. He was sure he'd hear Sally on the other end, just like last time.

He didn't. "I—I used the towels. They're ruined. I used them to s-soak up the blood. There w-was so-so-so much. S-so much blood." It was his own voice he heard on the line, distant through time and a little less weathered and gravelly, but his voice all the same. This came with a sharp, vivid image of a sunny day, Sally's tiny blonde head in a quickly spreading corona of blood. The air smelled like apple blossoms, and the sun felt hot, making him sweat down his neck and back and under his arms and behind his knees, hot and guilty and helpless. Sally's eyes stayed closed long after he thought she should have gotten up. Only her skinny little chest moved, and even then, only in shallow, irregular hitches that didn't sound right or normal, even to a nine-year-old boy.

He remembered calling for his mother, thinking the frantic, terrified squeak would never reach her, but worried at the same time that if he left his sister something even worse might happen, and then he'd really be in trouble. He also remembered his mother running across the backyard. She looked at him as if he'd failed her, failed his mother and Sally both. It had been the first, but not the only, time she had looked at him like that.

"It was an accident." He mouthed the words along with the mental image of his nine-year-old self.

He also remembered the way the lady next door kept a chilly wall of disapproval between her and him. No comfort, no hugs, no reassurances that Sally wasn't going to bleed dry all over the ambulance. She glared down over the tip of her nose at him like he was some hooligan, fatherless and directionless and by all accounts Godless, a mere nine years away from prison and maybe only five away from some juvenile detention facility. Even her words were crusty, brittle with the sureness that he'd pushed Sally on purpose. Like he'd hurt her on purpose. Like he was always pushing her right into the path of trouble.

He'd sneaked out late to mop up the blood. Knowing it was out there, soaking into the wood, staining the concrete, drove him crazy. If he had to look at those blood stains every time he played out there, he'd smack his own head senseless.

He'd used his mother's towels. They were ruined, stained a sickening purple-red. He even mopped up a couple stray blonde hairs. She'd smacked him for ruining her towels. Never once did she ever tell him it wasn't his fault. And she'd never said Sally was okay.

Dave was about to say he was sorry into the little black toy telephone when there was a click like call-waiting, and then another voice got on the line.

"I'm so cold, Dave, so cold all over. Help me. My feet are frozen. And my legs hurt so, so bad . . ." Cheryl. Hearing her voice brought immediate tears to his eyes.

Dave blinked to clear his vision. He couldn't find words to respond.

"Dave, tell me there are no more Hollowers. Tell me that one will never come back. Tell me we're free."

"Cheryl, I—" his voice cracked.

"Tell me that underneath all that fucked up, cowardly, self-pitying, self-centered, drunken bullshit, there's a man that might be able to satisfy me once in a while, that might be able to keep up with me, that might actually be able to protect me and provide for me. Tell me you'll do more for me than you ever did for your mother or sister."

Dave couldn't tell her those things. Even now—especially now—he couldn't reassure her. His eyes felt heavy, the tears solid, like pebbles in his sockets. He held the receiver of the toy telephone to his ear and his chest heaved, but the tears didn't fall, and he couldn't make a sound.

"The only thing you've ever done right," Cheryl's voice said in a maliciously calm, precise way, "is realize you ought to just do yourself in. But you're too stupid to have picked any way faster than alcohol. Now Erik, he had the right idea. Your new friend Jake, too. Your new cop friend, well, it was just a matter of time before someone kicked the life out of him. Oh, I love that shuddery little sound you make when you can't quite draw in enough air to breathe, when all kinds of things are broken and jagged inside you, puncturing your lungs like balloons and tearing holes into those blood bags you call organs. But then you die all the same, don't you? You all do. That stupid fat cow you're hanging with nowadays was as dense as you. Still, once I cut through the fat . . ." The voice changed as she spoke, becoming an all too familiar kaleidoscope of highs and lows and overlapping timbres. She (it) laughed, a deep bass unlike anything Cheryl's voice had ever produced. "If you think you can help them, you're wrong. They're dead already, every one of them—all the ones you fought with before and all the ones you brought with you to-night. All the silly self-help tricks in the world couldn't save those sorry lots of meat. So now, it's only you. All by your lonesome. All by yourself. Everyone's been taken away from you, so *why don't you just die?*"

"How?" The word came out dry, rusty.

"Telephone cord will hold up to asphyxiation. Or take the razor out of the table drawer. I sharpened it just for you."

Dave opened the little drawer of the desk, beneath the phone. There was indeed a straight razor in the drawer, along with three unmarked orange bottles of pills. He picked one up, shook it, and it rattled. He put it back in the drawer.

"You can go fuck yourself," Dave said quietly, and hung up the phone.

He turned to walk away when it rang again, sounding a little more shrill in his ear, he thought, with each ring. He hesitated a moment and then picked the receiver back up. Elevator music filled his ear, some mournful Michael Bolton–esque sax version of John Lennon's "Imagine." After a moment, the music paused, and a voice said, "We're sorry. All operators are currently unavailable. But your death is important to us. Please stay on the line, and the next available representative will take your call. Thank you. We're sorry. All friends are currently unavailable. But your—"

He slammed the phone down, but the elevator music started up again. He could hear it through the receiver, a faint echoing strain of saxophone that sounded soulless between the walls of the tunnel. He closed his eyes. "You'll have to try harder."

When he opened them, both phone and table were gone, the music already fading. He pressed forward into the encompassing black.

He'd gone about a hundred feet or so farther down when the ground fell away from him. The air rushed out of his lungs in a panic as he fell. Every once in a while, the wall would grow brighter, like someone was adjusting a television set, and he'd see flashes of words. He was falling fast enough that he didn't have time to read any of it, really, and could only guess at the names, parts of phrases, and beginnings of Biblical quotes based on the little he did see and the connections his own brain made.

He did catch one word, though, just before he connected with solid earth.

HOLLOW.

CHAPTER THIRTEEN

Erik was alone in the tunnel. He took a deep breath and swallowed the panic. This couldn't be happening. Not again. Not here. Not now.

He was pretty sure it wouldn't be like the last time, and that scared the hell out of him. This Hollower wasn't looking to tease and torment them. It wanted them to give up completely. It wanted to crack them open like walnuts and chew up their despair.

He walked forward. Moving would give him a rhythm, a purpose, a sense of direction, at least. It would help him think.

All around him, the darkness swallowed up the tunnel. He couldn't see where he was going. More often than not, he tripped over a bump in the ground. Loose pieces of rock, he assumed. Sometimes his foot dipped into a crater and his heart jumped, a tingling feeling traveling up his body from his misplaced feet in anticipation of a fall. In those moments, his thoughts turned to dark wells and shafts and the very real possibility that he might plunge headlong as Sally had into a black pit in which maybe even the Hollower wouldn't be able to find him.

He slowed, feeling his way with feet and hands.

By degrees, the diffused light of the tunnel increased somehow, enough so that the first forms and outlines his hands brushed against made him jump, and it took both his eyes and his brain a few seconds to register them as drawings on the wall and not actual beings. In the sharp, carved contour of rock, Erik saw other worlds.

Garish paint, like overdone makeup, was smeared all over some of the carvings, accentuating the crude and almost primitive violence of some and the outlandishness of others. One scene depicted a scarecrow of some sort slicing off a naked woman's face with a large hunting knife. In another, a man was peeling strips of his own skin off his arms, chest, and calves and laying them in a pile while a shadowy figure in a hat lurked in the background. In yet another farther down, a cave beneath a forest, lit only by firelight, contained a child with pain-glazed eyes whose head bled from the nose down, while a hideous figure added small lips to a wall of hanging mouths, dried like parallel worms and arranged as hunting trophies. Erik felt a little sick.

The painted bas-relief got more bizarre and more disturbing as he followed the corridor down. Another showed a stampede of a strange race of tripod beings, their pyramid faces shrieking and wide-eyed as they poured down a hill. Behind them, a city suspended in the sky rained grotesque skeletal beasts down on them. The beasts tore them apart, devouring pieces of some and doing other unspeakable acts to others as they lay mangled, maimed, and dying, abandoned and half-trampled by their own. Another showed a small village with tears in the dimensional fabric causing ugly lesions across the landscape. From these, long fingers curled out, along with the first curves of heads, the first scissor-blade of a leg or the tip of a crablike claw. Dead bodies, split open down the middle as if overripe, lay strewn about the grass in between the buildings.

Erik's hand passed over these, feeling not just the cold scrape of the stone from which they were made, but also something else, some sense of the abject terror the subjects of the paintings must have felt. He also got a dreadful sense of a bigger picture, a broader spectrum of hate, an awful sinking recognition of what the pictures represented not just for his world, but evidently for others in other dimensions, other places like and even not so like his own.

The Hollowers were everywhere. And, if the illustrations on the walls were correct, they were only one of many races that preyed on worlds like Erik's.

Even entertaining the vaguest notion that putting this Hollower down might not even begin to cover other doorways and other invasions of unspeakable things was too much. Erik turned away, the thought too horrible to let surface.

Sprinkled around the hasty portraits, terrible alien landscapes, and off-kilter still lifes were all manner of painted and carved symbols—Egyptian hieroglyphics, graffiti, even tick marks. Some of them, strange symbols that curved in and swam out of each other, extended out into the tunnel. As Erik continued, the crammed art (he couldn't quite think of those paintings and carvings as art without grimacing in disgust) grew few and far between until the rock smoothed out. The sporadic gaping mouth or blind eye would draw his attention, but he blocked most of it out, refusing even to touch the wall as a guide through the dark.

A spray-painted stick figure whose face had been rubbed off caught his attention. Erik stopped to look at that one. The artist had endowed it with an impossibly large cock, which it held up over the head of another stick figure whose circle eyes bled red paint down the flat round cheeks. Beneath the lower figure was a name:

Casey.

There was another one a little farther down that made Erik cringe to look at. It was a crude painting, faded now, of a dead Confederate soldier, his skeletal horse rearing up, his gun raised high in victory. And more so than the other things he'd seen portrayed on the walls so far, that one made him feel sick to his stomach.

Erik reached out and touched it. The chalkiness of the colors got on his fingertips. He rubbed them vigorously against his jeans, but the red stained.

He backed away from the painting. It dredged up a memory from his childhood, but rather than let that take hold, his mind slipped him instead a recollection of when the Hollower first split them up. He remembered the awful panic at finding himself alone, making his way down what he thought was Feinstein's upstairs hallway. The terrible sinking feeling returned as Erik recalled seeing his father in the sweat-darkened T-shirt, faded from black to a dull gray, sitting on a couch in an almost bare room—a slice of the past removed and re-pasted onto the present, out of sync, out of time. His dead father with the meaty hands and rough elbows and big, tattooed arms.

He remembered the tattoo on his father's bicep. A dead Confederate soldier whose skeletal horse reared up over the massive plane of skin. He used to focus on that tattoo, to concentrate his strength, his will not to cry when his father rained blows down on him. He'd grown to loathe that tattoo and what it meant. He feared it. It meant pain. It was the threat of death.

Erik continued down the dark corridor, hypersensitive, listening for sounds ahead of him, behind him. Once he thought he heard a laugh track, and once, the snap of a belt. Once, he thought he heard the beer-soaked sound of his father's laugh.

"Erik . . ." The voice beside his ear made him jump and wheel around, but no one was there. The voice continued.

"I know you still want to get high, Erik. I can feel it all over you. You can't help Jake. You can't help anyone. You're just as useless as you were before. Every bit as much of a lazy, useless no good sonuvabitch. Admit it. Just tell me you still want to get high."

"No, I don't," Erik said to the heavy air and walked faster, afraid to run into the unfathomable black before him. Still, the voice followed.

"You're lying. I don't like liars, Erik." It was his father's voice; same timbre, same tone, everything. It sent a shiver of cold across his skin, and Erik almost stopped. The unspoken command to obey, to stand there until his father was done with him, hung in the air all around him.

He didn't stop, though. Feeling along the wall, Erik moved faster.

"You still can't touch me," Erik whispered.

"Yes, I can," the Hollower replied. "Oh, yes, I can."

Suddenly, flashes of memory, clips of sound and sight and even smell bombarded his senses, forcing him to a stop, dropping him to his knees.

He saw the blood on the bed he and Casey shared, saw blood on her leg, which was just visible from the floor on the far side of the bedroom.

Flash.

The sound of his father bellowing throughout the house.

Flash.

Casey crying blood down the front of her white tank top, stinking of overturned things in the earth.

Flash.

Cocaine in long, brilliantly white rows on a polished mahogany table.

The taste of it. The smell of it. The tingle of it in his nose.

Flash. He tried to stand.

A room with pale green sheets, a picture of Casey tacked to one of the plain white walls. Metal bars on the windows, scuffed tiles on the floor.

The floor was a snowfall of cocaine. It kicked up in little puffs around his feet as he walked.

He stopped. The dark tunnel was gone. He really *was* in that room. From the other side of the wall, he could hear a boy crying, begging someone to let him out, begging for a little smack to get him through the morning. The irregular sobs melded into a wail that tapered off and became the fiendish mumbling of words. They slowed into almost a chant, and Erik could make out some of the words:

"Tell me you wanna get high wanna get high got drugs got ups got downs crack cocaine heroin get high wanna get high, wanna die die die so high wanna cocaine gonna swim in it, gonna drown in it, gonna ride it right up to the ceiling and be sooo hiiigh . . ."

Erik tried to turn, to move toward the door, and found he couldn't. He looked down. The cocaine was up to his knees.

He felt a surge of panic, not only in being unable to move his legs, but in the quietly suggestive voice just beneath that told him not to bother.

"Relax. It could be worse."

He closed his eyes, employing an old stabilizing trick. *Ten . . . nine . . . eight . . . floor beneath my feet . . . seven . . . six . . . light on my face . . . five . . . four . . .*

His counting, the sound and sensation of his breathing, helped steady him, eclipsing the other, more suggestive voice.

The soft rustle of cocaine against denim drew his attention. He opened his eyes and looked down. Now it was up to his groin.

The Hollower was going to bury him right up to his nose in cocaine! Panic fired alarms all over his head, and yet his body didn't respond. Somewhere in the back of his head (this sounded crazy, but even so), the thought of being buried over in cocaine seemed a good way to go. Fitting. Exciting. A culmination of all his greatest moments.

He laughed, and then realizing what he was doing, stopped. But it took a few moments to get the giggles under control.

Death by laughter. He died laughing. Busted a gut. Split a seam and he spilled out all over. Seasoned all his inside organs in white powder like flour like filets when Casey breads them then cooks them and—

He dropped the train of thought. He had to get out of there. The cocaine was up to his waist. His arms were free, and good *God* it was so fucking close, and it would be so easy, so damned easy, to just pinch a little off the mound in front of him and—

He remembered Casey, and all the other thoughts pulled back.

Erik had come past this point in his life. He didn't need coke, and he didn't want it. He needed Casey. He wanted her. And he promised her he'd come back.

Erik made swimming motions, pushing the cocaine out of his way. More spilled a little into the valley he created, but he wriggled and pushed and kicked and pushed until he'd managed at least a little leeway. The sensation of it, of so much of it sliding between his fingers and over his skin made him moan. The top half of the door—and, thank your Higher Power of Choice, the doorknob—were visible and just about at arm's reach. He grabbed for the knob and used it to pull himself closer. He twisted it, and at first it wouldn't budge.

He was about to attempt to throw some elbow into it when the door flew open and he spilled out on a landslide of cocaine. He rolled on the ground, came to a stop, and then sat up.

The lightest dust of the drug frosted the tops of the grass blades like powdered sugar. Otherwise, looking behind and all around him, all traces of the door he'd fallen through and the room he'd left behind were gone.

Alone in the tunnel, Jake yelled out names—Dorrie's, Erik's. He yelled for help, feeling the panic-sweat under his arms and across his back, the dread spreading hot-cold waves up his neck and into his gut. He was in trouble now—big, bad-assed trouble. Extending his hands into the darkness, he felt his way forward until he came to something solid, cold, and smooth. His hands slid down its length and came to what felt like a metal handle. He pulled, and the solid thing—a door, he guessed—gave in his direction. A pale glow poured into the tunnel from the other side. Jake went through the opening and found himself in a room.

Overhead speakers cranked out some saxophone instrumental song that Jake vaguely recognized the melody of. He glanced behind him in the tunnel, lit a cigarette, and turned around to find himself in a hospital waiting room. The cigarette hung from his mouth, forgotten.

A large white desk, spotlit from lamps at either end, stood in front of the nurses' station. Behind it, charts and files stuck haphazardly from labeled bins. A clipboard sat on the counter surface. On the far wall was a window boarded up. Between it and him, a series of upholstered benches formed a Grecian pattern across the floor. All of these but one were immaculately white and intact. The standout one in the center of the room was rust colored, with springs poking through the upholstery like thin bones through skin. The white and gray tiles on the floor followed the same pattern as the benches. A fan of dust motes hung in the air, visible through the stark, white light that seemed to have no direction or origin. It gave the whole place a sterile, scrubbed raw kind of feel. Jake also got the sense of the place not quite having completed the transition to total emptiness—a feeling that there had just been bodies there moments before he'd walked in kicking up the dust motes, that if he went and felt the seats of the benches he'd find them still warm.

Medication time, Mr. Dylan. Jake shivered.

The music paused. "Excuse me, sir," a pleasant woman's voice talked down to him from a speaker somewhere in the hazy white blur where the ceiling should have been. "This is a no-smoking facility. Please put out your cigarette."

Jake looked up, then back around the empty room in dumb shock. At first he wasn't sure what the woman was talking about, but then a tendril of smoke rose up into his eye. He plucked the cigarette from his mouth, dropped it on the floor, and stepped on it to put it out.

"Hello? Anybody here?" It seemed a silly thing to say into the sanitary stillness, but it filled the emptiness a little and gave him a modicum of strength. He hated hospitals—always had. He'd had pneumonia when he was five, and he'd spent days in a hospital bed alone, except when his big brother could come and visit. Mostly, though, he just inhaled the air circulated by the sick, listened to the machine beeps and bloops and the hurried chatter of doctors and nurses, and sucked in more air that just didn't go anywhere, air that died in his mouth without satisfying his chest. The room had a television, at least, but it only got a handful of channels. They left cartoons on; the laughter and bright colors made his room seem a little more alive. But still, he couldn't wait to go home.

His mother and father had died in a hospital, after the accident. His aunt, too, when the drinking and the cigarettes had given up toying with her health and decided to take her permanently. And he'd ridden in the ambulance when it came and got Chloe. That might have been the worst trip of all. With the others, he'd been party to the hushed hallway discussions about quality of life and care termination at the worst and abrupt ushering of family and friends out of the way so that medicine could be administered at best. But with Chloe, there was no next of kin to sign the papers and no strong and certain brother-type to make decisions about funeral arrangements.

Standing there in the waiting room with all the helplessness and pain flooding back, he wanted very much to get high. The thought of welcome oblivion, the death flow of a heroin high, gripped him tightly.

He turned to the nurses' station. On the counter was

a little paper cup that hadn't been there before. It reminded him of the methadone they gave him in rehab, and his chest ached.

Maybe rehab had been the worst hospital experience he had.

He crossed over to the nurses' station and looked down into the cup. A dark reddish-brown liquid filled it halfway. Frustrated, he turned his attention to the clipboard, and he felt another ache in his chest, as well as a surreal sense of misplacement at seeing what was written there. In Chloe's handwriting—he was sure it was hers—were scribbled a few words. It wasn't signed, but Chloe had rarely signed any of the fridge notes or Post-its she'd left for him all over the house. Sometimes they were reminders, or requests. Sometimes they were just love notes, back when things were good. Absently, he rubbed his chest, reading the words again.

"Got you a present. Go look on the seat. Like old times."

XOXO

Jake felt a little sick but turned slowly to the waiting area, to the one blot in an otherwise clean room. It had to be that seat she meant (it meant), and he fully expected a needle filled with heroin to be waiting for him. He didn't have a good view of the cushion itself or what was on it until he made his way around a few other benches and came upon it. He looked down, and tears filled his eyes.

He was wrong about the needle. Amidst a clutter of

old razor blades and scattered pills was one of her eyes. Next to that looked like a shriveled corner of her mouth, and beneath them, a few of her black-nailed fingers and toes. Jake collapsed onto the floor, holding onto the next seat over, and dry heaved at the tiles.

The pleasant woman's voice came down through the invisible speakers in the obscured ceiling. "You tore her apart, Jake."

The voice filled the room, filled his head. He closed his eyes.

"Tore her up from the inside out."

"Stop," he whispered.

"Just like I'm going to do to you." And the brassy laughter that followed reverberated through the speaker, sounding fake (*borrowed, not yours, that voice and those memories aren't yours, you bastard*), and Jake swallowed several times to keep his stomach in check and the solid sense of realness in his head.

"I didn't kill her."

"You don't really believe that, now do you? It's all your fault, Jake. Much like everything else, it's all your fault. It has always been all your fault."

"Shut up." He thought about it, though. He knew he didn't put his parents' car in harm's way any more than he fed booze and cigarettes to his aunt. But those things had always felt like they were his fault. Either he hadn't listened the night before or he'd mouthed off or brought home a note from the teacher, and it was like clockwork. Shortly after, something bad happened. It was child logic, child inference, but of all the things in his life he'd had trouble shaking, child logic had proved the hardest. Old habits, as they said, died hard. And old ways of thinking even harder.

He thought of Dorrie. A week ago, he never would have imagined someone as wonderful as her in his life. She looked at him with almost frantic intensity. When he'd been in bed with her, she had needed him, wanted him. She'd done everything to make him feel like he mattered, and he'd realized after, cuddling with her, that she might have been the first to ever make him feel that way. Even Chloe, as much as he'd loved her, even in the beginning when things were good, had made him feel insubstantial.

Or maybe he'd always made himself feel that way. Until Dorrie. There had never been a purpose, a person to protect, a reason *not* to get high, until last night.

He opened his eyes and looked at the chair. The drugs and the body parts were gone. On the seat was a jagged piece of rock, like a broken-off piece of concrete. One edge was very sharp.

"You could slice your neck with that," the woman's voice said through the speaker. "Probably wouldn't even hurt much. You'd be doing yourself a favor. And that girl, too. She doesn't need someone like you."

He rose onto shaky legs and picked up the rock. It felt cold, heavy, and abrasive in his hand. He looked up. A low hum came from the speaker, wherever it was above him, as if the nurse-voice was waiting for him to make his decision.

Jake did. With an effortful grunt, he threw the rock upward with all his strength, straight at where he imagined the voice was coming from.

The speaker emitted a flatline sound, and the perfect white of the room began to peel away, like flakes of paint, like old dead skin, portions of white pulling away from the wall, drying to black and fluttering to the ground. Jake breathed hard, his panicked gaze darting around the rotting room. He wasn't sure what to do, where to go, so he stood by and watched the illusion of a hospital meant to hurt him fall apart. And when it had fallen away, Jake found himself back in the tunnel. He followed it for a while, still breathing hard, badly shaken, until he came to another door. This one gave him a little more trouble, creaking protest as he slid it along the concrete floor. He managed to get it open enough to slip through. It was still dark, but he noticed the change in the air immediately.

Fighting very hard not to hyperventilate, Dorrie stumbled blindly through the dark of the tunnel, very much aware that the others were gone. She was afraid to call out to them, afraid that it might hear her and come looking for her, alone. Maybe do things to her like it had done to Steve. Maybe worse things.

She started forward in the tunnel, and as she did, the darkness grew steadily lighter. The ground loosened up into pebbles beneath her feet, and the air lost some of its musty closeness. In fact, she thought, as long, thin shapes loomed ahead in the duskiness, the air carried the smell of pine trees and lake water.

Dorrie was outside. The gravelly path fell away beneath her hurrying feet, and she was quite sure she could make out the trees surrounding the path around the lake where she'd first seen the Hollower. She thought she even heard crickets.

"What the—how . . . ?" Alert, looking for signs of anything that might be trouble, her head swiveled, her eyes darting, her breath tight in her lungs. She continued around the curve, the water lapping against the shoreline, the leaves rustling overhead. The path stretched out ahead of her, running straight where her feet were used to turning, but she followed it anyway. The long, black branches reached down into the pathway, overstepping their friendly canopy. On the lake path she was used to, the trees didn't encroach so far into her territory, the land of the paved and made-for-man.

Here the crickets and tree frogs made strangled, painful croaks and chirps, like sadistic fists were catching hold of them and crushing them methodically in the hidden places between the trees.

She glanced behind her and discovered the path being eaten by the same kind of murkiness as in the tunnel. She couldn't bear to go back, not now. Pressing forward through the wooded path couldn't possibly be as bad as that. She turned forward then and stopped short.

A large wooden door in a doorframe stood in the center of the path. Trees grown up to either side prevented sidestepping it, and it took up the entire width of the pathway.

She approached it with caution, leaning forward a little to listen. No sound came from the other side. She tried to peer around it but couldn't quite angle herself to see past it between the trees. She touched it with a finger, and then with all her fingers, feeling the even, polished wood.

She knocked. No one answered. No one knocked back.

Dorrie checked behind her. The gloom ate up the path at a steady rate. It was getting closer, obliterating everywhere she'd just been. She felt a surge of panic as she turned back to the door. She grabbed the knob, but it wouldn't turn. She shook it, begged with it under her breath to give. Behind her, the dark got closer. It made a whirring sound like a garbage disposal, chopping up the illusion of the woods.

Dorrie shook the knob harder, her hands sweating and slipping over the brass. Grabbing a corner of her shirt, she grabbed the knob hard and gave it a sharp twist.

The door opened, and she tumbled through, banging her shoulder against the doorframe. Behind her, the door slammed shut and blacked out her entire view.

The darkness inside was oppressive again, giving her the impression of a small room claustrophobically tight. The kind of room that big girls never felt comfortable in, because they always thought they took up too much space. By instinct, she felt upward, and a thin chain dangled against her hand. She grabbed it and pulled, and a sickly brown light came on.

Dorrie found herself in a small room lit only by a bare bulb hanging from a socket near the chain she'd found. Occasionally it flickered, threatening to go out, and during those brief blinks of dimness, Dorrie's heart skittered in her chest. She looked around and determined that she was in some kind of storeroom. There were metal bracer poles that formed racks with shelves to either side wall and along the back. On these were mostly boxes, big brown moving boxes like she'd used when she first moved out and into her place on Cerver Street. In fact—she squinted in the poor light, frowning as she approached one of the boxes—it looked like her handwriting, scrawled in loopy script on the cardboard sides. However, instead of labels such as KITCHEN or BEDROOM or even BOOKS, the boxes closest to her were marked NEW THIGHS, EXTRA HEADS, and stranger things: WHERE THE LIGHTS GO WHEN THEY GO OUT. ENDS. PORTABLE PORTALS.

She frowned, reaching a hesitant hand toward the nearest box, one marked DECORATIONS. She pulled it toward her. It came toward her so fast that it seemed as if another force from the other side gave it a push, and surprised, she let go of the corner she held. The box spilled over onto the floor, and the "decorations" tumbled out.

She covered her mouth with her hand to keep from gagging and stepped back, horrified that one of them might roll toward her feet. Globs of something yellowish and congealed and veined with white and red lay scattered about the floor. Tiny ornament hooks speared the globs, and a whitish crust that Dorrie couldn't help thinking was skin seemed to seal them inside the globs, as if they had begun to heal and grow around the hooks.

Oh God. Oh my God, it's fat. Chunks of fat. Balls and beads and bubbles of fat. Baubles of fat. The reiterated thought drove bile up into her throat. Dorrie took several long breaths to fight the nausea.

Behind her, she heard stiff movement, the scuffing of something inflexible on the floor, and cruel giggling. She turned and jumped, a strangled little cry escaping her throat, and staggered back a little against the box-lined shelves.

The mannequins that were crowded at the far end of the room—there were four of them, and they took up a significant part of the small room's space—regarded her with cold, painted eyes. *Not unseeing eyes*, she thought with dread. *They see me, all right. They're watching me.*

Judging me, she was tempted to think. A stupid thought, but it seemed right, all the same. The cool, naked forms, cream-colored, composed of bald heads, curving breasts, tiny waists, and small hips, posed, waiting. Each of them was propped up on long legs. One had no arms. Another sported only the bent arm, whose hand, connected by a seam at the wrist, rested on the hip. The third had two arms, at least down to the elbow, and the fourth had one long bent leg coming out of the shoulder socket. From everywhere that body part met body part, they bled out from the seams. In the quiet that hung between them, Dorrie could hear the blood droplets hitting the concrete floor, making little starbursts of red at their feet.

They stood in what were likely habitual display poses from their respective department store days, the flattering stances of supermodels and actresses. Their placement suggested a private conversation, an exclusive meeting of the beautiful people, a chick session of hen-pecking, catfighting, backstabbing, and two-faced, double-edged sweet talk. Dorrie had been the outside conversation subject of many of these groups, from grammar school straight through college. Cheerleaders, sorority sisters, prom queens, and princesses with perfect bodies and beautiful faces and their pick of any boy around—girls who found her weight first a thing of disgust and ridicule as a child, then a thing of abject horror as teenagers, and finally, a thing of hushed and whispered pity as college coeds. Her self-conscious loathing of those girls had first begun to finally dissipate, ironically enough, with her neighbor Cheryl, who seemed above needing to remind the world that fat women made her look thinner, or needing to maintain someone else's discomfort to lessen her own. But she remembered the stances, the conspiratorial whispers and nods of the head, the look of superiority in their eyes. Her mother told her once that all girls were insecure and that all teasing was only to draw attention away from those insecurities from the safety of mob mentality.

Maybe that was true of some. Some were just bitches.

She'd come to find the world did contain women like Cheryl, who moved with unassuming grace, whose beauty seemed present but immaterial. She'd thought that maybe she'd reached a point in life where she was willing to attribute those qualities to other beautiful women, to make all modelesque women less powerful monsters and more vulnerable human beings. And to reinforce that idea, Dave had told them a little about his ex-girlfriend in the car on the way to Oak Hill, how she worried that people wouldn't think she was smart enough or capable enough, how it made her feel like a helpless little girl when men leered at her, but how in spite of those things, she stumbled through. She tried to make informed decisions, tried to read the paper to learn about things to talk about (she also encountered, more often than not, people utterly uninterested in actually *talking* to her about anything important, or hearing what she had to say.) Maybe women like Cheryl felt insecure and scared and unsure of themselves.

But the looks on the faces of the mannequins masked no fears and insecurities of their own. Those looks, which seemed to observe and ultimately despise every part of her without any movement whatsoever of the eyes, chilled her. Those looks of hate meant retribution. They meant cruel pranks and torments that sometimes bordered on dangerous. They wanted to, in a sense, eat her alive with their hate.

And they stood between Dorrie and the only door out of the store room.

Without taking her eyes off the mannequins, she reached behind her, feeling for the top of one of the boxes, and stuck her hand in, hoping for (*Oh God, anything, anything at all but blood and guts and body parts and—*) something to use as a weapon. Her hand closed around something cold and hard, and she pulled out a tire iron.

Oh, thank God.

"Aren't you going to cry, Dorrie?" The mouth of the mannequin with no arms didn't move, but its voice, eerily muffled, rattled around its insides, trapped, a vicious animal waiting to spring. It sounded, Dorrie thought, vaguely familiar, from another time and place.

Ashley. Ashley Tiller from middle school, blonde and blue-eyed—a girl whose power was secured through whispers behind the backs of hands and displays of callousness in the lunchroom.

"Uh . . . excuse me?"

The mannequin with the leg in its shoulder socket tilted its head with a stiff scuffing sound. "You were always such a crybaby. Whiny little Dorrie with her fat ass and her hurt feelings, bitching about why everyone was always so mean to her." Natalie Romanieri from high school, the beautiful dark-haired cheerleader, the girl who only dated college boys, whose locker was more treacherous to navigate past than any girls' room or gym locker room in the school.

Heat flushed Dorrie's face. All the powerless anger and insecurity drove her free hand into a fist, set her eyes alight. There were a hundred things she wanted to say—almost twenty years' worth of comebacks and insults running around in her head. But when she opened her mouth to speak, none of them came out.

"Do you have something to say to us, Dorrie? No? I didn't think so. You never did. Your mouth was always full." That one hit home with aching familiarity, down to the words verbatim. Jennifer Rossler, another high school girl, pretty, popular, wild, and looking to lash out at anyone that she could showboat over to draw more attention to herself.

A fresh wave of angry heat washed over Dorrie. She swung the tire iron in front of her.

The one with upper arms laughed. "What do you think you're going to do with that, Dorrie? Really, this unhealthy, I daresay borderline obsessive, hostility you have toward women who have everything you don't is just sad, frankly. Do you really intend to swing a tire iron at us?" And finally, Madison Monroe, from Seton Hall University, with her double-edged kindness and her pitying eyes. By then, even if Madison had actually possessed a single genuine bone in her body, Dorrie would have hated her. She was the woman that girls like Ashley and Natalie and Jennifer grew into.

"I will," Dorrie said, "if you don't let me out that door."

The one she'd come to think of as Natalie shook her head. "Not likely. You can't fit." She kicked her shoulder-leg out toward the door. "Not a lard-ass like you."

Dorrie looked at the door. It did look smaller—a lot smaller. Not so small that she couldn't squeeze, maybe, but . . . smaller, definitely. She felt acutely aware of her body and its dimensions, her hips, all the places of her that billowed out enough to be a potential problem.

She surprised herself by answering, "I'll get out that door if I have to ram one of you through the wall to widen it. One way or another, ladies."

With jerking steps, Madison moved toward her. "How about you try that?"

Dorrie took a few wide steps around it and headed toward the door. Madison stepped in front of her, moving surprisingly fast on such stilted legs.

"Oh, uh, Dorrie?" Jennifer said sweetly. "Why don't you let us give you a makeover? Girls to girl. First, we'll rip all the fat off you. Then we'll stretch your legs and puff up your lips and paint your face. Let us play."

Dorrie was absolutely terrified. She knew that tone; she knew they meant to do everything they said. For the second time that night, she surprised herself by swinging the tire iron into Madison's perfectly curved fiberglass waist. It cracked, caving in a little.

Madison swung one of her upper arms and smacked Dorrie hard across the face. The pain sent white sparks across her eyes. The mannequin dropped another blow down on the dip between her shoulder and neck. Sharp pain flared out into her neck and back. She swung up, the tire iron catching Madison in the jaw, and the face first cracked then caved in. The empty cavity behind the face filled with blood, which spilled out onto the floor. The mannequin wailed in pain and sank to the ground.

The mannequins still standing collectively sent up a wail to join with Madison's. It sounded to her like a siren. Blood poured out of their seams where the body parts met, streaming down their bodies and puddling on the floor.

Dorrie quickly stepped over the puddles to the door and yanked it open. Gagging, she tumbled out.

And she found herself on the quad.

CHAPTER FOURTEEN

Dave looked around the quad for his friends. Dorrie leaned against a corner where the buildings came together, her hand on her heart, catching her breath. Jake, his whole body shaking, crouched on his knees over by the gate where they'd come in. Steve sat slumped against the bench where the paper creatures had beaten him unconscious, bleeding and breathing in huge gasps. And Erik rose slowly to his feet in the center of the quad, in the dip where the hills sloped down into a little valley, away from the buildings.

"Hey, you all okay?" he called out to them, and, seeming to notice each other for the first time, the pain and uncertainty on their faces eased. They weren't alone anymore. They rose with effort and made their way toward each other.

They all met in the middle by Erik.

"I'm confused," Jake said. "Why did it bump us all out here?"

Erik shrugged. "I have to admit, I kind of thought it would try to bury us alive in there."

"So, what, is that it? Did we have our trial by fire?"

Jake shoved his hands in his jeans pockets. He looked very washed-out. "Are we done?"

A creaking sound in the sky, like something about to fall over, drew their attention upward. Overhead, stars hung scattered across the sky, but they could also see dark and swirling spots, huge vortexes that ate the stars. A trail of black spun out behind them, spitting out the processed light as glittering dust. Directly above them, strange flat islands floated across the night. They measured maybe fifty feet long and dropped sprays of dirt and sand into their hair. On many of them, black trunks and branches grew, and grotesque organic shapes with eyes and teeth in all the wrong places peered down at them from the branches.

"I don't think so," Dave said. He took a few steps and looked around. The last time a Hollower had put them in the middle of a dimensional crossroads like this, it had been hurt, maybe dying, and it just cranked out whatever odd images were in its head. The physical stuff—the houses with meat peeling off their frames, the lawnful of faces, the geysers of blood and rocketing jets of bone—that had all been what the Hollower itself was afraid of. He was sure they hadn't hurt this one, or even ruffled it very much. So what was it doing? Experimenting? This . . . this was like the Hollower was still tapping into collective memory and smearing its own across that, a layer of its experiences over theirs. Maybe in doing that, it could accomplish what probing their fears couldn't.

"What is this place?" Dorrie drew closer to Jake.

Before anyone could answer, a rumble like thunder

nearly shook them off balance. One of the islands stopped overhead, and it took a moment before they realized they should—

"Run!" Dave said, and, dragging Steve, hurried up the side of the hill. They scattered, but the impact of the island knocked them over.

"Okay, okay. Everybody, let's just go over by the catacomb door and figure out what we should do ne—" The words died in his throat as Dave stood up and turned around.

They were in the parking lot. Dave glanced back to the entrance they had used. Huge chains with thick links threaded in and out of the gate, with padlocks sporadically gathering and locking the chains. Curling barbed wire spiraled along the top. Wooden boards completely covered the windows. A broken-off piece of board, hanging from a rusted chain, said, "One more game."

"What the hell?" Erik came up alongside him. "What's it doing?"

Steve, with the help of Jake and Dorrie, limped up to join them. "It kicked us out? That doesn't make any sense. I find it hard to believe it's just going to let us walk out of here."

"I don't think it is," Dorrie said. "Look at that sign. It's still messing with us."

"Well, I've got nothing." Jake indicated the gate with a wave of the hand. "If it won't let us back inside, I can't see how we're supposed to find it."

"Dave!"

Dave felt his skin grow cold. It was Cheryl's voice.

He turned to the car—his car. It looked like someone sat in his passenger seat. The dark hair hung from the bowed head, obscuring the face, but he thought he recognized her anyway. He jogged and then broke into a run, the others following behind him. He vaguely heard a warning from Erik that it wasn't Cheryl, but he dismissed it. He had to know. Had to see.

When he got to the car, though, the figure was gone—no trace of anyone in the passenger seat or anywhere else in the car. Dave slumped a little where he stood, and Steve clapped a hand on his shoulder. "Who was it?"

"Cheryl," he said. "It was Cheryl. Well, it was something that looked and sounded like Cheryl."

"Uh, guys?" Jake tapped them on the back, and they turned to see what had drawn Jake's attention. The paved parking lot was melting. The few other cars in the lot groaned as they sank into the spreading ocean of liquid blacktop.

"We have to go," Dave said.

"We can't! Who knows if we'll get another chance at this thing?"

Dave turned on Steve. "We won't have any chance if the parking lot drowns us where we stand." He dug in the pocket for his keys and made his way around to the driver's side. Erik took the shotgun seat.

"This is what it wants," Dorrie said. "If we get in that car—"

"If we don't, baby," Jake interrupted gently as Steve climbed in the backseat, "we might be in bigger trouble. It's the lesser of the two evils." He tugged her to the car. "I promise it'll be okay."

She smiled at him, but she looked sad. "You can't promise that." But she got in the car anyway, and he followed.

Steve groaned as he watched his own car, traded with the police cruiser before he drove over, disappear beneath a wave of asphalt.

"Hurry," Erik said through tight lips as Dave tried the ignition.

The car started, and he threw it into drive, heading for the hill and the main road that ran parallel to the bottom of it. A sheet of pavement heaved in front of him, and he swerved around it, narrowly missing the floe in the liquid mess of the parking lot. They all cried out when the car jumped, the back wheels pulling out of road reduced to tar right under them.

Dave's car shot through the open gate and out onto the main road, heading by instinct to the Olde Mill Tavern.

After a moment, Erik said, "Okay, what in blue hell was that?"

"It wanted us out," Dorrie said. "Although I can't imagine . . ." Her sentence trailed off. They all noticed it at about the same time.

There were no other cars on the road. Normally that would not have been so odd at that hour of the night, except that there were none in the parking lots, none on the street, none anywhere. There were no lights in any of the store or diner windows, no signs lit up, and the street lamps winked out as they drove by each one. The street signs glowed, though; they hung slanted on the posts, the names a series of black smudges across their luminous faces.

The most unsettling part about the whole thing—the thing that made it abundantly clear that even though they'd driven away, they hadn't really gotten away—was that there were people out on the street, walking, sitting, staring at the car as it drove by, going in and out of restaurants and diners. And none of them had a face. Not a one. None of them moved. They looked like mannequins, positioned to simulate life in a place that didn't exist, a place devoid of anything human besides them.

"It's never going to let us go," Dorrie finally said. "We could drive out to California, drive right out into the damn Pacific Ocean, and it would twist the fish into sea monsters on our way to the bottom."

"Look, maybe we should turn—"

A jaw-thudding recoil as the car suddenly lost the road sent them flying in their seats before the car pitched downward and stopped moving. The walls of a hole about four feet deep rose up around them on all sides. Dirt, rock, and chucks of street pavement tumbled down on top of the hood of the car.

After several groaning moments, Dave and the others came around, rubbing bruised foreheads and elbows. "Anybody hurt? Is . . . are we . . . ow!" Dave tried to open the driver's side door, but it wouldn't budge. The dirt and rock caved in around it filled in too much space between the door and the slope of the hole. He rolled the window down and clumsily climbed out while Erik and the others got out on the passenger side. Pulling each other up onto the hood and then the roof of the car, they had enough leverage to climb out of the hole.

They stopped where they stood.

About fifteen or twenty of the faceless folks stood poised close to the hole, blind witnesses gathered maybe a hundred feet or so away. They didn't move, but among them was a kind of menacing stillness, like cats crouched and ready to pounce on their prey. In the frozen clutching hands, they held knives and scalpels.

"I think we can get past them," Jake whispered. "I don't think they can see us. And even if they can," his voice dropped to a conspiratorial whisper, "we have joints and muscles. We can probably move faster."

Steve, leaning on Erik, said, "I'm just . . . so tired."

"Hang in there, Steve. We'll get out of this." Dorrie didn't look at him, but her tone suggested there could be no argument.

Dave wasn't sure how they'd managed it, but the mannequins had closed some of the distance. Now a hundred feet seemed more like sixty.

"Take them," Dave said to Erik. "I'll distract these things. Get the others out of here."

"We're not leaving you behind," Dorrie said.

"There are more of them than there are of us. Just go."

"Not without you."

From the looks on the others' faces, they seemed to all stand in agreement.

"Dorrie, I appreciate—"

"Look, I know you're hurt and you've lost a lot. But we need you. We can't do this without you."

"You don't need me. I haven't done one damn thing this whole time to help any one of you. I've dragged you deeper and deeper into the twisted folds and layers of this bastard's mind and now . . ." He threw up his hands. It took every ounce of will not to mist up. "Now we're in the middle of someplace that doesn't even really exist, with no plan of action, no clue where to go, and . . ." He noticed a group of faceless teenaged mannequins with switchblades milling around outside a 7-Eleven across the street. Where in God's name had *they* come from? One had a cigarette glued to the place where its mouth should have been. A stream of smoke rose up. Dave heard Jake light up a cigarette behind him. "And no one to help us."

"We don't need help," Erik said stubbornly. "We're going to find it and kill it."

Dave sighed. "Where? How? It seems to have just stranded us out here."

"It won't leave us alone out here for long."

"We don't know what this one will do. It wants us to suffer. It wants us to hurt. It wants to wear us down until we give up, and it's starting to work." Dave turned away in disgust.

After a while, Steve said, "Why don't we head back? I mean, if we're more or less in agreement that it's going to make its presence known no matter which direction we head in, well, then . . . I say we go back to the heart of darkness, so to speak."

"You can't make the walk," Dave told him. "You can barely walk as it is. We've gone at least a mile, maybe two."

Steve waved him away. "I've done worse at the Academy. Don't worry about me. Let's just go."

Dave shrugged and said, "Okay. Okay, let's try. I guess—"

"Damn it." Erik saw it, too—they all did. While they had been arguing, the colors of the buildings had run off. In fact, the very buildings themselves sagged and dripped at odd angles. The people, frozen in the postures of everyday life, had also slid into smeared disarray. Many had melded into each other, preventing any kind of access into or around any of the buildings. The hole into which Dave had driven his car had filled in until only a corner of the trunk poked up through the new asphalt like a newly discovered bone of an ancient behemoth. There was one road out, and it led in the opposite direction of Oak Hill.

"This reminds me of a very bad dream I had once," Erik muttered.

"I don't like this," said Dorrie as they headed down the road. The air around them blew chilly across their skin. As they covered ground, the buildings became scarce. The periodic gnarled things that might have passed for trees suggested tortured shapes—one feminine form cut off at the shins, another a broken little rag doll–type whose neck bent at terribly wrong angles and whose body looked contorted in unnatural ways. Dave rubbed his eyes. The battle with the first Hollower, the swipes that death took at every one of them, seemed nothing compared to this endless feeling of being lost, of being tormented by the past, of always worrying about imminent danger and never being sure when, exactly, it was going to strike. Dave imagined that this was very much what it felt like being in hell.

They trudged along in silence, and Dave realized that if it was hell, it was also, to a much more magnified degree, just what it felt like being him, on an average day.

After a while they came to a railroad tunnel. It rose like a massive yawning mouth of mud-colored rock; the pings of something liquid dripped in its interior and echoed out to them. No other sounds issued from the opening—no laughter, no derisive layers of voices, no other indication of the Hollower's presence whatsoever. For some reason, this struck Dave as more terrible. It was like waiting for his mother to get home to yell at or punish him, waiting for a test you know you failed, waiting for that phone call that you knew in your heart meant the relationship was over and she was never coming back. It was a terrible feeling of anticipation. If the Hollower wasn't in the tunnel, then it was surely waiting for them on the other side.

The ground beneath their feet rose up in a simulation of tracks that disappeared into the sable curtain of air beyond.

"Now what?" Erik shook his head.

"No light to go into," Jake muttered. "Thought there was supposed to be a light."

Dorrie frowned at him but took his hand. With her other, she grabbed Erik's hand. Steve grabbed his and then Dave's.

They plunged into the darkness.

There were many things it could have done, wanted to do in the tunnel. It populated the lightlessness with blind and hairless things that gaped and bore razor teeth and shuddered and slithered and skittered across the ceiling on soundless feet, drooping long feelers and flicking barbed tails silently all around the meats. It considered letting those things hit them, bite them, scare them, send them fleeing, just as blind, down the remainder of the tunnel. It had grown impatient, and the anticipation of feeding on their dying Despair had set the voids inside it roiling and churning. It burned with hunger and the desire for Vengeance, burned to hurt, to destroy.

But it found the Fear of silence, the silence itself, a torture to them. For ones whose every moment was cacophonous with the obsessive replay of Insecurity and Anxiety, the silence, pregnant with horrors, was more delightful than any contact with the pets of its imagination could provide. It stretched the tunnel wide, very wide, as wide as its dwindling patience would allow.

The tunnel, which the senses beyond sight implied to them was fairly constricted, maybe just a breadth away from being claustrophobically so, widened about halfway down. The dark, too, seemed to lighten to reveal walls, first rough-hewn and rocky, but smoothing out by various degrees to a smooth cement finish.

Dave thought it before Jake said it.

"I think . . . I think we're back in the catacombs. I think we're in a catacomb tunnel." The defeat he fought hard to keep from weighing his words down hung between them in the poor light. He was right, by their estimation. They were back in the catacombs. It was a very likely possibility that they had never left.

The cement all around them felt like a tomb. They

pressed on. The ammonia smell, stronger than the smell of dust and stale air, and that leaden quality that made the air feel like bricks in his chest made his heart sink. That confirmed it.

"No! No no no. We're back in the fucking catacombs?" Steve ran his hands over his face. "Why is it doing all this?"

"It's tired of wearing us down. It's brought us back to its lair to finish things," Erik said.

"Where . . . where are we?" Jake looked around.

"Beats me if I know," Steve said, the fight in him faded some. "The map won't do any good now." He shrugged, and then winced from the pain. "I'm not even sure I could get us back to the entrance now."

"So we're stuck down here? With . . . it?"

"Plan's no different than it was before," Erik said. "We find it and kill it. Or, it finds us and we kill it."

"Or it finds us and—" Jake said.

"No!" Erik held up a warning finger to Jake. "No. There are no other options."

"Erik, I think—" Dave began.

"No."

"I think we have to look at the fact—"

"No."

"—that maybe we're stuck. Maybe it won."

"No . . ."

"Erik," Dave said.

"No!" The look on Erik's face silenced them. "No," he said, quieter. The desperation in his face told Dave everything he needed to know. Erik was thinking of Casey, who he'd promised to return to. "We're going to find it and kill it." He turned and started walking, adding over his shoulder, "Or it will find us. And we'll kill it."

Dave nodded. "Okay. Okay. We'll find it and kill it." And he started following Erik.

Jake looked at Dorrie and then Steve, then he shrugged and followed after. "Or it will find us."

"Either way, we'll kill the bastard," Steve said, and he and Dorrie hurried to catch up.

They followed a long tunnel in almost absolute darkness, saying very little other than commenting about foods they'd like to have when they got out, wines and beers and shots they'd like to drink at the Tavern, hot baths, warm clothes, Monday Night Football. They didn't talk about what they'd seen in the catacombs the first time. They didn't talk about the Hollower. It was enough that it hung over their heads, the impending fight. None of them had any idea what to do when they found it again, but they were fairly sure it would eventually tire of toying with them, as Erik said, and actually try to kill them.

Dave estimated that they'd been walking for about an hour when they came across a cavernous room. Strangely enough, bare-bulb light filled the room. Wiring stapled to wooden beams ran across the ceiling. A washer and drier set stood in the far corner across the room from them, and the casing for the furnace and the water heater stood in another corner off to the right. The floor beneath their feet crackled as they crossed the room. Dave looked down and found a crimson stain spread out across the better part of the floor.

"This . . . can't be . . ."

Dave turned and saw a staircase that ran up into the gloom of the ceiling above them. He jogged over to it and looked up. It was just like he remembered.

The door at the top looked smeared, as if someone had taken a damp thumb to an ink picture. Exactly like it had looked last time.

"Oh, hot damn," Dave said, rejoining the group.

"No way," Erik said. "No fucking way."

"What?" Steve looked from one to the other. "Fill us in."

"It's Feinstein's basement," Dave told them.

"Huh?"

"Max Feinstein," Erik explained. "It's Max Feinstein's basement. Where we found the Hollower. Where we . . . hurt it."

"Oh." Jake sounded worried.

"Well," Dorrie said, "I guess we know which plan to follow. The one where it finds us."

"Found you."

They all jumped and turned.

It stood there, taking up the center of the room, its presence—its *will*, Dave thought—weighting the air all around them.

It had found them. And this time, Dave was sure it didn't intend to let them go.

CHAPTER FIFTEEN

Up close, it looked just like the other one, just like Dave remembered. The blank surface of the face was not entirely empty. The movements of countless tiny fractal threads of ash-gray in the white formed subtle expressions—suggestion, amusement, anger, triumph. Dave thought that beneath that black trench coat, its hate churned like a storm, driving it, moving it forward. And he hated it right back. This thing that had taken everything from him—he loathed it. Despised it. He wanted it dead.

It stood in the center of the basement by the stairs, right about where the first one had stood. He half expected it to change. He remembered how the first one looked there in Feinstein's basement, shooting up into the air to a terrible height and throwing off the trench coat like a sheath of dead skin. He'd watched as its body pulled backward and the upper torso elongated to form a long goose neck on which the faceless head hung. The lump of a body had split four ways so that two pairs of long, lean scissor blades could serve as legs and propel it around. The horror Dave felt at seeing the discs of bone that swam in and out of the curve of its back was nothing compared to its series of whips, which ran along the length of the body to either side, their segmented bony spikes dangling like dungeon chains. It shook something awful, its head and its body twitching with every movement.

It had hurt them very badly with those whips. It had touched them. And yet, when it was physical, it was vulnerable. They'd been able to hurt it. They'd brought it down out of the untouchable realm of nightmares and into the everyday world of things that have reason and explanation. And they'd been able to kill it.

It was then that Dave remembered the mirror, the one he'd bought at CVS, just in case. He'd tucked it into a back pocket and forgotten about it, but now, in the simulation of Feinstein's basement, it seemed worth a shot. Maybe if he could take some of its power away, they could take it down, kill it like the first one. Maybe there was still a chance. He pulled it out of his pocket and with the blood from the car accident, still tacky from the palm of his hand, he smeared a basic smiley face on the mirror. Then he turned it on the Hollower.

For a moment it shrank back, the white faceless surface curving and wrinkling in what appeared to Dave to be a frown. He wondered what it was they saw, the Hollowers, when they looked into mirrors—the frothing hate, the voids inside them, the elements of their own fears and insecurities, if they even had such things? He liked to think maybe they saw all the stolen faces of the people they hurt, all the expressions of surprise and pain and despair. At the thought, he smiled.

But the Hollower surprised him. Its black glove swiped

the air between them and the mirror shattered. The pieces fell like crystal rain onto the hard floor, but didn't stay there. A moment or so passed, and the Hollower made a noise that was unlike anything Dave had ever heard, a whistle of air passing through something empty and forgotten, and the glass leaped up and flew at them. Dave felt a cool slice of pain against his cheek before he threw up his hands to protect his face. From the shouts and cries of the others, he assumed they were being cut as well. Cuts opened up through his sleeves, biting into his forearms, his shoulders, his stomach, and legs. There couldn't possibly be so many pieces of glass, and yet jabs of pain kept coming.

And then suddenly, they stopped.

Dave dropped his arms and looked around. Steve's cuts glittered with shards and dust of glass. Tiny cuts formed irregular lattices over Dorrie's cheek, neck, and bare arms. Jake had a piece of glass embedded deep in his hand. And Erik . . .

Dave felt a little sick when he looked at Erik, whose nose and cheekbone bled and whose bloody knuckles were tight fists. A large piece of glass had buried its tip an inch or two into Erik's side, and a burgundy stain spread quickly all around it.

"Erik," he said, but Erik waved a hand away.

"I'm okay." He swallowed. "Okay."

But Dave already felt awful. Once again, he'd allowed his friends to get hurt. Once again, it was undeniably his fault.

They were going to die in those catacombs and no one would ever find them, and the reek of their rotting bodies would join the must and ammonia and the flesh of them would fall away and the hard bones would turn to dust and blow away to mix with the dust of the basement and—

Those weren't entirely his thoughts. He glared at the monster.

In response, the Hollower's laughter bounced off the walls and filled the basement room to an almost deafening level. It threw back its head, soaking up their fear and pain.

Dave felt a hot flash of rage. *No.*

It stopped laughing but seemed to have trouble containing stray giggles. "They are coming. I have called them."

It raised a black-gloved hand, and with the other, plucked off the glove, which took an indistinct animal shape with wings and fluttered off. A glinting silvery claw reminiscent of a crab's waved where a hand should have been. The Hollower chattered the claw a little and then swiped at the air next to him.

With a sudden sizzling sound, a black bolt of what reminded Dave of lightning cut through the air right next to the Hollower. The bolt folded in on itself, seeming to indent the very fabric of the reality around them in a jagged, crackling cut. It spread to about six feet from top to bottom and then pulled itself open. Beyond the fluttering edges of the rip, a gaping blackness yawned.

"They will come, and we will devour you all."

It took Dave a few moments to realize what the Hollower had done. But it wasn't until it tilted back its head and a siren wail filled the valley between the Oak Hill buildings that Dave really understood what the Hollower meant to have happen.

It meant to have other Hollowers pour through, just like what he'd seen on his television that night. It occurred to Dave that, unlike the other Hollower, this one wasn't willing to risk death just for sustenance. This one wanted vengeance, and it was willing to give up its meats just to see them all destroyed.

Its thought-answer felt like a sharp pain behind his eye. *No. You're mine. The others will come and destroy everyone that any of you have ever loved, everyone connected to you, everyone whose lives you've ever touched. They will find ways to hunt them all down and wipe them all out. Any trace that you all ever existed, and any ripple outward through your Likekind, mine will obliterate.*

From the looks on the others' faces, he knew that they had heard this, too, in their heads.

"You can't do that," Dave said out loud.

"Yes, I can," it told him. "I can make it like you never were at all." And it giggled again, high-pitched and manic.

Dave felt all the guilt, the frustration, the anger—everything he couldn't do for Sally, everything he couldn't be for Cheryl—all of it, and something snapped inside him. His whole body felt hot and tingly, a pins-and-needles sensation of getting the feeling back in a limb that has fallen asleep. His vision blurred a little and grew white around the edges, like he was going to faint, but he knew he wasn't; he'd never felt so strong, so alive. He'd never felt so powerful. So in control. He knew that no matter what happened, however it all turned out, no feeling in the world would ever be able to top this one moment.

Dave knew the Hollower wasn't going to hurt any more of his friends. Simply, he wouldn't let it.

Dave not only saw but also felt the Hollower, which, poised with confidence on the edge of the rip, awaited its kin. He felt its anticipated triumph, its hate, and Dave's own senses, particularly the ones above and beyond his basic five, sang with energy. A bellow of rage and determination rose up from the soul of him, the marrow of his bones, the blood in his veins.

No.

He remembered seeing the Hollower he'd killed stringing up his sister in its barbs and whips, a thing they'd made physical, ugly, weak. He remembered thinking deep down that he couldn't save her, that he never had been able to save her, and the sheer rage toward the beast that was hurting her. And toward himself, for not knowing how to have protected her in the first place.

A low, quick sound, like a horn that hasn't actually fully realized its tone, the sense of a sound about to crescendo, stirred the air. It was coming from the rip. Somehow, it was more horrible a sound than growling or screaming or crying, because it suggested what was to come. It meant they were coming, and the very notion of a thousand or even a hundred Hollowers, hell the thought of even one more of them coming through that rip was absolutely unbearable.

No.

He didn't know if he'd ever been much good to anyone in his life, but he'd be damned if he didn't at least try to stop it. It would not, would *never* so long as he breathed hurt another one of his friends again. The sentiment was a pull, undeniable, useless to fight against, and he let it sweep him up in its intensity.

No.

He charged the Hollower head on, tackling it with arms gripped around the torso, and for just a moment, he expected to fall straight through it, like passing through smoke, and into the rip, down, down into the blackness beyond. But he connected with something, not quite solid, but not exactly lacking substance, either.

Like a torrent of blood was the thought that came into his mind. It felt like hitting a wall of something, a liquid surface that the image of thickening blood seemed to capture just right.

They both tumbled backward, back through the rip and into the dark, he and the Primary, the Hollower, struggling in his grasp. He could see just enough to make out both himself and the monster, as if they were illuminated from within, but nothing beyond.

Then the cold started in on him. It felt like freezer burn on the places where his exposed skin made contact with the Hollower's body. The cloth of his shirt against his chest felt stiff, uncomfortable, even painful. The Hollower struggled against him, looking to Dave to be worse off than he was. Where Dave touched it, it rippled and even vibrated as if caught in a terribly strong and concentrated wind. He could feel nothing but the cold, and yet, somehow, he could sense where the forces pressing against the Hollower came from—the volatile, the unstable, the ever unbalanced vacuums inside it.

Dave shivered, the cold sinking so low into his body that it made him numb and heavy. He found it difficult to move at all, to even blink, and eventually the shivering slowed and stopped, too. So did the pain. He felt insubstantial, less *there*. Dave, whose body was never meant for a place in between dimensions, could, however, still feel the shuddering of the beast in his arms, and with the last of his strength, he let it go.

It drifted away from him in their free fall. It wailed, a siren sound he'd heard once before from the depths of another Hollower, a death-wail that only by the sheer power of it carried at all through the nothingness around them. Then, whatever unstable vacuum was inside it punched through—around the middle, where Dave's arms had been, a blackness several shades deeper than the nothing-space around them, darker than anything Dave had ever seen, sucked at the Hollower's pretended clothes, its pretended form, and pulled them into itself.

The wail crescendoed for several moments while it struggled, and then the Primary Hollower simply winked out of existence. Its death siren carried for a few seconds after that, and then it, too, faded out.

It was not just a matter of there never having been corporeal bodies in this place. There could be no physicality there. Dave was sure of that. His solidness, his realness, had polluted the Hollower. And now he could feel that solidness unraveling and dissolving all over. It didn't hurt. In fact, it didn't feel much like anything at all.

Dave smiled—or at least, that was the sentiment behind the movement, although he was past the point of knowing or caring whether he'd been successful in achieving it. He had a moment to wonder where he'd go once he winked out of existence, too, and then he thought of Sally, waiting.

He'd fixed it. He'd fixed all of it. *Not bad, Kohlar. Not bad.*

Then, with perhaps the only truly contended exhalation of breath in his entire adult life, Dave Kohlar faded out of being, too.

Dorrie screamed when Dave made contact with the Hollower and watched in horror as they stumbled backward, locked in hate, and fell through the rip.

It sealed up behind them with a faint pop that the cavernous walls of the catacombs bounced back and forth above their heads.

Dorrie, Erik, Jake, and Steve half ran, half limped (and in Steve's case, was half dragged) to the spot where the rip had been, feeling the air with outstretched hands, hoping to grab some part of Dave still left in this world.

But he was gone.

Dorrie's tears came fast and heavy, her sobs echoing on the heels of their movements. Jake pulled her close and held her, blinking and finally wiping the blood out of his eye. Erik sank to the ground beside Steve, both of them stunned and in too much pain to stand. With effort, Steve clapped a hand on Erik's shoulder, and for a moment, he thought he would crumble beneath the modest weight of it. Erik did buckle a little but remained upright.

"He did a brave thing," Steve said softly. "Sally would have been proud. His girl Cheryl, too."

Erik didn't turn to look at him. In fact, he didn't move at all. Steve didn't think Erik heard him until his words, thick, saturated with the heavy threat of tears, drifted back over the clapped shoulder.

"For once, I hope he was proud of himself. He should have been."

"You're talking about him like he's . . ." Dorrie broke off and buried her face in Jake's shoulder.

"He's dead," Erik said in that same thick tone, a certain note of inarguable sureness in it that left the others silent. "Him, and that thing with him." He rose, offering Steve a hand to get up. "It's done now."

EPILOGUE

At the close of his first day back to work, Steve found himself in a fairly empty police station with Bennie Mendez. The other detective had ribbed him some about looking all beat up, but not as much as Steve expected. Something in Mendez's eyes, sublimating even the warm easiness of his smile, suggested that he knew Steve's injuries were not a matter of jest.

As Steve picked up his car keys, he spied the folder labeled "Feinstein, Maxwell—Suicide" and picked it up. He crossed the room to Mendez's desk. The detective didn't look up, so Steve just slid the folder neatly on top of a pile of folders.

"Spun, signed, and done with."

"Really?" Mendez kept his eyes on his paperwork.

"You can tell her we killed it. It isn't coming back."

Mendez didn't answer. Steve moved away with a small smile, and it wasn't until he reached the door that the other detective called his name.

Steve turned around. Mendez regarded him with an almost apologetic look. "I'll tell her. Thanks, Steve."

Detective Steven Corimar nodded. "My pleasure." And he headed out into the night.

★ ★ ★

It had always been Erik's habit to order a Diet Coke at the Olde Mill Tavern. He didn't drink, as it came too close to using a drug for the likes of either him or his sponsor, but he liked the atmosphere, the noisy crowd of pretty, tight-clothed women and muscle-heads trying to pick them up, the jukebox music, the bleeps of that near-to-ancient Outrun arcade video game. He liked watching people with their different personalities, their different levels of control, their celebrations and good, hearty laughs, quiet smiles, and jealous observances. He liked watching how many times a guy would approach a girl's back and turn away, and he'd bet to himself on whether the guy would have the guts, and if he did, whether he'd strike out.

It was a social society he would never quite be a part of, but that was okay. It soothed him, being outside and yet able to observe their lives. It was like watching an old familiar sitcom whose set design, characters, and canned laughter gave the comforting appearance of simple resolutions, of happy endings, of nothing ever being too much to handle or too hard to fix. It was escapist, coming to that bar, drinking those Diet Cokes, and Erik needed that.

After the first Hollower, he and Dave had made it quite a habit, going to the bar to escape things. Diet Cokes for Erik, and a shot of tequila—Jose Cuervo—and a Killians for Dave.

After Dave's death, Erik thought of asking Jake but thought better of it. He might understand about the Diet Cokes, and his sponsor, Gary, might understand, but there was no way that he, as a sponsor himself, could, in good conscience, invite his own recovering addict charge to a bar, virgin drinks or not. Besides, nowadays Jake and Dorrie spent a lot of time together. They'd even talked of moving in together, as that house on Cerver Street gave Dorrie the creeps and Jake was tired of sharing his own house with ghosts.

Erik's going to the Olde Mill was a man thing, he always thought—man versus the elements, man versus himself, man conquering temptation and ruin, that sort of thing. So asking Casey was out.

Since Dave's death—really, since the night of his funeral—Erik had developed a new habit. It seemed to skirt close to the edge of good recovering-addict behavior, but the bartender never cared because he still got the money and Gary had been swayed to Erik's way of thinking when it had been explained.

Several weeks after they'd climbed sweating and bleeding and bruised all to hell out of the catacombs, Erik went to the bar alone. And as was his new habit, he ordered a Diet Coke, a shot of Jose Cuervo, and a Killians. The latter two he didn't touch at all, nor did he let the bartender sweep them up with the empties and forgotten drinks of the night. He didn't let any of the jostling, half-crocked jocks that often frequented the place scoop them up either. They sat untouched, slightly to the right of his Diet Coke as if waiting for the one to drink them to return from the men's room, say, or from the Outrun game. In Erik's mind, they were for Dave, and they stayed that way until closing time, until Erik walked out that door. He never turned around. He never watched the bartender swipe the glasses and dump the booze, untouched. He didn't have the heart to.

But that night several weeks after the catacombs was different. Erik sat there, sipping his nonalcoholic drink and watching an old man put the moves on a very drunk, somewhat chunky blonde in her early forties, whose eyes were half-closed and whose V-neck sweater was crooked enough that when she leaned over to hear what the old man was saying he got full view straight down. Behind Erik, the door opened and closed, and the unoccupied stool next to him was fitted with a familiar form.

"Steve." Erik nodded at him. "How are ya?"

Steve nodded back. "Off duty tonight. First night off since . . ." He waved it off, letting the obvious dangle between them. "Looking to get good and drunk."

Erik considered this for a moment and then slid the shot and the Killians in front of the police officer.

"First of the night. On me. Drink up."

Steve looked at the drinks skeptically. Erik supposed he was trying to figure out why he even had those drinks to dispense with in the first place.

"Seriously?"

Erik felt a lump in his throat, but nodded. "I . . . yeah, I think so."

"Thanks." Steve downed the shot and then kicked back the Killians. "God, I needed that." He grinned brightly at Erik.

With a small smile, Erik turned back to his Diet Coke. "Do you like movies, father?"

"Huh?"

"Nothing. Line from an old movie."

From the corner of his eye, Erik saw Steve nod, confused. "Ah. Well, for the record, I do like movies."

"Yeah, me too."

"We could catch one some time." Steve held his hand up when Erik looked at him and seemed to tense a little. "Not as a date."

Erik grinned. "So you're not going to pay?"

Steve visibly relaxed. "Well, I was figuring that after the drinks, you were the paying type."

"Hey, you asked me out. Although, I do consider myself a gentleman, of course . . ."

After that, the conversation was easy, even comfortable. They talked about the Mets and the Giants, they talked about places they'd traveled, about movies that sucked and movies they loved and their jobs and their high school days and psycho exes and what it might be like to spend a weekend partying with Derek Jeter. Steve introduced his attraction to men casually, off-handedly, and Erik acknowledged it by simply taking it in stride. They talked about books and Erik's wedding plans and whether the old man was going to bag the chunky blonde. They even talked about Dave. The Hollower, though, never came up once—not because of an empty superstition of bringing them back through a new rip between worlds, but because, maybe for the first time, the subject finally seemed done and closed.

Steve got up to leave, and Erik said, "Still wanna catch a movie?"

The police officer nodded. "I know where to find you."

"Long arm of the law."

Steve grinned, considered something for a moment, then said in a conspiratorial lean, "Not just my arm."

Erik laughed, and Steve looked relieved when he opened the door and tipped out into the night.

An hour later, as the Olde Mill Tavern was winding down, Erik got up to leave, too. The night had grown cooler, but not uncomfortably so. He walked toward his car, and a glint of something white and round and smooth caught his eye. He looked up and to the woods, in the direction of the thing, and saw an old hubcap, which had caught moonlight.

The breath Erik hadn't realized he'd been holding seeped out in relief.

They weren't coming back. It was done. They were gone.

Erik breathed in the night air, and when the rest of him believed that, he smiled to himself, got into his car, and drove home to his girl.

Behind him, in the woods, in the night air, in the quiet over the lake, on the empty streets of the suburban neighborhoods of Lakehaven, New Jersey, there hung the air of regrets, of lies, of fears and insecurities, but they were not Erik's nor Jake's, not Dorrie's nor Steve's, and nothing, sensing those things, came to find them.

From Horror's greatest talents comes

THE NEW FACE OF FEAR.

Terrifying, sexy, dangerous and deadly.

And they are hunting for YOU . . .

WEREWOLVES

SHAPESHIFTER by J. F. GONZALEZ

THE NIGHTWALKER by THOMAS TESSIER

RAVENOUS by RAY GARTON

WOLF'S TRAP by W. D. GAGLIANI

Available Now!
Get them before they get you…

To order and to learn more visit
www.dorchesterpub.com
or call **1-800-481-9191**

Master of terror

RICHARD
LAYMON

has one word of advice for you:

BEWARE

Elsie knew something weird was happening in her small supermarket when she saw the meat cleaver fly through the air all by itself. Everyone else realized it when they found Elsie on the butcher's slab the next morning—neatly jointed and wrapped. An unseen horror has come to town, and its victims are about to learn a terrifying lesson: what you can't see can very definitely hurt you.

ISBN 13: 978-0-8439-6137-9

UNCUT VERSION!
IN PAPERBACK FOR THE FIRST TIME!

THE
PINES

Deep within the desolate Pine Barrens, a series of macabre murders draws ever nearer to an isolated farmhouse where a woman struggles to raise her disturbed son. The boy has a psychic connection to something in the dark forest, something unseen... and evil.

The old-timers in the region know the truth of the legendary creature that stalks these woods. And they know the savagery it's capable of.

ROBERT
DUNBAR

ISBN 13: 978-0-8439-6165-2
